For
Gary & Grace—

D1496109

BEFORE
SHE WAS
A FINLEY

Thanks
for coming
to my book
launch—

A NOVEL

Enjoy

CAROL HOENIG

ALL NIGHT
BOOKS

Paperback ISBN 978-1-63226-144-1
eBook ISBN 978-1-63226-145-8

Published by All Night Books
An imprint of Easton Studio Press
PO Box 3131
Westport, CT 06880
(203) 349-8413
www.allnightbooks.com

Book and cover design by Alexia Garaventa
Manufactured in the United States of America

Words of Praise for *Without Grace*

"We need more North Country novels like *Without Grace*, novels with a keen sense of place."   —North Country Public Radio

"I so completely enjoyed your novel. Got completely hooked on it, loved Vicky especially—of course with my food obsessions, of course I would—but got very involved with her journey. She's a wonderful heroine and the ultimate encounter with her mother is powerful. Congratulations to you for writing such a moving book."
                    —Delia Ephron, author of *Siracusa*

"Like Scout Finch and Mattie Ross and Ellen Foster before her, Vicky Finley has grit and will and insight, a wry eye for the world around her, and a deeply engaging way of finding there a place of her own."   —Michael Malone, author of *Handling Sin*

"*Without Grace* is the story of a girl's search for her mother, a subject that cannot help but make the reader, and this reader, wonder what is going to happen next."
                    —Rona Jaffe, author of *The Best of Everything*

"If you begin reading Carol Hoenig's *Without Grace* at the start of the workday, you might as well call and tell your boss that you are engaged in a work that transcends the day. A meal, it is as smooth as lobster bisque, a grand main course, and what a dessert! What more can we want in a book? Get it and plan to take the day off."
                    —Malachy McCourt, author of *A Monk Swimming*

"*Without Grace* is a story of tragic loss and subsequent self-discovery. Vicky Finley's tale is haunting and unforgettable, as Hoenig's narrative deftly draws us into the drama of her character's life."
                    —Susan Shapiro Barash, author of *The New Wife*

"Searching, soulful . . . *Without Grace* is a heartfelt exploration of that small town in all of us, our bittersweet Place of Angels."
—Arthur Kent, journalist, filmmaker and author of *Risk and Redemption*

"This book is dynamite—literature as it was meant to be: at its finest. Keep your eye on this one—that is, when they're not glued to the pages inside."
—PODDY Mouth

"All the while I was reading, I kept thinking this is as good, if not better, than Isaac Bashevis Singer. You took life, and articulated it as if you were one of Robert Heinlens, "Fair Witnesses." It was about the evolution of a human being, and the sometimes agonizing decisions we are forced to make on our drives to center ourselves."
—Shawn Phillips, award-winning rock pioneer

Words of Praise for *Of Little Faith*

"Two sisters and a brother are bound to a dark past by their shared interest in the family home. Painful memories render them unable to come to an agreement that would open the door to the possibility of healing. Hoenig skillfully shifts between four narrators to tell this gripping story, avoiding excess sentimentality. A real page-turner I found hard to put down."
—Anna Jean Mayhew, author of *The Dry Grass of August*

"Brutally frank and devastatingly real, this exceptional novel explores the dynamics of a dysfunctional family while calling attention to hypocritical behavior."
—*Foreword Reviews*

"Serious and heartfelt, and highly readable."
                    —Meredith Sue Willis, author of *A Space Apart*

"Reactions by this novel's readers may depend on one's beliefs or lack thereof, but it cannot be denied that the essence of compassion is the theme brilliantly shining through this poignant story. The reader's feelings evolve parallel to those of the characters. Change and honest caring were the by-products of the '60s, all of which the reader experiences in a wondrous way that remains long after the story and its afterword are finished. Excellent historical fiction and highly recommended."
                    —Historical Novel Society

This novel is dedicated to my fellow Wildflowers podcasters, Judith Vaughan and Peggy Zieran, who helped bring *Before She Was a Finley* to where it needed to be. Their encouragement, friendship, and support is something every writer should experience.

PROLOGUE

It was the first assignment for Adele Thibeau's summer journalism workshop. There were only seven students in the course, though it had begun with eleven. The call of the warm breeze and rhythmic lake's laps were so enticing that some of the students dropped out to enjoy the short season in Upstate New York; summers always seemed brief in the rural area skirting the Canadian border. But Adele refused to be distracted. Instead, she envisioned receiving the Pulitzer for reporting one day, and, even though she wasn't terribly intrigued by what the teacher assigned, she figured she'd make the best of it.

With her notepad and pen at the ready, Adele waved goodbye to her father as he drove away and walked through the main doors of Franklin County Nursing Home with a sense of purpose. She'd never been in such a place before. Not only that, but at seventeen years old, she'd never had much cause for talking to old people, or they with her, if she was honest with herself. She went up to the front desk where a woman was seated, her head bent over paperwork.

"Excuse me," Adele said.

The woman looked up, giving her the once-over. Adele, in her ripped jeans and loose-fitting t-shirt, knew she didn't look the part of any journalist she'd seen on camera, but since she wasn't going to be on camera, she figured her appearance wouldn't matter. After all, that's what Mr. Wilson had told her when she'd asked how she should dress to do the interviews.

"Half of the people there are probably blind, so I don't think it matters much," he'd said.

"Are you sure there's nothing else I can write about?" she'd whined. *How could she possibly earn an A with such an assignment?*

"Well, find a local business and see how they started out, if you prefer," Mr. Wilson replied.

Since she had to rely on her father to drive her, she decided it would be easier going to one location instead of trying to seek out a business that would be willing enough to be interviewed, so she took the nursing home assignment.

"Yes?" the woman from behind the desk said.

"I'm Adele Thibeau. Mr. Wilson sent me here to interview some of the patients for a class assignment."

Looking over the top of her glasses, the woman said, "Well, they aren't *patients*."

"They aren't?"

"No. We refer to them as guests."

"Oh," Adele said, tucking a strand of curly dark hair behind her ear.

"Patients are sick. These people are just old."

Adele liked the quote and mentally took note.

"So, who are you here to see?"

Adele shrugged. "I don't know." Mr. Wilson had told her to find out if any of the people at the nursing home had fought in the war. She wasn't sure which war that would be.

"Or maybe they suffered a major loss and had to start from

scratch," Mr. Wilson continued. "That happened to a lot of the farmers around here." He must have seen Adele's dubious expression because he said, "Or maybe finding out how they were affected by how fast the world was changing."

"In what way?" Adele had said.

Growing exasperated, Mr. Wilson said, "Believe it or not, Miss Thibeau, there was a time women couldn't even entertain the thought of working outside the home and had to depend on a man to support them. Women were, well, second-class citizens." He scooped up his papers, and as he walked out of the classroom, snapped, "It's up to you to find the story and write about it."

Now she said, "I'm looking to interview someone who had an interesting life." When the woman looked confused, Adele added, "I want to be a journalist," as if this would suddenly make everything clear.

Just then a middle-aged man dressed in all white came around the corner pushing an old man slumped in a wheelchair. As they passed by, the woman behind the desk said, "That's Earl Duprey. Not the orderly, but the old man. He loves to talk."

"Oh!" Adele said. "Would it be okay, if—"

"—Go right ahead," the woman said with a chuckle.

Adele dashed down the hall chasing after the orderly. "Excuse me! Excuse me!" she called out, waving her notepad and pen. "That lady told me I could interview him." Adele pointed to Earl.

The orderly looked from Adele to the old man and down the hall toward where the lady was sitting behind the desk. "She did?"

Adele nodded, hoping Earl Duprey would be a "get" and her story would be written in no time. Then she'd be able to join her friends at the lake.

"Follow me. I'm bringing him to the solarium." As the orderly started to roll the wheelchair down the hall, he said loudly, "Earl, this pretty young thing is here to talk to you!"

Earl began mumbling and, to hear what he was saying, Adele had to practically run to stay abreast of the rolling wheelchair. She scribbled the date on the first page of her notebook: July 9, 2013.

"Thing is they gotta be milked twice a day. Otherwise, they die."

"Excuse me?" Adele said, leaning in so he could see her.

"Buddy, be sure to lock up tonight."

Adele looked at the orderly, who said, "Oh, he'll talk all right. Never makes any sense, though. I think June was pulling your leg."

"Who's June?" Adele asked.

The orderly nodded back down the hall. "The woman at the desk. Earl ain't made a lick a sense since he's been here."

"How long has that been?" Adele asked.

"Going on about three years."

Adele studied the old man as he continued to mumble, slumping further into his wheelchair while the orderly brought him into the solarium. He parked him near a table next to several other elderly people and nodded at Adele before leaving Earl in the warm sunlight streaming in through a large window.

Adele turned to survey the room. There were two women sitting in front of a television, though neither of them seemed interested in the soap opera that was playing. There was another man, who didn't look as old as the others, sitting at a table with a deck of cards spread out in front of him. Another elderly woman was nearby, but she was being entertained by a young child calling her Grandma. Adele figured it was useless to get any sort of story from the confused man in the wheelchair, so she went over to the man who was playing cards and introduced herself.

"Adele?" he repeated. "That's a pretty name. You're pretty. Wanna go out tonight?"

She laughed and said no, but once she rebuffed his advances, he wanted nothing to do with her and wouldn't answer any of her questions. It seemed none of the people that were in the room wanted any sort of interruption to their day. She then decided to check out the place. After all, she would need to give the reader of her article a sense of the surroundings. However, if she had to describe it, one word came to mind: depressing. It soon became apparent that for the *guests* there was only one means of escape.

She wandered out of the solarium, leaving Mr. Duprey mumbling about nothing that made sense to her, and took a right. The smell of disinfectant mixed with stale odors filled the air as she strolled down the hall. She passed one room after the next, reading the names in the little slots in the wall outside each door. After peeking inside, she would then keep going. Some had a television blasting, others were curled up in bed, their mouths slack, eyes closed. She couldn't help but wonder how Leslie Stahl and Cokie Roberts got their stories. Getting her assignment complete so she could enjoy some time at the lake might take longer than she'd hoped.

She reached room 120 and looked in to see a woman in a wheelchair facing a window. Her hair looked to be nothing more than thin white fluff, and Adele studied her for a few moments, the woman unmoving, perhaps gazing at the empty field beyond the window. It was also possible that she was sleeping. Adele poked her head in further, noticing that someone else was in the bed closest to the door, the nightstand covered with photos and cards.

Adele stepped back out into the hallway and read the two names next to the entranceway: Mary Patnode and Grace Dormand.

"Margaret, that you?"

Adele took a hesitant step into the room. The woman in the bed sat up, her eyes wide open, anticipating.

Adele replied, "No, no, I'm Adele Thibeau."

"Oh, thought you might be my daughter, but come on in!" The woman shifted as if to make herself more comfortable for a visitor.

"I'm doing a story for my journalism class."

The woman leaned to one side. "What kind of story?"

Adele wasn't sure how to answer, but said, "Just something people would want to read about." Adele pointed to a chair next to the woman's bed. "May I sit?"

"Oh, that'd be nice," the woman said, reaching around and plumping up her pillow.

Adele glanced over to the other side of the room, noticing that the woman with white fluffy hair hadn't budged, leaving her to wonder if she'd already begun making her journey into the afterlife. Adele took a chair and said, "Which one are you? Mary or—"

"Oh, I'm Mary. Mary Patnode. I got nine, no, ten or more grandchildren. Five great grandchildren."

Adele started writing on her notepad, even though Mary hadn't said much of anything worth writing about yet. She went on to say that she'd raised her kids and took care of her husband who had worked at the aluminum plant in Massena. "Traveled back and forth every day, no matter the weather. Died September 26, 1994. Sure do miss him." Despite this detail, Mary's life didn't seem all that remarkable. Adele decided to nudge her a little.

"Did you ever do anything out of the ordinary?"

Mary squinted, thinking. "Once when I went to town, I bought myself two pairs of the same shoes 'cuz I liked them so much. Figured when one pair wore out, I'd have a second."

Adele smiled and then pushed a bit harder. "Well, did you do anything that most women back then didn't normally do? Or did you ever want to?"

"Like what?"

Adele shrugged. "I don't know. Did you have a job?"

"A job!" Mary snorted. "I had five children to take care of. One of them so slow, I had to keep him home."

"Where is he now?"

"Living with his sister in Ellenburg. People loved my banana nut bread. I used to make about twelve loaves every Christmas and give 'em as gifts." Mary stopped and studied Adele. "You're not writing."

"I . . . I'm looking for more of a *story*. I mean, something with some drama."

"Drama?" While Mary took a moment to consider this, the fluffy white-haired woman wheeled herself around and stared at Adele.

Adele felt as though the woman wanted to say something, so she said, "How about you?"

The woman's expression was hard, but her voice weak and quivery when she replied, "Drama? Like walking out on your two babies and husband?"

Adele gazed at her, stunned.

"That's Grace Dormand," Mary said. "That's the first I ever heard her speak."

Part One

CHAPTER 1

It had been about a week since that young girl first barged into the room and began nosing around and she hadn't stopped since. When Mary had been quick to ask, "What kind of mother would do something like that?" Grace wasn't sure why she'd volunteered such a reply in the first place, especially when she hadn't been spoken to; not right away, anyway. She never talked of her past and tried to avoid thinking about it. So she turned around to face the window again, but it wasn't enough to make the girl leave her alone.

"Ma'am?"

Even at her age, Grace never considered herself old enough to be called "Ma'am." However, maybe it had been the need to unload the guilt she'd been carrying all these years, so when the girl kept returning day after day prodding, "May I ask you a couple of questions," Grace started to wonder if her answers would be her penance. Perhaps that's why she hadn't died yet. Maybe she wasn't going to be allowed to go to her grave without first acknowledging her sins.

She turned her wheelchair around. "What did you say your name was?"

"Adele. Adele Thibeau."

Thibeau was a surname she'd recognized. She probably knew of Adele's family, or the ones who'd passed on, anyway. "Adele," she mumbled, "what do you wanna know?"

Adele edged down onto a chair that was in the corner. She turned a page in her notebook, and said, "So, you, um . . . left your family?"

Grace stared off and then nodded.

"Why?" Adele said.

Grace looked away. She'd never given voice to the real reason and still wasn't sure she could.

"Um," Adele said, "where'd you go? What'd you do?"

"*Do?* I played my guitar in different honkytonks."

Adele had her notebook opened and pen ready. She looked up. "Honky *what*?"

Mary called over from her side of the room. "That's another name for a bar that has live music."

Adele acknowledged Mary's reply with a nod, then noticed a scratched-up guitar in the corner, on Grace's side of the room.

Grace said, "Some better than others." She saw the young girl start to scribble, noticing some hesitation, or was that judgment of her?

Adele cleared her throat and didn't make eye contact when she said, "So, you had two children?"

Grace paused, blinked, and said in barely more than a whisper, "A son and a daughter. More, if you count . . . ," she trailed off.

"Oh, I'm sorry." Adele scowled, turning the pages of her notebook. "I thought you'd said two children and a husband."

Grace nodded. "I did." She looked over her shoulder to see that Mary was sitting on the edge of her bed at full attention. "Maybe we should stop here."

Adele looked up, wide-eyed. "*Stop?*"

Grace turned back toward the window.

"How about I ask some easier questions? I mean, for instance, how old are you?"

After a long pause, Grace said, "Somewhere in my eighties."

"You don't know your exact age?"

Grace shrugged. "My aunt raised me and didn't provide a whole lotta information for me back then. I eventually found proof, but I suppose I just stopped counting at some point or another."

"Your aunt raised you? So, where were your parents?"

Grace never much liked talking about that part of her life. Still didn't.

"Mrs. Dormand?" the young girl nudged.

"Don't call me that." Barely above a whisper, she added, "You can call me Grace."

Adele paused, then said, "Okay, Grace, where were your parents?"

"I need a smoke," Grace said, turning her wheelchair around and heading out of the room. She passed Mary, who shouted, "Supper will be coming soon. Maybe you shouldn't leave just now."

Ignoring Mary, Grace headed to the solarium, and rolled up to a glass door. On the other side was a patio. She looked up at Adele, motioning toward the outside.

Adele ran over, opening the door. Grace rolled through and parked. The old woman took out a pack of cigarettes and a book of matches from her pocket. Once she had lit a cigarette, she took a deep pull before the smoke swirled from her thin lips.

"They don't let us smoke inside," she said, sounding disgusted. "It's hell in the winter. Could catch a death of cold out here." She held out her pack of cigarettes, offering Adele one.

"No thank you," Adele said.

Grace looked up at the sky, blue without a cloud. There was a field that bordered the nursing home property, then a copse of pine trees beyond that.

"How old are *you*?" Grace said.

"Seventeen," Adele replied, dragging a chair next to Grace. She sat down and opened her notebook.

"Do boys like you?"

Adele started jiggling her foot. "I think they like pretty petite blondes better. And that isn't me." She waved a hand across her body. She wasn't heavy, more big-boned, with a round full face. Without an ounce of makeup, she didn't look as if her appearance was all that important to her.

"Vicky was blonde and beautiful," Grace muttered.

"Vicky?" Adele said.

Grace turned her gaze out toward the field. "Of course, she was just a baby when I left her." Then she stopped talking, her face scrunched up as if she were in pain. She mumbled, "I said too much already."

Tapping her pen on the notepad, Adele said, "So, you were going to tell me about your parents." She flipped to an open page.

"Not much to tell, really. I can't say that I knew them."

"Why?" Adele said.

"They were," she paused before saying, "dead."

"What? They were *both* dead?"

"I didn't want to go into it in front of miss nosy pants back there in the room."

"So how old were you when—"

"Just a baby. Never had a memory of them."

Adele hesitated as if respecting the weight of the reply before continuing. "How . . . how did they die?"

"Gunshots," Grace blurted. "My father killed my mother then put a bullet in himself." Grace tightened her grip on her bathrobe and looked directly at Adele. "Bet you didn't think you'd hear any kind of story like that, huh? Is that drama enough for you?"

Adele stared at Grace for a moment before she mumbled, "I'm so sorry." She straightened herself, then asked, "Where did you live? I mean, with your aunt?"

"Coyote Hill."

Adele repeated it, wrote it down, then added, "Where's that?"

"Not sure you'd ever find it on any map. Somewhere up in the mountains, in the Adirondacks."

Grace never had much of an appetite but was relieved when the orderly appeared outside and announced supper would be served in ten minutes in the dining hall.

"That's that," she said, tossing her cigarette on the ground, and turning her wheelchair around to go back inside.

Adele jumped up. "Um, could I come back? Maybe tomorrow?"

"Do what you want," Grace said, "but I'm not talking. Said more than enough already."

When Adele returned the next day, she found Grace sitting by the window in her room watching the rain come down. Adele took the chair from the corner, pulled it close to the old woman, and sat down. She was grateful that Mary wasn't in the room just then.

"What'd I tell you yesterday?"

"I was hoping you changed your mind." Adele looked around, noticing that Mary's side of the room was filled with photos on the walls, flowers in a vase, and a pretty Afghan on her bed. Grace's side was devoid of any expression of love or family. There was only the guitar in the corner. It made Adele all the more curious.

"So, you'd mentioned Vicky yesterday. Can you tell me anything about her?" Adele asked.

Grudgingly, Grace replied, "My baby girl. She grew up to be a beautiful young woman."

Adele looked up. "You went back?"

Grace chuckled sarcastically. "No, couldn't ever do that. She found me."

"Oh, that must've been so amazing. Was your son with her?"

Grace stiffened, and her voice became strained. She shook her head. "Kevin? No. He was dead by then. Well, murdered."

Adele stopped writing. "Oh my gosh. You've had a lot of violent deaths in your life. Who . . . who . . . killed him?"

Grace's sights were on the rain as it came down.

"Mrs. Dor . . . Grace," Adele prodded, "did they ever find out who killed your son?"

"Not sure."

Adele spotted Mary standing quietly in the doorway, hoping Grace wouldn't see her and stop talking.

"But I know who did," Grace said.

"You do?"

Rigidly, and with a coldness, Grace replied, "It was me. I killed my son."

Just then, from across the room, came the words, "merciful heavens!"

CHAPTER 2

Adele wasn't sure what to make of Grace Finley and wondered if she should report her confession to the police. The next day she ran into the high school, hurrying to her classroom. Most of the other students were already in their seats. Without waiting to be acknowledged, she approached Mr. Wilson, who was casually sitting on the edge of his desk and told him what she had learned.

"Well, what do you think *you* should do?" he replied.

Eddie, one of the other students in the class, overheard the discussion and interrupted, saying, "She sounds like a whack job. Did she say how she killed her son?"

Adele said, "No. And I'm not really sure she did. She said she walked out on everybody years earlier."

"Well," Mr. Wilson said, motioning for Adele to take her seat, "it might be wise to do some investigating before you run to the police."

"But it would've happened so long ago," Diane said. Her assignment was to write about the wind turbines that were cropping up on many local farms, a controversial topic since some were untroubled by the intrusive sight that changed the landscape while others were against it. The ones for it were making a nice profit by leasing their property while those against it weren't able to take advantage of the money-making opportunity since their land wasn't in an ideal location to be of value to the leasing company. Diane had told Mr. Wilson she was close to finishing her assignment, making Adele jealous.

Mr. Wilson focused his attention on Adele. "You do know that the library recently installed a massive computer system, right?"

Adele nodded and Eddie shouted, "And you could find copies of old newspapers there!"

"That's right," Mr. Wilson said. "Maybe you'll find some answers there."

Adele's eyes widened. "Can I go now?"

Mr. Wilson gave her the go ahead while the other students protested, saying they wanted to go and do their research, too, but he wouldn't have it.

Before long, Adele was sitting in front of a computer, referencing her notes. She typed in the name Kevin Dormand, along with the years 1950 to 1970, into the search bar. Nothing came up for Coyote Hill, which was where Grace said she'd lived. However, the name Churubusco came up. Adele lived about twenty miles from Churubusco but had no memory of ever being there. She supposed there'd be no reason. She then leaned in to read a headline. "Rabble Rouser Kevin Finley Protests Farmers Selling Their Property to Scoleri Enterprise" popped up from a local paper titled *Chateaugay Record*. Chateaugay was about thirteen miles from where Adele lived.

Finley? But Grace's last name was Dormand. She read the article that had a grainy picture of a distraught-looking young guy standing in front of a crowd. He had apparently caused a scene at a town meeting. He didn't want a company called Scoleri

Enterprise to buy farmland bordering Benny's Lake. Adele then came across another brief article from the same paper. "Finley Arrested for Refusing to Leave Sold Property." There was a quote from someone named Brad Hunt: "He's always been a little off."

Adele kept scrolling until she came across this:

Snowmobile Accident Takes Young Man's Life

Kevin Finley, 23, died after driving into a barbed wire fence while snowmobiling. Neighbor Fred Scott said it was pitch dark and Finley quite likely never saw the fence that had only recently been posted. "He got a call from his sister needing help. She was babysitting. He never reached her." By the time his body was discovered, it was too late to save him. According to medics who were called, Finley lost too much blood. He is survived by his grandfather, Gerald Finley, father, Jack Finley, and sister, Vicky Finley. His grandmother, Simone LaBarge Finley, predeceased him.

The article made no mention of Grace—neither Dormand nor Finley.

"If it was the same Kevin, she didn't kill him," Adele muttered to herself, immediately putting Grace's name in the search engine and came across an article in the *Press Republican* with a headline, "Local Farmer's Wife Disappears." The article quoted Jack Finley saying, "'She was a hell of a singer. Wanted to get on "Country Hoedown." She was supposed to call me when she got to Montreal, but the phone hasn't rung yet.' Gerald Finley, Jack's father, said, 'She's a sweet girl but has had a lot of issues in her life.' Jack's mother, Simone Finley, added, 'She's a Dormand, after all.' Authorities suspect possible foul play and ask the public to let them know if they saw anything suspicious. Keeping his children next to him, Jack Finley said all that he wanted was for his wife to come back home." Printed beneath the article was a photo of a smiling pretty blonde-haired woman with the name Grace Finley.

Adele then searched for the name Vicky Finley, finding some articles in the *Press Republican* about her being a proprietor of a resort called Lake in the Woods, which was located in Churubusco. That was over thirty years ago. Then there was another article. This one from Long Island *Newsday*: "Vincent Scoleri of Scoleri Enterprise Marries Country Gal." There was an adjoining photo of the newlyweds, Vincent and Vicky Scoleri.

"Wow," Adele said aloud. The couple looked like they belonged in a fashion magazine. The article stated that they were making their home in Upstate New York so that they could run their business.

Adele sat in front of the computer, staring at the screen. So much about this story made her curious. There were too many coincidences for it not to be the same Kevin, but why had she said she murdered her son when it had been an accident with no mention of her at all? Adele planned to find out.

The next day, she ran through the doors of the nursing home. Some of the staff smiled in recognition of her. She went directly to Grace's room to find only Mary there.

"She went to have a smoke," Mary said.

Adele headed to the patio, spotting Grace in her wheelchair, a cigarette between her fingers, her hands, with blue veins protruding, resting on the wheelchair's handles. She was the only one on the patio. Adele wandered over, pulling out a bench from the picnic table nearby, and sitting down.

Grace knew she wasn't alone. She brought the cigarette to her mouth, inhaling and exhaling slowly.

"Was your son Kevin *Finley*?"

The young reporter didn't waste any time to start the inquisition again making Grace wish she'd never said anything to begin with. Her memories were bringing her back in time, keeping her awake at night.

"He died in a snowmobile accident," Adele added.

Grace looked over at her. "What makes you so sure?"

"I found the article." Adele had printed out a copy and handed it over to Grace.

Grace held the paper, gazing at it. The print was too small to read, but she didn't need to. She said, "It doesn't tell everything." Grace noticed her cigarette had burned down to the nub. She looked up to see Adele sitting there, staring at her, waiting.

"It's my fault Kevin died. That's all I know." Grace dropped the butt on the concrete and pulled a pack of cigarettes and a lighter from her pocket. She tamped out another smoke and lit it, taking a strong pull. "These were supposed to kill me a long time ago, but I guess my punishment is having to live with what I did."

"I also found an article about you going missing," Adele said. "Did you remarry?"

"Remarry? Why?"

"Well, your last name is Dormand, but weren't you a Finley?"

Grace stared at the young girl. *Did it matter anymore if people knew who she really was?*

"I . . . I don't understand," Adele persisted.

"And you probably never will." Grace wheeled her chair around so that her back was to the young journalist.

After several minutes passed where Grace refused to answer any more questions, the girl cleared her throat, mumbled a thank you, and went into the hall. She took out her cell phone and called her mother. "I'm done for the day. Can you come and get me?"

That afternoon, Adele shambled into Mr. Wilson's classroom discouraged. "I'm going to have to find someone else," she said.

"Why's that?" Mr. Wilson said.

"I already told you this isn't the kind of story I wanted to do. It's too hard."

Mr. Wilson sat on the edge of his desk, studying her. "So that's what you think a reporter is supposed to do? Tailor their story to make it an easy fit with what they want to write?"

Just then the other students began coming in for class. She wondered if she should have taken one of the topics they were covering. Besides the wind turbines that Diane was writing about, Dave was doing an article on the Almanzo Wilder Homestead that was just a few miles away, and Marilyn was doing a story about the chasms where a paper mill once existed. They all seemed like they'd be easy stories to write without needing to pull information from difficult interviewees, unlike hers.

"Did you ever speculate who this woman was as a young girl?" Mr. Wilson said. "She's given you some great information to follow up on. Her parents were a murder-suicide. And just where is Coyote Hill?"

"I . . . I don't—"

"Why did she leave her family?"

"She won't talk much!"

"Well, Adele, it's too late to change topics now. If you don't stick with it, you're going to fail this course."

"But that's not fair! I need this credit for college!" She was hoping for an easy A.

Mr. Wilson shrugged. "Get busy. I want to know more about this Grace Dormand." He cocked his head. "And something tells me you're afraid."

"Afraid of what?" She riffled the pages to her notebook, refusing to make eye contact with her teacher.

"Just what you might discover about this woman . . . and yourself."

CHAPTER 3

In the dead of night, when the nursing home seemed still, Grace lay in bed unable to sleep. For so many years she'd fought her memories by pushing them away. But ever since that girl showed up it was as if she were forced to face her past, keeping her awake at night, tossing and turning, sighing and heaving. But there it was, the memory of the first time she'd laid eyes on Jack Finley; she thought she'd die, he was so handsome. She couldn't have been more than eight or nine, and he a couple of years older, but something about him made her go all warm inside.

It was the first day of school. A rickety bus had driven up the back roads to come and cart her off several miles away. There'd have been no school for her if the sheriff's car hadn't rambled into the yard, which wasn't too long after strangers found her at her aunt's place up in the hills and took what they called a census. As clear as day, she could see her Aunt Gladys walking out onto the broken-down porch asking what brought the law to her place. Grace hid behind her, but when she peered out, the sheriff pointed at her and said that she was required to attend school.

"Who says?" her aunt's tone challenging. When he explained, she replied, "Too much government getting into our business these days."

But several days later, Grace was climbing up the steps of the yellow school bus, carrying a small burlap bag holding a tin cup and brown sugar sandwich, and bundled in a heavy coat and leather laced-up shoes. It was September and her aunt called it an Indian summer, but she wanted to be sure that Grace was warm enough. Her aunt had also written Grace's full name, Grace Cooke, on a scrap piece of paper and pinned it to her dress, telling her in a strict voice not to take it off. "You're a Cooke, remember that."

As she took her first step onto that bus, she looked back to see her cat, Snowball, sitting next to her aunt, who was standing by the shack, her arms crossed. She was shaking her head, still disapproving of Grace being forced to leave her for the day. There was no recollection of her aunt telling her to be brave or what to expect, except that the bus would be bringing her home before dark. She also pointed out that with the child being gone for the day, she'd have to do all the chores herself. They had a cow that needed milking in the morning and late afternoon. Chickens that needed to be fed, their eggs collected before any other creature got to them. A garden that required tending, the vegetables canned. So, taking what felt like a leisurely ride on the bus and seeing children her own age didn't seem so bad to Grace.

"Well, come on," the man driving the bus had said.

The steps were steep, so Grace had to take big strides before she got to where the driver was sitting. She then looked down the aisle. She saw a couple of boys sitting all the way in the back staring at her, but there was no one else on that bus.

"Well, find yourself a seat," the driver, a burly man with a welcoming smile, instructed.

Grace scooted into one of the seats and before long the bus was rumbling along the narrow, rutted path while she gazed out the window, bouncing this way and that, looking at the trees surrounding them on either side. She'd been living with her aunt as long as she could remember. On occasion, they'd take the long walk down that path to a main road, which eventually led to a store where they would get stuff they couldn't grow or make from the land. For instance, the shoes she wore were bought from that store. They were practically new since she wasn't allowed to wear them while doing her chores; they needed to last through-out the winter, she had been told. She wasn't sure how that was going to work since they were already squeezing her toes.

Soon, after they reached a main stretch of road, the seats began to fill up with kids of all shapes, sizes, and ages. From her window seat, Grace could see where many of them lived; some in shanties similar to hers, while most lived in big farmhouses in wide open fields. Everyone seemed to know each other, and no one said a word to her, although they kept looking in her direction with curious expressions.

The bus pulled up to a two-story white building then squawked to a stop. Everyone stood, crowding each other in the aisle until the driver opened the door. That's when they began pouring out. Grace followed suit.

When Grace's aunt had said the night before that she'd be learning a lot of rubbish, she also mentioned that the school had once been a training center for soldiers. Her aunt knew this because her brother had been there in 1916. Grace didn't know what World War I was but thought it sounded scary.

"Are they still there?" Grace had said to her aunt.

"Who?" her aunt snapped as she pulled a brush through Grace's just-washed head of hair.

"The soldiers."

"Don't be foolish. The war is over. That one anyway."

"Where's your brother now?"

Her aunt's reply was nothing more than a shrug.

Her aunt also said that Grace would be right across the street from the church they went to on Christmas Eve and Easter. She and her aunt would walk down to the main road, no matter how cold or how much snow there was, and relied on the kindness of a passerby to take them the rest of the way. Then once church was over, they'd get a ride back to the path that led up to the mountains where they lived, and hike back to the shanty. By the time they'd get home, Grace would drop onto her tick mattress and fall fast asleep. The next morning she'd wake up just like she had every other morning. Even though it was Christmas Day, nothing felt special about it. It wasn't until she was in school that she found out that a man named Santa Claus would visit children in the night and bring them a doll, a fire truck, or some other surprise while they were asleep. When she'd asked her aunt about such things, she said it was hogwash. That was the beginning of Grace being curious about anything beyond her little shack in the mountains. It was also around the time when she started taking notice of one particular boy.

Once she climbed down the steps from the bus, she spotted the church just across the road. Another bus pulled up alongside hers and opened its doors and more kids came thundering out. Two older women emerged from the building, shouting orders to the kids. Depending on how old they were, children were directed to different lines. Anyone who was in the upper grades was told to go directly into the building and head to their classroom. But Grace's problem was that she wasn't sure just how old she was. Her aunt couldn't recall if she was eight or nine, or even the day she was born. But, thankfully, when one of the women called out, "If you are from eight to ten years old, file up here," Grace made her way over to that particular line. That was when she spotted the cute boy. He was standing in the line for those who were ten to twelve. She was mad at herself because she would've said she was ten and gone over to his line had she noticed. She couldn't help but stare at him. He stood about a head taller than her and had hair that was golden brown.

"Whatchu looking at?" he sputtered in her direction after another boy nudged him and motioned toward Grace.

Hastily she looked away, feeling her face burn.

"This way," called one of the women at the head of her line. Grace followed, marching into a room. She saw that the other line went into the room across the hall and wondered when she'd see that boy again. Everyone was then instructed to be quiet and take a seat at a desk. Grace took one in the middle and then looked at everyone and everything around her in amazement. They all seemed to know what to do.

"Please pay attention," the woman at the front of the classroom said, looking directly at Grace before she began writing on the board. She then underlined what she'd written and said, "Can anyone tell me what this says?"

Two hands went up. She motioned toward the girl sitting in front of Grace and said, "Jean, can you tell us what this says?" She took a stick and pointed at the board with the letters.

"It's your name!" Jean said.

"Right. And can you tell the class what my name is?"

"Mrs. Lagree."

"Yes. I am Mrs. Lagree and I will be your teacher. Now, can you guess what this says?" She aimed her pointer at the other words on the board. When no one replied, she said, "It's the name of the month, day, and year. It's September Third, 1941." She then went over to her desk at the front of the room and said she was going to take roll call, and when she said our name, we were to call out "here."

"Charles Boomhower."

"Here."

"Robert Brady."

"Here."

"Mary Campbell."

"Here."

Each time someone replied, "Here," Mrs. Lagree marked something in the book in front of her.

"Grace Dormand."

Everybody waited but no one replied.

She repeated, "Grace Dormand."

She stood, looking at Grace. "What's your name?"

"Grace," she replied.

"So you are a Dormand."

Some of the students began to whisper and point at Grace.

Barely above a whisper, she said, "My aunt said to tell you that my name is Grace Cooke." She then patted the piece of paper her aunt had pinned to her dress to verify as much.

Mrs. Lagree scowled and one of the boys in the back shouted, "No, you're not. You're a Dormand and your father killed—"

"Stop that right now!" Mrs. Lagree called out. She then looked back at her. "Okay, Grace, thank you." She then continued, "John Hoomans."

"Here."

"Jean LaFrancis."

"Here."

"Helen Poupore."

"Here."

"Simon Thibeau."

Grace barely heard the rest of the names called, feeling all the eyes on her.

Once Mrs. Lagree was finished, with seventeen students in all, she said, "Now everyone take out your pencils and paper that are in the desk in front of you and see if you can copy what I wrote on the board."

Grace watched those around her do as the teacher had instructed and did the same, though she had no idea how to form the letters that were written. Sometimes when her aunt didn't have her helping, she would take a stick and try to draw in the dirt, or if it was winter, try to do the same in the snow, but she had no idea how to write the teacher's name on the paper in front of her. But she tried, wrapping her fist around the thin pencil and pressing down. The end broke off. She looked at the other students vigorously writing on their papers and began to cry. She wanted to go home.

"What's wrong, honey?"

Grace saw that Mrs. Lagree was crouched down next to her. She sputtered, "I broke it. Now I can't do it."

Mrs. Lagree took the broken pencil and Grace's hand, leading her to the front of the room. There was some sort of gadget on the wall and she put the pencil in it and began cranking. Moments later, she pulled the pencil out and it was fixed. Grace wiped the tears from her face and smiled.

"Whenever your pencil breaks, you can do what I just did." She bent down and whispered, "Since you missed so much school already, you'll need to catch up, but you'll be able to write and read in no time."

After they practiced what Mrs. Lagree called penmanship, with the teacher showing Grace the correct way to hold the pencil so it wouldn't break so easily, she passed out books and said it was time for a reading lesson. The book was about two children named Dick and Jane. They had a dog named Spot and a cat named Puff. Grace listened as the students around her sounded out the words but had little idea how they did it.

Helen read, "Dick said, 'Look. Look.'"

When everyone turned the page, Grace did too, though she didn't know why.

"Okay," Mrs. Lagree said, "since you all worked so hard, you can have a fifteen-minute recess. When the weather isn't nice like it is today, you will play in the gym, but today you may go outside in the yard. When the bell rings, you come back in."

They were then instructed to form a single line and walk quietly outside to play, but Mrs. Lagree pulled Grace aside before she got to the door. After everyone was outside, she said that they were going to sit together every day so that she could help her learn what the others already were doing. "In order to catch up." The teacher smiled and said, "Okay?"

Grace nodded but wondered if she was being punished. The teacher then instructed her to go outside and play but that the next day she would have to miss recess so they could work together.

As soon as she reached the last step to go into the yard, one of the boys said something about her father being a bad man. *How would he know my father?* she wondered. Aunt Gladys had told her that her parents were killed in an accident but wouldn't go into detail, even when she pressed her for more information.

Grace ran around to the side of the building, watching two girls go up and down on some long board. There was a swing set and boys were taking turns pumping their legs to see who could go the highest. It looked like fun, but Grace was too afraid to go over and be among them. She had never played with any other children before. The only person she was ever with was her aunt.

Moments later, she heard more kids come down the steps and run over toward the others. *And there he was.* As slyly as she could so he wouldn't see her, Grace watched *him.* Then before long, the bell rang.

Once everyone was back at their desks, the teacher tried to show the students how to tell time by the clock on the wall and said that when both the big hand and little hand were on the three, they would be excused and could go home. Grace stared at that clock all afternoon, eager to see those hands land on that three, with Mrs. Lagree often reminding her to pay attention. It wasn't that she was eager to get home but was hoping to see that boy from across the hall again.

When the time came though, and they were all lined up to get on the buses, he was nowhere to be found. Disheartened, Grace went up the steps to the bus, trying to figure out where to sit when Helen, the girl from her class, scooted over and motioned for her to sit with her. She had curly brown hair and brown eyes to match. At first, she didn't say anything but then asked Grace, "Where do you live?"

Grace wasn't sure how to answer, so she just pointed down the road.

From the back of the bus, one of the boys shouted, "Hey, Gracie, what did your mother do to your father that he wanted to shoot her?"

Another boy started cackling, "And then kill 'imself!"

Helen turned around and told them to shut up. She then turned back to Grace and said, "They're mean. Don't pay them any mind."

Grace scowled. "Why are they saying that?"

"What do you mean?"

"My daddy didn't kill anybody. He died in an accident. With my mom."

Helen shook her head. "No, that's not true."

The bus pulled away from the school and headed down the road. She said, "See those woods?"

Grace looked and nodded.

"That's where it happened."

"What?" she asked.

"Where your father killed your mother and himself. That's where you used to live."

Grace shook her head, refusing to believe what Helen was saying, but it didn't stop her from speaking.

"Everybody still talks about it," Helen said. "You were just a baby. My dad found you on the floor. And he found . . . *them*. It was awful. He said he sometimes has bad dreams about it."

The bus came to a stop and Helen jumped up out of her seat. "See you tomorrow!"

Grace watched as Helen got off the bus and walked toward her house. A younger boy, who'd also been on the bus, was walking alongside her. The house looked big and friendly, but Grace wasn't sure she liked Helen.

The minute she got back to the shack, she told Aunt Gladys what the kids had told her, and her aunt started slamming the cupboard doors and pacing around the small space. "I knew sending you to school would cause problems. Don't you listen to that nonsense!" she yelled. "It's all lies!"

The following morning, her aunt marched right up to the bus and shouted at the driver that if her niece heard any more lies about what happened to her mother, she would report it.

Grace squeezed by her aunt to get on the bus.

"Who you gonna report it to?" the driver said.

That seemed to stop her aunt for a minute. She sputtered, saying, "Don't you worry about it."

Grace climbed up the steps, and rushed to her seat, hearing the driver say, "She's gonna find out the truth sooner or later. One of the biggest stories in these parts." He then closed the door and drove off. Grace saw her aunt stomping her feet and waving her fists until they reached a bend in the road, and then she was out of sight.

CHAPTER 4

Grace liked school better than she thought she would. Mrs. Lagree did begin keeping her inside during recess to help her with the alphabet, and teach her how to read, write, and add up numbers. She didn't mind that she was missing playtime since it meant she wasn't being hounded by the other kids. There was a strange curiosity about who she was, although the one person who didn't seem all that curious about her was Jack Finley. Eventually, she'd found out that was the cute boy's name and would whisper it to herself under her breath. He rarely looked her way, but he also never joined in with the other kids picking on her for being what they called an orphan. Yet, when the taunting did finally stop, she wanted to believe it was because he defended her but found out otherwise when one day Mrs. Lagree pushed aside the book she was helping Grace read and said, "Sweetie, it wasn't your fault what happened to you. Your father was a very troubled man. I told the students to stop talking about it—or they'll be punished."

"Aunt Gladys told me they died in an accident." Even Grace could hear the hesitation in her own voice, wondering if her aunt had been lying to her all these years.

Mrs. Lagree paused, then said, "Well, that's fine. We all have to deal with tragedy in our own way. Now, why don't we get back to finding out where Spot went?" She put the book back in front of Grace and continued having her sound out the words.

Soon, the class was drawing pumpkins on paper and then cutting them out to decorate the room. Snow had already fallen. Mr. Prevo, her bus driver, had warned her aunt that if the snow was too deep, he wouldn't be able to pick Grace up in front of her shack. "She'll have to walk to the main road. I'll pick her up there," he'd said. So far that hadn't been an issue since they'd only gotten a couple of inches every now and then.

As time went by, Grace wanted to know more about her parents and what really happened to them but was too afraid to ask. When her aunt had scolded the bus driver those months ago, she'd mentioned being her mother's sister. Grace wanted to know more about that. How long were her parents married? Did they love her? There were so many questions and so far she had found no answers.

Finally, Grace could join the others at recess because Mrs. Lagree said she no longer needed extra help since she had caught up "quite nicely." It was too cold to play outside, however, so the children were sent to the gym. Grace would go off to a corner with her friend, Helen, and they'd try to figure out the truth about her parents, a topic that Helen liked to discuss all the time. She said that her parents answered some of her questions but that they didn't really know the Dormands all that well. According to the information that Helen had, "The Dormands pretty much kept to themselves." But "Dormand" was a name never spoken by her aunt who insisted Grace was a Cooke and that was that.

"Uncle Henry's come to stay with us," Aunt Gladys said one day when Grace got home from school. She looked over at the man sitting in the rocking chair near the wood-burning stove. She wanted to run over to it to get warm, but with him sitting there, a cigar dangling from his mouth and his shirt struggling to stay buttoned, she just wriggled out of her coat, kicked off her boots and brought her homework to the table. No one had ever stayed with them before. Snowball ran up to her, mewing. She crouched down to pet him while sneaking a look at the stranger, who had hair sprouting in different directions from his round head and a grizzly looking face. He also smelled weird.

"He's my brother," Aunt Gladys said. "I told you about him. He's the one who'd fought in the war. He'll be here for Thanksgiving."

Grace kept petting Snowball without saying a word.

"It'll be good to have an extra set of hands around to help with the chores," Aunt Gladys said.

Uncle Henry sniffed and replied, "Remember my back, Sister. Limits what I can do."

As time went by, all he ever seemed to be able to do was pick up a fork and shove food in his mouth or light another cigar, as far as Grace was concerned.

One night, while the wind was howling and the snow coming down hard, Grace sat with her aunt and uncle at the table eating beef stew. She'd missed school that day because the bus couldn't get up into the mountains due to the high snowdrifts. Grace wanted to walk to the main road, but her aunt wouldn't allow it, despite how much she begged, even suggesting that

Uncle Henry could bring her to the main road. He just chuckled at that and said she could stay put. "Missing one day's lessons won't put you too far back," he added.

But it wasn't so much the lessons that Grace missed. She wanted to see Helen and learn about things beyond Coyote Hill. She also missed Jack Finley. He never talked to her, but she would listen as he talked to the other boys during recess. He talked about his ma and pa, working on the farm and music he liked. He especially liked someone by the name of Gene Autry, said he liked the way he played the guitar. Then the other students, most anyway, spoke about their home lives and it became apparent that hers was lacking in some way. That night between bites of stew, she looked at Aunt Gladys and said, "How come you never got married?"

"Too ugly," Uncle Henry said, before breaking into laughter, and spitting a piece of potato across the table from his gap-toothed mouth.

Aunt Gladys reached over and smacked him on the arm, but she seemed to find what he'd said funny. "Look who's calling the kettle black," she said. "You'll be single forever!"

Grace never thought her aunt pretty or ugly. She was just Aunt Gladys. She'd told Grace a while ago that she was somewhere in her thirties, as far as she could recall.

Just then, Uncle Henry looked straight at Grace and said, "I'll tell you why she never married. To take care of you. She missed out because of—"

Aunt Gladys didn't let him finish the thought. "Never found the right man, Grace," she interrupted. "That's all."

Something about the way Uncle Henry looked at her aunt when she said that made Grace feel weird. Normally, he slept on the cot in the living room, since that was the only place to put him, but that night with just a makeshift wall separating her sleeping area from her aunt's, Grace was awakened to the sounds of grunts and heavy breathing. Snowball was curled up next to her but leapt off the bed as Grace lunged up and squinted, peering between the planks' slats. Uncle Henry was on top of her aunt, making her cry out. Grace jumped from her bed and ran to her aunt's side of the room, shouting for him to stop.

Her aunt screamed, "Get out! Get out!" But she wasn't screaming at her uncle. She was screaming at the little girl who raced back to her room and pulled the covers over her head, trying to make sense of what she'd seen.

The next morning, sun was pouring through the windows. The snowstorm had passed, but that didn't mean the path to their place was accessible; however, that wasn't going to stop her. Grace bundled up and decided to walk the mile or so to the main road by herself to catch the bus. She didn't care what her aunt said. She needed to get out of that shanty, even though she wasn't quite sure why. While her aunt was out milking the cow and Uncle Henry inside snoring like a wild sow, Grace headed out, trudging through snow so deep it was past her knees. As far as she was concerned, Thanksgiving couldn't come fast enough; assuming he'd come for Thanksgiving, he'd be leaving after.

With her notepad and pen, Adele said, "So, was he *really* her brother?" She tried to hide her expression of shock. She had to be careful. Mr. Wilson told her she'd need to get the woman to trust her before she could press her for details. So far Adele just listened while Grace seemed to be talking to no one in particular. When Grace had gone to the bathroom, Mary motioned Adele to her side of the room and whispered that it was as if the floodgates had been opened ever since she appeared. "She talks all the time," Mary said. "Some of it makes sense, but not much."

Instead of wishing she were with her friends at the lake, Adele now tried to get to the nursing home as often as possible so as not to miss something Grace would reveal. There was something about this woman that kept Adele awake at night, eager to find out more.

Grace scowled. "Of course, he was her brother. There just weren't many options in the mountains to satisfy what the body yearned."

Adele was an only child, but even if she weren't, she couldn't imagine a brother doing to her what he was doing to Grace's aunt. It took some time for Adele to collect herself before she said, "So, uh, did he leave after Thanksgiving?"

Grace shook her head. "I ended up leaving for good before he did. But that was some time later." Her eyes then took on that far away expression that Adele was becoming familiar with, which meant Grace was going to shut down for now.

Adele's father wasn't due to pick her up from the nursing home for at least another hour and she didn't want the time spent sitting in silence. Cautiously, she asked, "So, did you and Jack Finley ever start dating? I mean, it must've been difficult living in such a remote place. So far away from everything and everyone."

Grace nodded and stared off. "I suppose. I was young, didn't know much about the way life worked, you know. I don't know what would've become of me if I hadn't gone to school. Kids finally forgot my past, or at least they didn't badger me about it, and school was a great escape for me."

"So did your uncle help at all with the chores?"

Grace huffed in anger. "He kept saying he had back problems, but you could've fooled me, the way he kept going after my aunt."

The image of what her aunt and uncle were often doing in the dark of night came back to her. As did the memory of how her aunt had been gaining weight, and then she recalled the day she got home from school and walked into the shanty to see her uncle come out of her aunt's bedroom, carrying something in a burlap sack. She thought she saw blood on it and heard what sounded like mewing. She was sure it was Snowball and screamed at him to put him down.

"Snowball's over there!" he shouted, motioning over to the pile of wood. Sure enough, Snowball was sprawled on top.

"What's that?" she pointed to the burlap bag.

"Nothing. Just mind your Ps and Qs." He carried the sack outside, with sounds of whimpering coming from inside it.

She ran over to the door and watched him go around the side of the shanty, grab a shovel, and go up the hill into the woods. It was late spring then, the ground soggy and soft.

Just then, Grace heard her name being called. It was her aunt. She went to her and saw that she was in bed, the covers over her. She was never in bed during the day. She looked doughy and sweaty.

"Get me a bunch of rags from the bag," her aunt mumbled.

"What happened?"

"Don't you fret 'bout it. Just do as I say."

She ran to the bag hanging under the sink, grabbed a bunch of rags—rags which were usually used to mop and clean—and brought them to her aunt. She didn't wait for Grace to leave but tossed the covers off and put those rags up between her legs. Grace gasped at the sight of the bloody blankets.

"Go on," she said. "I'll be okay." She tried to shoo Grace away but she just stood there gaping until her aunt threatened to use the switch on her, even though she didn't look like she had strength to do any such thing.

Later, after Uncle Henry came back, he went to check on his sister before lighting up his cigar and settling into the rocking chair without offering any sort of explanation. He said, "Supper'll be up to you. Your aunt needs to rest."

After they ate slabs of pork with bread, Grace sat at the table finding it impossible to concentrate on the arithmetic problems that Mrs. Lagree had given her for homework. She kept looking toward her aunt's room. She'd only been sick one other time that Grace remembered and that was with a hacking cough. There'd been no blood involved that time.

The following morning her aunt was awake and told Grace to get ready for school. It didn't take her much time to do so, and Grace was relieved to see her aunt up and about, even if she was moving a little slower.

"Aunt Gladys?" Grace said, as she stood by the door waiting for the bus, and hearing her uncle's snores coming from the cot. "What was Uncle Henry carrying in that bag?"

"I don't know what you're talking about." Her aunt pulled a chair out from the kitchen table and dropped down onto it, her eyes filling with tears.

"Yesterday when I came home, something was making sounds in a bag he was carrying. I thought it was Snowball—"

Sounding defeated and drained, her aunt replied, "It was nothing." She then mumbled, "God help us."

Just then her uncle sat up with a grunt at the same time that Grace saw the school bus approaching. She would need to stop with the questions and go outside.

Adele hadn't written a word for a while but stared off, thinking she might vomit. Had she heard correctly? She didn't know what to say, too stunned to speak. Grace had stopped speaking just then and pushed her wheelchair to her bed. Her whole body, looking to be not much more than skin and bones beneath her nightgown, trembled as she climbed under the sheets and lay down, her back to Adele, signaling she wasn't willing to say much else.

Adele looked at her watch, realizing her father must be waiting outside for her. She stood and one glance over at Mary's side of the room she realized by her horrified expression Mary had heard what she'd heard. She rushed by her without making eye contact and headed down the hall and out the front doors. As she thought, her father was sitting in his Toyota pickup waiting for her.

"How'd it go?"

She replied that it went fine but didn't say another word for the twenty-minute ride until they were almost home. Then she said, "Dad, do you know where Coyote Hill is?"

"Coyote Hill?" He looked to be thinking.

"When I asked Mr. Wilson, he had me look at a map but we couldn't find anything by that name on it in the area."

"That's where she's from, right?"

"I wish I could find it. I'd like to go and see what it looks like," Adele said.

"Probably overgrown by now if it's in the mountains. Doubtful anyone lives up there." Her father pulled the truck in the driveway and said, "Your mom's made lasagna for supper."

But Adele didn't have an appetite for lasagna or much else and told her mother she just wanted to go to bed, even though it was only six o'clock. As she walked up the stairs to her bedroom, she overheard her father say, "Something's got her shook up."

The following day, her mother drove her to the nursing home. She'd asked Adele how the interview was going. Adele felt the weight of what Grace had revealed but couldn't talk about it with her mother. Mr. Wilson had stressed to the students not to share their projects with anyone until he had a chance to grade them.

When Adele got to Grace's room, she wasn't there. Neither was Mary. She eventually found them, along with other guests, sitting in the solarium listening to a group of kids singing "Somewhere over the Rainbow." Mary was surrounded by some members of her family that Adele recognized from times she was interviewing Grace. She spotted Grace sitting in the back by herself. Adele walked over and stood next to her. Grace didn't seem to notice but was listening to the singing with all her attention. Once the kids were finished, Grace looked up at her.

"You're back," she announced without any inflection.

Adele nodded.

"I need a cigarette," Grace said, maneuvering her wheelchair to head outside. Adele followed her. Most everyone else stayed in the solarium to share in some refreshments with the kids.

Adele sat down on a bench nearby and watched as Grace lit her cigarette and took a pull on it before she said, "Grace, did you ever tell anyone what you saw your uncle do with that sack?"

Grace scowled, appearing to be confused, until she suddenly looked to have recalled what Adele meant. "How'd you know about that?"

"You told me. Yesterday. I was just wondering . . ."

Grace paused, finished her cigarette, and then said, "I couldn't wait to get to school to talk about it with Helen. We'd become best friends and she always liked to figure things out."

The school library, as small as it was, had copies of Nancy Drew books and Helen devoured them. But it turned out that Helen had other things on her mind that day. It was her birthday, and she could hardly contain her excitement. It wasn't until she'd started school that Grace found birthdays were a cause for celebration. Her aunt never made mention of them. For Helen, though, her birthday was a big deal. She kept bragging that she was no longer in the single digits. She had turned ten years old.

"What do you want for your birthday?" Jean asked while they were playing outside. It was a warm spring day and they were glad not to be in the stuffy gym for recess.

"A Shirley Temple doll," Helen said. "But Mom says they're hard to get now."

Grace didn't understand anything about birthdays or getting something you wanted on that special day, but if she did get something she wanted she knew what it would be. More than once, she'd overheard Jack talking to his friends about some singer who played the guitar "real good," Jack's tone admiring. Before she had a chance to give what she'd want a voice, the bell rang, and they had to go back inside where Mrs. Lagree instructed everyone to take out their McGuffey Readers and turn to page twenty-five. There'd been no opportunity to tell Helen what she'd witnessed, especially since Helen's mother picked her up early that day from school to go to Malone for a special birthday treat.

That night when she got home, Grace went through the door looking for her aunt.

"Don't bother her," Uncle Henry said. "She's still 'cuperatin'."

"But I have to ask her something."

"Well, ask me," he said.

"You wouldn't know," she replied.

"Give me a try."

Grace put her books on the table, then said, "I don't know when my birthday is."

"What brought this on?"

"It was Helen's birthday today. Mrs. Lagree had us all sing 'Happy Birthday' to her. She's my best friend and she's going to have cake and ice cream tonight. And she might even get a special doll."

He studied Grace for a moment. "The way I remember it, you were born sometime in the summer."

Snowball came running over to her, rubbing his body against her leg. She bent down to pet him, remembering the sounds coming from the burlap sack.

"Uncle Henry," she said, "what was in that bag yesterday?"

"You're a nosy little thing, aren't you?" he snapped. "Told you yesterday it was nothin'." Then before she could say anything else, he said, "So what would you want for your birthday? A doll, like your friend?"

She didn't have to think long about what she wanted. "No. A guitar."

Uncle Henry sputtered, "A guitar! You don't even know how to play."

"I could learn."

Just then, Aunt Gladys appeared in the doorway. She leaned against the wall and said, "Grace, could you go in the cellar and get me a chicken and some potatoes to fry up?"

She said, "Aunt Gladys, when's my birthday?"

Her aunt scowled, and stumbled over to the table, mumbling, "I don't have time for that nonsense." She dragged out a chair and collapsed onto it.

Sitting in the rocking chair, one he'd claimed for himself, Uncle Henry gazed at Grace. "Better get going on supper."

She grabbed the kerosene lantern from the shelf, lit it with a match, and went to the back of the shanty. Lifting the handle on the floorboard, she climbed down into the cellar where provisions were kept. The smell was a combination of mustiness and rot. Grace rarely went into the cellar and when she did, always found it creepy. She trembled as she put down the lantern and picked through the potatoes, putting several that didn't feel too soft in the bucket next to the bin. She then went over to where a plucked chicken was hanging by a rope from the low ceiling, and after managing to get it free, rested it on top of the potatoes. She couldn't carry both the bucket and lantern back up the ladder at the same time so she climbed up with what would be supper and then went back for the lantern. Once she got back up and closed the floorboard, she saw that Uncle Henry was rocking back and forth in the chair, a cigar pursed between his lips.

Aunt Gladys patted the table, motioning for her to bring the chicken and potatoes to her. "And get me a knife," she said. "Oh, and the cow needs milkin'."

Grace looked over at Uncle Henry who didn't budge before she headed out to the cowshed.

Sometime later, with fresh milk on the table, and some in a small bowl on the floor for Snowball, they were eating fried chicken and roasted potatoes. Aunt Gladys picked at her food and kept sighing. Grace's gut told her it wasn't a good idea to bother her aunt, but she just had to know when her birthday was. While Uncle Henry began licking his plate clean, she asked.

Aunt Gladys pushed herself away from the table. Grace thought she saw tears in her eyes. "Pity that I don't remember. Evelyn would've."

"Who's Evelyn?"

"That was your mother's name," Aunt Gladys said.

Evelyn? Grace couldn't wait to tell Helen she had a piece to the puzzle.

"Gladys, stop that sputtering," Uncle Henry said. "No use crying. What's done is done."

Aunt Gladys pulled on the sleeve of her dress and wiped her face. "I s'pose."

"Don't cry, Aunt Gladys," Grace said. "There's got to be a way to find out."

Her aunt looked over at her in a daze. "Find out what?"

"When my birthday is."

Aunt Gladys pushed herself away from the table. "I need to get more rest. Grace, you clean up and get to bed." She walked over to the bag under the sink, pulled out more rags and lumbered back to her room.

CHAPTER 5

Eventually, Aunt Gladys was back to being herself. At least that's how she appeared to Grace. The only difference now was how she and Uncle Henry would constantly bicker. Grace no longer heard him in her aunt's bedroom again, but she did catch how her aunt pushed him away when he'd sidle up behind her, trying to hug her. She'd tell him to get away and he'd get all nasty and say, "What's a man to do!"

"Go take care of yourself!" she'd yell back at him.

Meanwhile, Grace looked forward to leaving their squabbling behind and going to school. She was now in third grade. Her favorite subject was geography. She gaped in amazement at how big the world was. It was hard to imagine there was much beyond the distance from her shanty to school. She now had a new teacher by the name of Mrs. Tregette and she talked a lot about what was happening in Germany and Poland while mentioning some of the young men from the area who went off to fight in the war.

Claire, who was seated across from Grace, shot her hand up so that Mrs. Tregette would call on her, which she did.

Claire said, "My brother is in the army. Mom's sick with worry because he hasn't sent a letter in weeks."

Mrs. Tregette hesitated before saying, "I'm sure your brother is safe. It takes a long time to get mail in these parts." She then pointed to another place on the map and said, "This is Pearl Harbor. Almost two years ago it was attacked by the Japs and President Roosevelt said it was a day that will live in infamy. And does anyone know what this schoolhouse used to be?"

Grace recalled her aunt telling her and shot her hand up, causing Mrs. Tregette to look surprised. Grace rarely offered an answer; only when she was called upon.

"What do you think, Grace?"

"A place where soldiers stayed?" she asked, suddenly realizing her aunt could have been wrong since she seemed to be wrong about a lot of things—like saying Uncle Henry would be moving out soon, but "soon" never came. But Mrs. Tregette smiled and said that Grace was almost right. "It was a training center for the soldiers."

When it was time to learn about all forty-eight states, Grace became particularly interested in Oklahoma because she'd overheard Jack say that was where Gene Autry grew up. He paid no attention to her and the only way she figured she could get him to look her way was by playing guitar. Every once in a while, she'd mention to her aunt that she wanted one, but her response was always the same.

"What do you know about guitars?"

Her aunt was right. She knew little about guitars or music, other than when Mrs. Tregette would give the class some songs to sing to help instill in them an appreciation for how to carry a tune. Still, Grace would continue to beg, hoping to wear her aunt down while trying to figure out other ways to get Jack's attention.

Every morning when the bus pulled up to the school, she'd hurry off, checking to see if Jack was hanging around outside until the bell rang. Some days he was there, others not. It all depended on the help his parents needed on the farm she'd overheard him tell his friends. The days that he did show up, he smelled of hay and sweat. She didn't mind this aroma, and tried getting as close to him as possible to breathe him in. However, she didn't let anyone know how she felt about him. Not even Helen.

Several times Helen had invited Grace to her home, but there was no way to get back and forth from Helen's home to her place, so she had to turn down her invitations. When Helen suggested maybe *she* could get a ride from her mom to Grace's place, Grace said her aunt wouldn't like that. When Helen pressed her, asking why, she had to make up a lie and say that her aunt was always under the weather and didn't like having people over. In reality, Grace wasn't sure if her aunt would like Helen coming over or not, but they were poor as dirt and Grace didn't want anyone else to know. She supposed that was foolish since anyone could tell by the way her aunt dressed her that she wasn't too well off. Then again, nobody was too well off where she was from, but there was poor and then there was *poor*. They were *poor*. So *poor* the idea of getting a guitar was nothing more than a silly notion.

"But you must've eventually got one."

Grace turned, realizing she'd been talking the whole time to that nosy young girl, Adele. The very idea stunned her. It seemed ever since that girl appeared, Grace's memories were stirred and couldn't be settled. It was as though she was watching a movie and the character, Grace, was on the screen, someone distant from Grace the old woman in a nursing home. *Had she really been talking aloud?*

"I mean," Adele continued, "you said earlier that you played at bars. So . . ."

Grace looked around. They were sitting outside. She looked up to see that the sky was filled with dark clouds. She didn't recall when she'd left her room but was grateful that she had. Now she could have a smoke. Her hand shaking, she took out a match and tried several times before the cigarette was lit.

Tapping her pen on her notebook, Adele said, "Winters must've been tough for you."

"Not as tough as summers," Grace replied.

"Really? Why?"

"That's when there was no school. I wouldn't see Helen, Jack, or anybody for those months we were off. It felt like forever. Besides, my aunt made sure I helped as much as I could with the gardening, canning, and taking care of the livestock."

"I'm guessing your uncle was still around," Adele said. She looked through her notes, adding, "And the war was over when you were about twelve or thirteen." Just then a raindrop hit her arm.

"We'd better get inside," Adele said.

Grace hurriedly finished her cigarette and then let Adele push her wheelchair into the solarium. She muttered, "Funny but I don't recall too much about what was going on outside my little world. I guess people were celebrating the war's end, but for me . . ."

"For *you*, what?" Adele said.

"I'm tired," Grace said. "I need to take a nap."

Adele blurted, "But I have so many more questions!"

"They'll have to wait," Grace said, starting to wheel herself down the hall, her slipper falling off her left foot.

"I'll get it," Adele said, bending down.

Grace protested while Adele began to put the slipper back on her foot, a foot missing a few toes, but not before she saw the shock on the young girl's face.

Sounding as though she were gagging, Adele sputtered, "What happened?"

"Just give it to me!" Grace snapped, reaching for the slipper, before hurriedly rolling away.

Grace entered her room, passing Mary who was in her bed, snoring. With some effort, Grace climbed into her bed and pulled the covers over herself. She hoped to sleep but her thoughts ran rampant.

By the time she was twelve, Grace was in sixth grade and once again had a new teacher. Meanwhile, her Uncle Henry wasn't too helpful around the place, and it appeared he had no intention of leaving. Any hope she had, which she'd kept to herself, of him going off to war was now over since Hitler had been defeated. So Grace and her aunt ran things while he'd sit in that damn rocker and watch as they butchered chickens and hogs, cleaned the cowshed and planted and weeded the vegetable garden. But he was always the first one at the supper table, a fork in his hand.

Around that time, she began to notice that he was eyeing her more than her aunt. By then, her breasts were filling out and she, too, had to take rags from the bag each month due to the blood that spilled out of her privates. During the school year, when it was that time of the month, she'd just stay home for a couple of days till the flow stopped. She had to justify her absence to Mrs. Smith, her sixth-grade teacher, and after she told her the first time why she couldn't go to school—she must've turned several shades of red—Mrs. Smith never called her absence into question again. She seemed to know. In fact, she seemed to know all the girls' times of the month, and no one got into trouble because of it. The boys often complained that it wasn't fair and once they found out why the girls weren't in class, they would tease them something awful when they returned.

Grace didn't like thinking about those times and eventually drifted off to sleep.

"So, how did you eventually learn to play the guitar?"

Grace looked up from her bed to see Adele sitting in the chair next to it. She saw from the window that the sun was shining. It must've been a new day. Then again, each day flowed into the next.

"I mean, it sounds like you didn't really have any access to music."

"Came across a Victrola," Grace replied.

"A vic . . . ?"

"Victrola."

"What's that?"

Grace looked at Adele and sniffed. "It played seventy-eights."

Adele looked confused.

"Records."

"But you didn't have electricity."

Grace sputtered, "Didn't need any. You just cranked it up."

"Oh," Adele replied, scratching on her notepad, muttering, "Research Victrola. So, did your aunt buy it for you finally?"

"Nope. It belonged to my mama."

Adele jerked her head up, her mouth dropped open. "So, how did you get the Victrola?" She waited for a reply while Grace gazed out the window.

One day she and Helen were playing outside during recess, when Helen asked if she had ever been back to her place, the place where she was born. Grace shook her head.

"Mom said she tried to be neighborly with your mom," Helen said. "My mom said your mom was no more than a kid herself when she was gonna have you. Your father did odd jobs to get by."

It startled Grace to hear Helen refer to her mother and father who were no more than strangers to her, making her more curious about where she'd once lived. "I don't remember any of it," she said.

"Oh, you wouldn't. Dad said he found you on the kitchen floor with a full diaper next to your mama. You were holding her hair. It was bloody."

"What do you mean?"

"Dad heard the gunshots, but just figured it was a hunter. But when he was out in the field, he heard howling. That was you. He said he was worried because it didn't sound like a regular baby cry. He found your mother on the floor in the kitchen and your dad out back. It was awful. He says he still has nightmares from what he saw. That poor little baby sobbing broke his heart." Helen paused before saying, "Sorry. I keep forgetting that baby was you."

Grace tried to absorb what she was being told, starting to believe Helen's story and not her aunt's. "I wonder what it looks like," Grace said.

"What?"

"The house. And I wonder who lives there now."

"Nobody lives there. It's all overgrown. Daddy said he can't imagine anyone wanting anything to do with it."

"I'd really like to see it," Grace said, "but my aunt would never take me there. She doesn't even like talking about my mother."

"I have an idea," Helen said.

That night, Grace told her aunt that Helen had invited her for a sleepover later that week. In a rush, before her aunt could say no, she added, "And it would be on a school night so you wouldn't have to get me there or anything."

"How would I do such a thing, anyway?" Aunt Gladys said.

"I don't know," Grace muttered.

Uncle Henry shouted, "What you got to do that for? Don't you see enough of your friends in school?"

When she thought her aunt might agree with him, Grace sputtered, "But we have a big spelling test coming up and it helps to have someone to study with."

After a long sigh, barely heard above Uncle Henry's protests, Aunt Gladys said, "I suppose, but don't make a habit of it."

All Grace could think about was the farmhouse where her mama was killed. During recess, she and Helen made plans for how they would get to it. Grace never thought Thursday would come.

Finally, when Thursday morning did come, Helen climbed onto the bus and ran down the aisle to where Grace was sitting. As she came closer, her friend gave her an odd look. "Where's your overnight bag?" Helen asked.

It hadn't occurred to Grace to bring an overnight bag with some spare clothes or pajamas. She sat there red-faced, certain she had messed things up, until Helen said, "That's okay. You can borrow a pair of my pajamas. You'll just have to wear the same clothes to school tomorrow."

Neither she nor Helen said as much, but Grace often wore the same clothes throughout the week since she didn't have much from which to choose. Her mind, though, was far from what she'd be wearing. All she kept thinking about was the house, and even got scolded a couple of times by Mrs. Smith when she wasn't paying attention. Finally, afternoon came, and class was dismissed.

As the bus rumbled along, Helen had Grace sit near the window, ready to point out where the infamous house was located. "You can't see it from the road," Helen said, "but it's right across from our field, over there."

Grace couldn't see a thing beyond the trees and overgrowth, frustrated that the bus driver was going too fast. Finally, the bus came to a stop.

"Come on!" Helen said.

Instead of watching Helen get off the bus along with her brother, Edwin, as she normally did, Grace jumped up from the seat and followed her. Edwin kept looking at Grace with a scowl but then took off like a shot up the long driveway toward the house, which rested on a hill.

"It's over there," Helen said, pointing across the field. Most of the snow had melted but there were still patches of it here and there. "But don't say anything about it in front of my mother. She probably wouldn't let us go if she knew."

There were milk and cookies waiting for them once they walked through the door. Grace was surprised to see that the kitchen alone was the size of her entire shanty. It was bright and cheerful, the aroma welcoming. Helen's mother used a soft, kind tone when she spoke to Grace. When Helen mentioned how Grace hadn't brought any pajamas, her mother clicked her tongue and muttered that her aunt should know better than to send her overnight without being prepared. But then she added, "No worries. You can borrow something from Helen."

Helen had twin brothers who were too young to go to school. They studied Grace the whole time while they all sat around the table having an afternoon snack, and she didn't know what to say to them. All she could think about was heading across the field to see where she had once lived as a baby.

After she took a final gulp of milk, Helen asked her mother if they could go out to the barn. "I want Grace to meet Molly."

"Okay, but don't get too close to her," her mother said.

They ran out the front door with Edwin following behind. "Eddie!" Helen said, "Leave us alone."

"Edwin," Helen's mother called, "you get back here and do your homework."

"Come on," Helen said to Grace, as she broke into a run toward the barn.

"Who's Molly?" Grace called, quickly following Helen.

"Our workhorse. We're not gonna really see her. Just follow me."

They ran behind the barn and cut across some fields, eventually wading through slush, tall grass, and then a small stand of trees. Their overboots squished as they pushed forward. Grace noticed a cabin in the distance. "That it?" she called, hoping it wasn't, since it didn't look nearly as big as Helen's farmhouse.

"Yup," Helen said, coming to a stop, but Grace kept going, wading through the brush and bramble. The grass and weeds were so tall that they almost went past her shoulders.

"Maybe we shouldn't go any further," Helen said. "Daddy says he thinks it's haunted."

Grace looked back at Helen. "Really? Like maybe my parents' spirits still live there?"

Helen stared at her wide-eyed. "Maybe we should go back. Mom might be getting—"

Grace paid her little attention. She hadn't lied to her aunt just to turn around now. She pushed back some more brambles until she got a better view. The house, if one could call it that, had a front open porch that slanted and a screen door that was tilted, hanging from its hinges. She pushed further and trudged through more grass, walking up two rickety steps onto the porch. Some slats were missing so she had to be careful where she stepped.

"Grace!" Helen squealed.

Grace went to the door, turned the knob, but it was stuck.

"I thought you just wanted to see it," Helen shouted, reaching the steps. "From the outside. I don't think we should go in."

"I can't believe this is where I once lived," Grace said. She touched the outside wall which was made of logs.

"I'm sure it was nicer then," Helen said.

Grace scrambled over to a window. She tried to peer in, but it was so dirty that it was impossible to see much of anything. She banged on the sash in an attempt to loosen it, but it wouldn't budge.

"Come on, let's go," Helen said. "We'll come back another time."

Another time? There was no guarantee that her aunt would let her sleep over again, so she wasn't going to waste this opportunity. She leapt off the porch and ran around to the back of the shanty in search of another door. She found one and turned the knob. The door squeaked and rubbed against the rough wood floor, but it opened enough so that she could see in. She stood there, gazing from the outside. Then she took a hesitant step inside, and said tentatively, "Hello?"

Helen appeared from behind. "Grace!"

Grace jumped and snapped, "Don't do that!"

Helen's voice quavered. "I didn't know you'd want to go inside. My dad'll kill me."

Grace turned and looked at Helen. "I don't recognize it."

"You were a baby."

She stepped further in; the walls were made of rough-hewn logs. There was a wood-burning stove and a sink with a hand pump. She wondered if the well still had water. There was also a small wooden table with four chairs. To one side, there was a metal chest of sorts, and she opened its door. "What's this?" she said aloud.

"That's an ice box," Helen said. "Don't you have one at your aunt's?"

She shook her head. They had a cellar that stayed cool year round, keeping their jarred vegetables and meat from spoiling.

She noticed a highchair in the corner. "I wish I knew what happened," she said.

"I told you," Helen replied.

"No, I mean before . . . before they . . . died."

There were shelves with some jarred vegetables covered in dust and dirt. Had her mother put the beans and carrots in those glass jars the way she and her aunt did every fall? On another shelf were some kerosene lamps.

"I guess they never got 'lectricty here," Helen said, trailing behind Grace who was making her way into an adjoining room. Inside, there was a beat-up couch and a rocking chair. Grace walked over and gave it a slight push, watching as it rocked back and forth on the pine wood floor. She took a deep breath, imagining her mother rocking her to sleep in it.

"Wow," Helen said, walking over to a corner. "My grandmother had one of these."

Grace looked over. "What is it?"

"It plays music." Helen opened a bottom cabinet and exclaimed, "And look at all these records!"

Grace crouched down. *There they were, her mother and father, dancing to the music while she sat on the floor clapping her hands.* At least that was what she imagined.

Are you lonesome tonight? When I kissed you and called you sweetheart . . .

Grace looked up to see that Helen was cranking a side handle, which was causing music to pour out. "This is wacky," Helen said.

Grace reached into the cabinet and took out the top record and read *Rye Whiskey* by Montana Slim. She pulled out another, *Break the News to Mother* by Shannon Four. She pulled out more, and held them in her arms.

"What're you doing?"

Grace stood there holding the records, realizing she couldn't bring them back home or she'd have to explain to her aunt how she got them.

"It's getting dark," Helen said. "We have to get back to my house."

Grace wanted to stay, but she didn't want to get Helen in trouble. She put the records back into the cabinet and shut it carefully. As they left, Grace pulled the back door shut as tightly as she could, hoping no one would discover the treasure inside.

All these years later, while she lay in bed in that nursing home, she couldn't help but think that day had changed the direction of her life. Some for the good, some not so good. She didn't like thinking about the not so good and soon drifted off.

Adele looked at her notes. It was as if Grace had been talking to herself, unaware that Adele was even in the room. But now she was lightly snoring. Some of the information she'd given her would make a good article, though much of it would have to be ditched. But when Adele had told Mr. Wilson as much the last time she was in class, he said not to discourage the old woman from talking. So she hadn't.

She stood up, pulled the cover over Grace's frail frame, and started to walk out of the room when Mary whispered, "Your coming here seems to have unsettled her somethin' awful."

Adele nodded, thinking the more Grace talked, the weaker she seemed to get, but there were still so many questions that required answers.

"See you tomorrow," Adele whispered and walked out. Grace's story had intrigued her and she was eager to hear more. She also wanted to see if she could find the property where

Grace had lived as a baby. The thing is, there was very little time left to investigate since the assignment would be due in a couple of weeks. She knew her friends had gone to Chateaugay Lake to swim that day, but she no longer cared.

CHAPTER 6

It had occurred to Grace that she would have to play hooky from school to visit the cabin again, though she'd also have to take the school bus to reach it. So after planning it out with Helen, she hid in the back of the bus once it got to school, waiting for Mr. Prevo to park. Once he got off, and she peeked out the window to see him walk over to McCann's Garage, she dashed out. She wouldn't be able to cross the fields from Helen's property for fear someone would catch her, so she took the main road where Helen had first pointed from so many months ago.

It was officially springtime, but there were still piles of snow here and there, the ground muddy. She'd worn her overboots with that in mind. Unlike approaching the cabin from the field, going toward it from the road wasn't quite as difficult, even though there wasn't a defined path, as far as she could tell. The tree limbs were still naked, allowing her to see the cabin through a clearing, the tall grass she'd waded through behind her.

Once she reached the cabin, she made her way around to the backdoor and pulled it open. Immediately, she ran to make sure that the Victrola was still there—it was—before she did more exploring. There were bird droppings on the roughhewn floorboards and feathers here and there, but as far as she could tell, no living creature was in the house. She stood in the middle of the small room just off the kitchen and tried to glean something to help her remember what had happened. She'd been very young but had no idea just how young. She had been surrounded by death, and this left her to wonder why she'd been spared.

She noticed a closed door in the corner of the living room. She hadn't seen it before. She went over and opened it to see a narrow stairway leading to a second level. Even though she didn't weigh very much, the steps groaned and creaked as she hesitantly took them up to the next level. When she reached the top, she saw a room to the left and one to the right. She was drawn to the room on the right. The sight of a crib made her gasp. *Her crib.* There were cobwebs woven around the slats. The room was nothing more than a square box; but there was a tiny window which allowed in a small stream of light that shined on something poking out from beneath the crib. She bent down and picked up a crocheted item, giving off a musty odor. There was one button for an eye. She assumed it had been a teddy bear. As dirty as it was, she still hugged it, hoping to conjure a memory. She wanted to take it home with her but wouldn't be able to get it past her aunt without raising suspicion. She placed it in the crib. There was little else in this room, so she went across the hall into the other room. She stopped and stared at an iron-frame bed, and a moth-eaten blanket on top of a mattress. There was a small stand next to it with an alarm clock. The time on it was twenty minutes after four. Learning how to tell time was something she'd been taught in school, a couple of grades earlier. She suddenly panicked, thinking she'd missed the bus home, until she realized time had stopped on that clock many years ago.

There was a dresser, the drawers partially opened. She looked into the top drawer, growing queasy to see men's handkerchiefs, a pocketknife, and a worn pair of suspenders, all belonging to the man who murdered her mother. She didn't want to touch any of it and shoved the drawer shut. Kids at school occasionally reminded her of what had happened, often looking at her as if she were the devil himself, as if she had some part in the horror.

She opened the drawer below, which held a lace dress, musty and moth eaten with age. She pulled it out, clutching it close to her, as she crumpled onto the floor. The realization that she'd been robbed of having what could have been a normal family, a family like Helen's, made her sob. Oh, how she longed to know more about her mother. Why wouldn't her aunt tell her about her own sister?

After a good cry, Grace got up and carefully put the dress back into the drawer and closed it. There was one more drawer. She had to tug on it before it finally opened. All that was inside were some yellowed papers. She leafed through them, coming across one folded in quarters. She unfolded it to see the words "Certificate of Birth" with her name, "Grace Erma Dormand." She studied it. Ernest Arthur Dormand was listed as her father. Her mother's name was Evelyn Frances Cooke. Then Grace saw the date she was born July 7, 1933. She had a birthday! Her place of birth was listed as Churubusco, New York. She then looked at the other paper. It was a baptism certificate. She'd been baptized on July 16, 1933, at St. Philomena by Father Landry. She did the math in her head. She was almost thirteen! She took the paper downstairs and put it in her burlap bag next to her sandwich that she now had no desire to eat.

She then went over to the Victrola. Recalling how Helen had made it work, she cranked the handle and then dropped the arm on the spinning record. Soon, a loud frantic squeaking sound filled the room, stunning her, and she hurriedly pulled the arm, scratching it across the record, her heart pounding. With the room silent again, she sat down onto the floor and began going through the records that were in the cabinet, searching for one in particular. There was The Dixie String Band, Harry Brady, Paul Whiteman and His Ambassador Orchestra, Golden and Hughes, and some others whose names she struggled to read. However, when she came across Gene Autry, she hooted in excitement! As far as she was concerned, she'd been given the best gift ever. The name of the song was "Black Bottom Blues." She took off the other record and put on Autry's. Her hand shook as she rested the needle on it. Grace stared at the Victrola while the singing filled the room:

If you go down in Black Bottom

Put your money in your shoes

The women in Black Bottom

Got them Black Bottom Blues.

Oh, good mama, your daddy's got them black bottom blues.

Grace listened to it over and over, even trying to mimic the yodeling before it dawned on her that the day was going by way too fast and she needed to get back to the school and sneak onto the bus without being spotted. She gently closed the cover to the Victrola, buttoned up her coat, and headed out the back door, wishing she had a key to lock out any possible intruders. As far as she was concerned, that cabin was filled with gold.

It started to rain so she tucked the burlap bag beneath her coat so her birth certificate wouldn't get wet. She slogged through the mud, reached the road, and got to school just as Mr. Prevo pulled the bus to the front. Grace hid around the side of the building, as the rain poured down. Then as quietly as she

could, stomped as much mud off her boots as she could until the
kids came barreling down the steps, some going to bus number
one or three while those on her route went to bus number two.
She got in line behind one of the eighth graders who was a head
taller than she was and snuck up the steps behind him to the
bus, as rainwater dripped from her. Helen was already on the
bus and called to her.

"You're soaked!" Helen said once she reached her.

Grace tried to dry herself off but was more concerned about
the burlap sack.

"How was it?" Helen said, shifting over to give Grace a seat.

"Amazing!" Grace said. "I found my birth certificate."

"Really?" Helen said. "Do you have it?"

Grace nodded. "I don't want to get it wet though." She patted her coat, indicating the precious document was underneath.

"Wow! Are you gonna show your aunt?"

"No way. She'd kill me if she knew where I went."

"Oh, yeah."

She told Helen what she'd done at the cabin until the bus
reached Helen's stop. For the rest of the ride, she kept thinking
about all that she'd discovered, wishing she could talk to her
aunt about it. Before long, the bus pulled up to her shanty. She
climbed out, still dripping wet and hurried inside.

"What in heaven's name?" her aunt exclaimed.

"Sorry," Grace said, rushing toward her room.

"You're goin' ta get your death of cold!" her aunt said.
"What is wrong with that school?"

"I'd send them a note, if I was you," Uncle Henry said. "If
she gets sick, sue 'em."

"It's not their fault," Grace replied. "It started raining before
the bus came." She pulled the blanket over, a makeshift curtain
for her privacy, and shrugged off her coat. She took the burlap
sack and shoved it beneath her mattress, then slipped out of her

wet clothes, draping them over a bench in her space, and put on dry ones. When she came back out into the kitchen, Uncle Henry stared at her, as if trying to glean the truth from her. She did her best to ignore him and headed out to milk the cow, the rain not having let up. This time, getting drenched, though, didn't seem to be a problem for her aunt or uncle.

With her notebook in her hand, Adele ran into the school an hour before her summer class was to begin and headed to the library. Once she was settled in front of a computer, she began her research by copying the names, Ernest Arthur Dormand and Evelyn Francis Cooke, into the database. It took several minutes but she finally found an article from the *Malone Telegram* dated November 12, 1934; the print was tiny, but she leaned in and began reading.

> ### Local Farmer Makes Grisly Discovery
>
> *Lionel Poupore discovered the murdered bodies of his neighbors adjacent to his Churubusco property. After hearing a baby's howls coming from Ernest Dormand's place, Poupore knew something was amiss and soon found the neighbors' hysterical infant daughter sitting on the kitchen floor, its fingers wrapped around the bloody hair of its mother, Evelyn Dormand nee Cooke.*
>
> *"I tried to make sense of what I saw," Poupore stated. "That's when I noticed the back door was opened and Ernie's body slumped near it."*
>
> *After Poupore brought the baby to his wife to watch, he went to get Sheriff Sears.*
>
> *"From all accounts," Sears said, "it looks like Dormand murdered his wife and then took his own life."*

Adele scanned the database and found other articles about the murder-suicide with neighbors claiming that Ernest "was an oddball" or "he couldn't hold down a job" or "he had bad blood." Another article stated that the baby was being cared for by a relative without saying who.

"Grace," Adele muttered. She printed out the articles to have them go with her report. With only a few days left before her assignment was due, she wanted to have something more conclusive to guarantee that A she wanted. If she admitted it to herself, though, getting a good grade was becoming less important to her as was just finding out how Grace ended up in the nursing home without ever having any visitors, unlike her roommate, Mary, who always had family or friends stopping by. Besides, she was eager to hear how Grace ended up marrying Jack Finley but then leaving him. She scooped up her materials and headed to class.

CHAPTER 7

Jack Finley wasn't in school for the next couple of days, which frustrated Grace, and then she had to miss school due to her time of the month, so it wasn't until about a week later that she saw him and was able to implement the plan she'd been working on.

It was a warm April day, so the students were allowed outside for recess. Unlike when they were younger, and the boys played tag and the girls jumped rope while sounds of laughter filled the playground, they now tended to mingle and gossip, the girls filling out into young women as the boys' voices became deeper. Grace would be going into eighth grade next fall while Jack would be going into ninth.

At first, her attempt to get Jack's attention failed, but she refused to give up and got closer and closer to where he was without it being too obvious. She started singing and it wasn't until she was in the middle of the second stanza when she noticed he was studying her. She pretended not to see him.

"If you go down in Black Bottom, just to have a little fun, have your sixteen dollars ready when that police wagon comes," she sang.

"How you know that song?"

Her mouth went dry. Her plan worked! She forced herself to act nonchalant and replied, "Who doesn't know Gene Autry?"

Just then the bell rang. Recess was over. Jack turned and ran up the steps into the school, and that was the extent of Grace's conversation with him. But she was determined there'd be more.

"Want me to ask him if he likes you?" Helen whispered in Grace's ear the next day after Grace finally confessed about the crush she had.

"No!" Grace said, afraid of what his answer might be. She wanted him to be attracted to her first, or think he was. And the way to do it, she believed, was through music, which meant she needed to get back to the cabin where the Victrola was to learn more songs.

The next day, she and Helen were sitting on the school's front steps during recess, trying to figure out how Grace could get back to her cabin. Cutting school was risky since the new requirement from the principal made it clear that the students needed a note from their parents as to why they missed any days. And then once school was over for the summer, the ways of getting to the house dwindled even more.

"You need a bicycle," Claire said. She was standing nearby, eager to be a part of Helen and Grace's clique. As they got older, it was becoming obvious that due to their figures and pretty faces, Grace and Helen were the most popular girls in their class. Conversely, Claire had mousy brown hair and a flat chest, so the boys just thought of her as one of them, if they thought of her at all.

"A bicycle?" Grace said, gazing over at Claire. "Why would I need a bi—?"

"You can have mine," she said.

Helen and Grace exchanged glances. "She needs a guitar, Claire," Helen said, rolling her eyes.

"But she said she wants to get back to the cabin and has no way to do it. I have a bicycle."

Suddenly, Claire had Grace's interest. "I don't have any money."

Claire shrugged. "It's free. I never use it. It was my older brother's. When he came back from the war, he said he didn't want it. He's too busy with his sawmill."

Now that the war was over, there seemed to be so many changes in people's lives, except for Grace's.

"It's kinda rusty, but still works," Claire added.

Even though Claire said it was free, Grace was sure it would cost her something. Quite likely, accepting the gift would mean Claire came with the deal, but Grace was willing to risk it since it might mean getting where she needed to be.

"Thank you," Grace said. "But where do you live?"

"In town."

"In town" meant just up the road. The town proper included a square block with McCann's Garage, St. Philomena's Catholic Church, the post office, Humphrey's grocery store, LeClair's Diner and the Summit Hotel, which was also a tavern. There were houses sprinkled in between the businesses.

"Maybe we could get it during recess tomorrow. It won't take too long."

The next day, Mr. Prevo helped Grace carry the rickety bike onto the school bus and then off the bus when he was dropping her back at the shanty. Uncle Henry was sitting outside on a stump eyeing the whole thing. He got up and approached her and the bus driver.

"Whatcha got there?"

"My friend gave it to me," Grace said. "Her brother doesn't want it anymore."

Mr. Prevo chuckled. "Can't blame him. Seems to be ready for the trash heap."

Uncle Henry drew closer to the bus. "What I wanna know is do you always make the kids wait out in the rain before they get on the bus?"

Mr. Prevo had a look of confusion.

"You're lucky we didn't sue. She could've gotten her death a cold."

"Come on, Uncle Henry," Grace said, panic in her voice. "Let's go show Aunt Gladys."

"Quiet down," he snapped at her.

Mr. Prevo climbed back onto the bus and called out, "Can't say I know what you're talkin' about."

"You're full a shit!" Uncle Henry shouted. "You didn't see how soaking wet she was the other day—"

Grace shouted, "Uncle Henry, that wasn't his fault!"

"Henry, what's going on?" Aunt Gladys had suddenly appeared.

"Look!" Grace shouted, rushing the bike over to her aunt in an attempt of keeping her from getting closer to the brewing situation. "Claire gave this to me."

"What in heaven's . . .?"

Thankfully, Aunt Gladys was more distracted by what Grace was rolling toward her than the verbal exchange going on between the bus driver and her brother.

"You said she *gave* it to you?"

Grace nodded, relieved to see that Mr. Prevo had closed the door and was driving off.

Uncle Henry came up alongside her. "He acted like he didn't know what the hell I was talkin' about."

"I . . . I . . . have to learn how to ride it. But I think I can do it," Grace said, attempting to redirect the conversation. It worked, since Uncle Henry said, "Where you plan on riding that thing, anyway?"

"I was thinking on the nice days I could ride it to school," Grace said.

"To school!" Aunt Gladys bellowed. "You'll have to get up at the crack a dawn to get there on time."

While Uncle Henry studied her, Grace pushed the bike over to the side of the shanty, leaning it there while she brought her knapsack inside. Moments later, she returned, ready to go about the business of learning to ride the bike and pushing it out onto the road.

"You'd better do your chores before doing that foolishness," Uncle Henry said.

"Why don't *you* do some chores around here?" Grace snapped.

Uncle Henry stomped over to her and sputtered, "Think you're getting too big to be spanked? I'll take you over my knee if you don't shut the hell up."

Grace gazed up at him, suddenly fearing him and what he might do. She brought the bike back to the shanty and went to do her chores. Once the cow was milked, the gutter clean, and chickens fed, dusk had already settled, but she brought her bike out to the road anyway. Eventually, her shins scraped and bleeding, she pedaled a half mile or so on the back road, learning to avoid the ruts, without falling once. She headed back home in the dark with a feeling of accomplishment. Now she had the means to get to where she needed. And when school was out for summer recess in a couple of months, she figured she'd have a lot more opportunities to do so.

CHAPTER 8

The following morning, she got up early, just as the sun was rising, well before her uncle usually got up, and rode her bike to school. Her breasts hurt as she rumbled along the rutted path down to the main road, using one hand for support in an attempt to prevent them from bouncing, while keeping the other hand on the handlebar where she'd fastened her knapsack. Helen had told her that she'd need a brassiere and showed Grace hers, but Grace had no idea how to get one. She wanted to ask her aunt but couldn't seem to get her alone without her uncle being nearby. Lately, the way he looked at her made her feel uncomfortable; something told her talking about breasts within his earshot would not be a good idea.

She rolled into the schoolyard before any of the buses arrived, but Claire, who walked to school, was already there on the swing. She jumped off once she spotted Grace.

"You like the bicycle?"

Grace nodded and thanked her again. "The chain came off a couple times, but I figured out how to put it back on."

"Maybe you can come to my house sometime now and we can play games or somethin'."

"Maybe," Grace said, pushing the bicycle to the side of the building and resting it there.

"Wanna play Simon Says?"

"Now?" Grace said, untying her knapsack from the handlebar. "I mean, aren't we getting kind of old for games like that?"

Claire shrugged, looking disappointed.

Not wanting to be unappreciative, Grace said, "Okay, but I gotta catch my breath first," which was true. Moments later, she said, "Okay, you can be Simon," but to her relief, one of the buses was heading toward the school. "Why don't we wait to see if anyone else wants to play?"

Claire scrunched up her nose and said, "I guess."

But once the bus door opened and the kids spilled out, the idea of playing Simon Says was forgotten. At least by Grace.

"Hey!" Helen called out as she ran over. "How'd you get here?"

Grace smiled. "I took my bicycle."

"Gee, maybe I should've kept it for myself," Claire said.

Grace whirled around, her eyes wide. "Why?"

"I don't know. I didn't realize it would be so much fun riding it."

"Oh, come on," Helen said, "don't be an Indian giver."

Grace blurted hurriedly, "But how will I get to your house in the summer so we can play games?"

Claire's face lit up. "Oh! True! When do you think you can come?"

"I'll have to get permission from my aunt," she said. "And then I'll let you know."

Before long it was the last day of school. Five students wouldn't be coming back in the fall; two girls because they planned to get married that summer and three boys who were needed to work on their families' farms. Grace was relieved to learn that Jack wasn't one of those boys. As excited as she was to have the means to get to her old house, summer recess meant not seeing Jack Finley for a couple of months. If only she had a guitar, she'd use that time to practice.

While the kids were whooping and hollering on the buses, Grace jumped on her bike with her report card tucked in her knapsack. She'd passed all her subjects and would be moving up in the fall but was more excited about heading toward her cabin. That's how she considered her first home: *her* cabin. She hadn't told her aunt that school would be let out early on the last day; that way she'd be able to go to her cabin without being questioned for getting home late.

"What're you gonna do there?" Helen said before climbing the steps onto the bus.

"I want to fix it up, clean the windows and stuff," she said. "And learn more of those songs!"

Helen laughed. "You should learn some new songs. Those records are pretty old."

Grace had little idea how to get her hands on new records, but was just as content to memorize the songs she imagined her mother having listened to. Grace fantasized that the small cabin had been a happy place filled with music . . . until that last day.

Mr. Prevo told Helen she'd better get on the bus or he'd be leaving without her. She called over to Grace, "I'll see you later!"

Grace waved goodbye, then started pedaling.

"Did you pass?"

She almost fell off the bike, stunned to hear Jack speaking to her. She came to a quick stop; he hadn't gotten on his bus. "Yeah, you?"

"Yup." He hesitated before saying, "So, where you off to?"

"Up the road a bit," she replied. "To my cabin. Where I was born."

"Really?" he said. "That safe to do?"

"Sure, why?"

"It's just I hope your bike holds up," he said, and started walking on Looby Road toward his farm.

She shrugged. "It better. It's all I got."

Jack stopped, turned, and shaded his eyes from the sun to see her better. "I heard you have a record player and lots of records."

Grace figured Helen had told him. She nodded, watching Jack scuff a foot, cough, and mumble something.

She blurted, "Wanna come and see it?"

"Can't. I gotta get home and help my pa."

"Don't you take the bus?"

"Sometimes, but it's a nice day and I thought I'd walk instead. It's not far."

She pushed her bike closer toward him, her heart pounding, wishing she wasn't all tongue-tied.

"Maybe some other time," he said, waving, then breaking into a run.

She wanted to ask when, but he was already too far away. Still, he had said *maybe*, and at that she rode off grinning.

Soon, she was pushing her bike along the rutted path, her legs getting scratched by the overgrown bramble, as she tried to avoid ripping her dress, the cotton material thin and worn. Once she got to the cabin, she dropped the bike on the ground and made her way around back while still thinking about Jack Finley. She'd gotten his attention!

Moments later, she cranked up the Victrola. While music filled the small space, she started straightening up. Now that Jack might be coming over, she was more determined to fix up the cabin. First, even though it was a struggle, she managed to get the front door opened. She would need to somehow fix the screen door, but for now she left the entranceway ajar to help air out the place. She then found a beat-up broom in the corner and swept while she learned the words to some of the songs pouring into the room. She recalled the time a few years ago when Mrs. Lagree had told her that she had a nice singing voice when the class had to learn the words to "Billy Boy." She only wished that Jack had been in her class and had heard the compliment.

Once the floors were swept, she decided to clean the small squares of glass that served as windows. There was a wash pan hanging on the kitchen wall. She took it down and went over to the water pump and started pumping with all her might. Finally, a small stream dribbled out, along with some rust, before more water started to flow. It was clear and cold, and after she splashed some on to her sweaty face, Grace had to use her dress to dry herself off. By then, she figured it was time to head back to her aunt's shanty.

Just as she was closing the back door, a "Hellooo!" startled Grace. She went around to the front of the cabin to see her friend standing on the rickety porch steps.

"Helen! What're you doing here?"

Helen whirled around and said, "I told you I'd see you later."

"I didn't know you meant today!" Grace ran over and gave her a welcoming hug. "Will your mom be mad?"

"I didn't tell her. She thinks I'm playing out in the barn." She peered into the window, squinting. "Wow, you got a lot of work to do here, huh?"

Grace shrugged. "I swept and I was gonna clean the windows, but I don't have anything to clean them with. And I want to fix that door." She motioned to the screen door off the porch. "I couldn't find any nails or a hammer."

"You're going to need a lot of stuff to fix up this place."

She agreed. "But I was just about ready to leave. It takes a while to get back to my aunt's."

"Will you be coming back tomorrow?"

"I'm gonna try and be here as many days as possible without raisin' my aunt's suspicion."

"Okay, if I don't have to watch my brothers, I'll try and come to help you. It'll be like our secret fort for girls!"

Grace laughed, and then said, "But Jack told me today that he'd like to come hear the records sometime."

Helen's mouth dropped open. "He did? He talked to you? Wow! Okay, then, it won't be just for girls."

Grace couldn't help but agree.

"I'll try to come tomorrow with some stuff to help fix things," Helen said. "This'll be so much fun."

Grace jumped on the rickety bike and said, "I just have to come up with some story to tell my aunt where I'll be."

"Say you're coming to my place!" Helen called as she ran through the woods to get to her property.

Later that night, while they were eating supper, Uncle Henry said, "You can bet your aunt is glad you don't be needin' to go back to school for a while. Lots to be done 'round here."

Grace looked across the table at him, deciding to trap him. "Like what?"

"Like what!" He sniffed, looking over at his sister with an incredulous expression. "That garden needs weedin', the cow needs milkin' morning and night, chickens' eggs collected, chickens slaughtered—"

She interrupted him. "And what will *you* be doing?"

Aunt Gladys snapped, "Grace!"

"No, I'm just wondering. He's been here for years now, and I haven't seen him do much."

Aunt Gladys pointed to the platter of trout. "Your uncle went fishing in the creek and got us supper."

Uncle Henry gave Grace a squinty-eyed look. "You know I hurt my back protectin' our country and you don't show an ounce of being grateful." He turned his attention to his sister, adding, "She's getting to be too big for her britches."

Grace dropped the topic, got up, and scraped some of her trout into Snowball's bowl.

"Don't go wastin' good fish on that goddamn cat," Uncle Henry shouted. "Don't know why Evelyn thought havin' a cat was necessary anyway," he added.

Grace turned around, thinking over what he'd said. "Snowball was Mom's cat?"

Aunt Gladys gave her brother a stern look.

"Is that how we got him?" Grace said.

"Couldn't very well leave him there," Aunt Gladys said. "Evelyn always had a soft spot for critters. Now, get busy cleaning those dishes." She turned to Uncle Henry and said, "And you learn to keep your mouth shut!"

After she cleaned the dishes and went to her room, Grace waited for night to come so she could take some items she'd need for the cabin. After her aunt went to bed and she could hear her uncle's snores, she crept into the kitchen, took some soap and wrapped rags around it. She then took an old canning jar and poured some vinegar in it before sneaking outside and hiding the items in the bushes. When she snuck back inside, Uncle Henry was standing in the kitchen, giving her a squinty-eyed look.

"What was that all about?"

"What do you mean?"

"What were you doing? Sounds like you were up to somethin'."

"I went to the outhouse," she said, trying to scoot by him, but he caught her by the elbow.

"Why you always trying to avoid me?"

Grace looked up to see his eyes bearing down on her. She used her free arm and clutched her shirt, hiding her cleavage.

He pulled her closer to himself, his putrid breath making her stomach turn. "Do boys like you at school?"

"Let go," she stammered, struggling to pull away.

He chuckled. "You're gettin' ta be a fiery little thing."

She pushed him off and headed directly to her bed, pulling the curtain as tight as she could even though it provided little protection.

The following morning, Grace got up and milked the cow, then helped her aunt work in the garden, pulling weeds. They were growing green beans, tomatoes, potatoes, and carrots. It seemed that her aunt made the garden bigger each year and she guessed it was due to their lodger who always showed up at the table ready to fill his expanding gut.

Once they were directly across from each other in the garden, Grace said to her aunt, "Does Uncle Henry ever plan on leaving?"

Her aunt yanked a weed out, wiped her sweaty brow, and then gave Grace a curious look. "He has no place else to go. Charity begins at home."

"His back doesn't seem to be botherin' him much," Grace said.

"Whatta you mean?"

Grace hesitated, then said, "Well, he could maybe milk the cow or sweep a floor once in a while."

Her aunt stood up and peered down at her. "Did you forget your place here? I didn't have to take you in. You could've been sent off to some orphanage."

Grace looked away and continued pulling the weeds aggressively without saying another word. But she did wonder if maybe an orphanage would have been the better option. By eleven in the morning, her chores were done. She said, "Claire wants me to come over and play with her."

"Play what?" her aunt replied.

"Dolls."

"Aren't you a little old for that?"

Grace shrugged. "She gave me the bike so . . ."

"So you feel obliged."

Grace said, "I guess."

Her aunt took a long sigh before saying, "Be back in time for supper."

Grace nodded and ran around to the side of the shanty to get her bike. She looked over her shoulder to make sure she wasn't being watched and grabbed the items from the bushes and shoved them inside her shirt. She knew she wouldn't have a lot of time to get everything done, and pedaled as hard and fast as she could, having to fix the chain a couple of times before finally reaching her cabin. She ran in and pumped a handful of water and gulped it down before going about the business of cleaning.

First, she cranked up the Victrola and put the needle on a record, then she wiped down the grimy kerosene lamps on the shelf, finding a box of matches next to them. Once the record was done, she took it off and put it back into the cabinet before taking out another, cranking the Victrola, and dropping the needle, enjoying the music as she pulled out the cabinet drawers, finding utensils. She cleaned them, too. There were some dishes in the cabinet, one a tin plate with the image of Little Red Riding Hood.

"Mine," she whispered, fighting back the tears.

She figured Helen had to babysit her brothers and wouldn't be coming so she worked with what she had. While playing one record after the next, liking some better than others, she then went upstairs, taking the feather tick mattress and shaking it with all her might, dust floating all around her. In one swoop, she gathered the items from what had to be her father's drawer and tossed the suspenders and handkerchiefs in a bucket she was using for trash. She decided to keep the pocketknife she found in there, thinking it might come in handy for something.

Next, she swept the floors and cleaned the upstairs window so that when she looked out, she saw nothing but woods.

She paid attention to where the sun was situated and by the time it was around four in the afternoon, she looked over the small two rooms on the first floor and felt a sense of satisfaction. The windows allowed in more light now that they were clean, and the floors were free of grime and bird droppings. She realized that she hadn't eaten all day and was eager to get back for supper. She jumped on her bike and headed home.

"How'd you get so filthy?" her aunt asked.

Grace looked down at her grimy dress, trying to come up with a reason.

"'Parently playin' with dolls is dirty work," Uncle Henry piped in. He was already sitting at the table waiting for supper to appear.

"We ended up playing tag and stuff," Grace muttered, brushing herself off.

"Well, help me get food on the table," her aunt said.

Soon, she was gobbling down chicken and biscuits, trying to ignore her uncle's eyes fixed steadily on her.

"Where's this friend of yours live?" he asked with a mouthful of biscuit.

"In town," she said.

"Must have a pretty messy place," he said with a snicker.

"I helped her clean her garage."

"You what?" her aunt said, giving her a stern glare.

Uncle Henry leaned in. "All that needs to be done here and you're helping a stranger?"

Grace realized she may have made a mistake. She mumbled, "She's not a stranger. And . . . and we were just trying to get some stuff to play with."

"Well, tomorrow you can get filthy here by helping out," Aunt Gladys said.

The next day she was back in the garden with her aunt. While she went up and down the rows, pulling more weeds, her birth certificate, which was still hidden under her mattress, weighed heavy on her mind, but she wasn't sure how to broach the subject with her aunt.

Finally, standing up and wiping the sweat from her brow, she said, "Aunt Gladys?"

"Hmm?" her aunt mumbled without looking at Grace.

"How could we find out when my birthday is?"

Her aunt continued weeding and hoeing without granting her a reply.

"I mean, it would be good to know the day I was born, even the year," Grace added. But she did know. The birth certificate told her she'd be fourteen, and that the special day would be approaching soon, although no one would be acknowledging it.

"What's putting all these thoughts in your head?" her aunt snapped.

"I don't know," she said. "It would be good to know how old I am. I was just wondering—"

"Stop your wonderin' and keep at what you're doing. Or . . . or you won't have time to go to your friend's today."

Grace looked up, surprised. She figured she'd have to wait a few days to ask to go anywhere after the response she'd gotten the night before.

"Don't look so godawful stupid," her aunt said. "Pretty much expected that was your intention."

Grace nodded, although she suspected it was her aunt's way of changing the subject and keeping her from pressing the issue of her birth. She then finished the weeding before running inside to wash up. After gobbling down a slice of bread with butter, Grace ran out to her bike.

Uncle Henry followed her. "Where you think you're going?"

"My friend's. Aunt Gladys said I could go."

He had a look of surprise mixed with curiosity. "Why you never bring any friends here?"

Grace decided to ignore him and got on her bike and pushed it toward the road.

"I'm talkin' to you!" he shouted. Then to his sister, "You're letting her go out again?"

Without giving her aunt any time to change her mind, Grace peddled hard and fast until she reached the main road. About a half hour later, she rode past the schoolhouse and took Looby Road, instead of heading to the cabin. She had no idea which farmhouse belonged to Jack's family, but she hoped maybe he'd be outside when she rode by. Each time she came to a driveway that led to a house, she slowed down. If no one was outside, she'd pick up speed. She did this until she saw some people plowing the field in the distance off Whalen Road.

It was hard to stay on the path while trying to make out if one of them was Jack, so she stopped and pretended to be fixing something on the chain of her bicycle. As the workhorses headed in her direction, she saw that the person on the plow was an older man who didn't seem to notice her as he kept the horses at a steady pace. Further down, someone looked to be picking stones from the field and tossing them onto a wagon. *Jack*? Her heart began to pound. Maybe she was just hoping. She got back on her bike and started pedaling again. She would ride for another mile or so before turning around but then the chain did come off, and she was forced to stop and fix it once again. While doing so, she heard huffing from behind. She glanced over her shoulder to see none other than Jack Finley pedaling toward her on his own bicycle.

"Hey," he called. "Where you going?"

She shrugged, knowing she couldn't tell him that she was looking for him. She said, "You live around here?"

He pedaled alongside her, sweat pouring off him. "Didn't you see me in the field back there? My pa was plowing over by the little house. We live in that bigger house," he said, pointing to the house closer to the road. "I was helping pick rocks."

"Oh, that was you?"

He nodded. "When I saw you, I asked my pa if I could meet up with you."

"You did?" Grace felt sure she was about to die. The chain fixed, she stood back up.

"I was wonderin'," he said, hesitating, "maybe you could show me that record player you got. Helen told me about it."

"Oh, sure!" she said. "Follow me." She felt like she was floating as she pedaled with Jack alongside her. As he passed his farm, he shouted toward the man in the field near the smaller house, "I'll be back in a little while."

The man acknowledged him with a wave.

Grace said, "You have two houses?"

"Yeah. My grandparents use to live there, but they're gone now, and it's pretty much empty."

Grace thought it amazing to have two houses on one's property. Even the little house looked much bigger than the cabin she was leading him to. Soon the path was so rough it caused the chain to fall off Grace's bike again. She stopped and began to fix it.

Jack stopped, dropping his bike, and walked over to hers. She liked how he went about taking over and repairing the chain. Several minutes later, the bike was back in working order.

Once they reached the cabin, she said, "We have to go around to the back."

"It's a log cabin!" Jack exclaimed. "Awesome!"

She felt grateful that she had made it somewhat presentable, saying, "I have to fix that door and stuff, but Helen and I are thinking about making it a secret fort."

They rested their bikes against the side of the cabin and went inside. She brought him directly to the Victrola. His eyes grew wide. He touched the stack of records and muttered, "All we got is a radio. How's it work?"

Feeling a sense of pride, Grace put on a record she knew Jack would like. He grinned as Gene Autry's voice filled the room. Once the song ended, he looked around and said, "So, this is now your place? I mean, ever since . . ."

Grace bit her lip, not knowing how to reply.

Jack looked directly at her. "Dad said it was the worst tragedy around here ever."

She nodded. "I was just a baby. I live with my aunt now. Nobody lives here."

"Why don't you take this stuff to your place?"

"Not really enough room," she said, which was true enough.

He looked around again, and said, "So you can come here whenever you want?"

"Sort of. I like to come and play the records."

"Don't blame you," he said going through the stack.

"You like music a real lot, don't you?" she said.

"Yeah. I can't play any instruments or anything, though," he said.

"I'm saving up to buy a guitar," she blurted, even though she didn't have a dime to her name and had no idea how she would even get one.

"You are? You know they're expensive. I saw one in Alix's once and it was thirty-five dollars."

"What's Alix's?" she said.

He gaped at her. "You know, in Chateaugay." When she didn't seem to understand, he added. "The five and ten."

She'd never been to Chateaugay, but knew it was a couple towns over. She just nodded, pretending to finally understand.

"It'll be nice to hear you play, though," he said. "You have a nice voice."

She felt her face go warm. "I do? How do you know?"

"I heard you during recess." He suddenly seemed embarrassed and while pulling a record from the stack, said, "Can we put this one on?"

After a while, Grace was getting the feeling that Jack Finley was more interested in the Victrola and music than her. Eventually, after they played several records, he said that he should get going.

"Okay," she said, even though she yearned to beg him to stay longer. "You can come here whenever you want, though."

He said a hasty thank you and headed out the back. Moments later, through the small front window, she could see him pushing his bike along the path, soon taking a bend out of sight.

Part of her was thrilled to have spent so much time with Jack Finley, but another part had become uneasy. She realized that she didn't want to leave her cabin and head back to the dreary shanty and her uncle's leering eyes, but knew she had little choice. At that moment, in spite of spending so much time with Jack, her life seemed hopeless.

Adele stopped taking notes, noticing Grace's eyes were glistening with the memory. It was as though the old woman was suddenly a smitten young girl.

Adele said, "He sounds like he was warming up to you."

Slowly, Grace, who was sitting in her wheelchair in her room, turned her head to look directly at Adele. She nodded and her expression then took on a look of pain. She said, "He shouldn't have. He would've been better off with someone else. His mother always thought I was trouble. Turns out she was right." She took a deep breath and said she was tired, wheeling herself to her bed, refusing Adele's help to get into it.

Adele noticed that Mary's daughter was sitting nearby with Mary. They'd been so quiet it occurred to Adele that they must have been eavesdropping. As she started to walk out the door, she stopped and said, "Are you familiar with the places she's speaking about?"

"Chateaugay? Churubusco?" Mary's daughter said. "Sure."

Mary added, "We lived in Fort Covington and the only reason we're familiar with Churubusco is that there was supposed to be a big concert there like at Woodstock. A lot of the locals call it 'busco. Anyway something fell apart and the concert never happened."

Adele nodded and walked out, hoping she wouldn't have to wait long for her mother to pick her up. She wanted to get home and type up her notes.

CHAPTER 9

In the few days since Grace had seen Jack, her aunt refused to let her go anywhere, saying she needed her help with the garden, cleaning the cow's gutter and the chicken coop, along with other things that had been let go far too long.

"With them taking you off to school all the time, I can't get the help I need," her aunt had said, and when she did, Grace glared directly at Uncle Henry, which still didn't change a thing. She guessed he'd talked her aunt into making her stay home so he didn't have to help in any way.

While Grace tended the garden in the sweltering heat and shoveled shit into a bucket, carrying it to the outhouse, and cleaned the chicken coop, Uncle Henry sat in the rocking chair. He'd dragged it to the porch and watched, while sipping fresh lemonade that Grace had made for her aunt and herself. It was bad enough hearing the back-and-forth squeaking of the rocker, but knowing his eyes were locked on her while she toiled was enough to make her scream. She only wished her aunt were as annoyed by his laziness as she was, but something about him going to war seemed to have given him a pass. He did not have to do much except eat, sleep, and rock. Well, that, and watch her with his lecherous eyes.

That night, it was too hot to eat anything other than a cold supper. The three of them sat at the table munching on ham sandwiches and pickles that had been canned the year before. Grace watched as her uncle poured the last of the lemonade from the jug into his cup. She was not only thirsty but exhausted from the nonstop workday. Maybe if there'd been some sort of conversation, she wouldn't have had to break the silence and suggest getting an allowance.

"A what?" Uncle Henry blurted.

Looking at her aunt, she said, "I want to buy a guitar, but I don't have the money for it and since I help out around here—"

Without giving Aunt Gladys a chance to respond, Uncle Henry sneered, "I never heard any dagburn idea so foolish. You're lucky you got a roof over your head."

"I'm not talking to you!" Grace shouted.

"Don't go disrespectin' me, young lady." He slammed his fist on the table causing the dishes to rattle. "You think it was easy for Gladys to take you in and raise you after what your father—"

"Henry!" Aunt Gladys yelled. "Shut your mouth."

"She needs to know, Gladys. Taking off all the time to who knows where, not having a care in the world. Ungrateful, I say!"

"I'm grateful," Grace replied barely above a whisper, her throat closing up. She got up to bring her plate and cup to the sink. She bent down to pet Snowball, his dish lapped clean of the milk she'd given him.

"Got a helluva way showin' it."

Tears started streaming down her face.

"Savin' for a guitar doesn't seem too wise," Aunt Gladys said. "Besides, I can't pay you for helping out."

Grace turned around. "Then maybe I could get a job."

"Job?" Aunt Gladys said. "There's enough around here to do, you don't need no job."

"Besides, where you gonna get one?" Uncle Henry said before taking a forceful bite from his sandwich.

"In town."

"Doing what?" he said, spattering chewed ham and bread onto the table.

"Whatever I can find," Grace replied.

"Your aunt said there's enough to do here!" he yelled.

"How would you know?" Grace screamed, warily glancing at her aunt.

Uncle Henry leaped out of his chair, knocking it over, lunging at the young girl, and yanking her by the arm.

"Henry, leave her alone!" Aunt Gladys cried.

"And let her take 'vantage of you?" he said.

Aunt Gladys covered her face with her hands and began to sob, sputtering, "Take your hands off that child."

When he did, he took his foot, and swung it, kicking Snowball clear across the room, causing the cat to yowl.

Grace screamed in protest, running after Snowball, but couldn't catch him as he ran out of the opened door.

"Why'd you do that?" Grace shouted.

"That critter serves no useful purpose," he sneered.

"He catches mice and that's more than I can say for you!" She ran to the door calling the cat, but he was nowhere in sight.

"Stop it, you two!" Aunt Gladys stomped her feet.

"No!" Grace said, feeling fire burn inside of her. "If he stays here, then I'm leaving."

Aunt Gladys didn't speak, but Uncle Henry said, "Then I guess we know what that means."

Grace felt she didn't have any other choice. She could stay and let things remain the same for who knows how long; or she could go and make her own way. If she didn't have the cabin to go to, she was sure she wouldn't have an option. She went to her room and gathered her few items of clothing and wrapped everything in a blanket. The two adults' eyes were on her when she walked out of her makeshift room.

"Where you going?" her aunt said, her voice quivering.

She almost told them where but stopped herself. She started out the door when she recalled what she'd hidden away under her mattress and ran back to get it, shoving it in with her clothes. She then walked past her aunt and uncle without saying another word and went to get her bike, overhearing her uncle say, "She won't get far. She'll be back."

She called for Snowball several times, before he appeared. She scooped him up, tucking him in with the clothes, trying to keep him from falling out. With one hand, she gripped the bike's handlebar while keeping the items, including Snowball, snug to her with the other hand.

At first, she was going to go to Helen's to tell her what happened, but then decided to keep going. By the time she got to the cabin, the sun had set. Somehow, she'd manage. Somehow, she'd make it on her own. At fourteen years of age, it wouldn't be easy, but she suddenly felt free, even as she had little idea of how she was going to survive.

With Snowball following her, she groped her way to the shelf, finding the kerosene lamp and matches, striking one and managing to catch the wick. She figured she had enough kerosene to last a couple of nights. Eerie light filled the room. She looked around, not sure what to do next. Then she realized the next day would be one where she needed to find a job, so decided a good night's sleep was in order.

Scooping up the blanket with her things, she brought it and the lamp up the narrow staircase. She went into the musty-smelling bedroom, grateful that she'd already cleaned the mattress. She opened the window to let in air. Thankfully, there was a light breeze. She pulled her few belongings from the blanket and placed them in the drawer that held her mother's items. Then Grace tossed the blanket over the mattress, put out the lamp, and lay down with Snowball next to her—though because the nighttime critters chattered and howled, sleep did not come for hours.

The following morning, Grace woke with daylight streaming in through the tiny bedroom window. She sat up, feeling hopeful but also hungry. Once she gave herself a quick sponge bath and changed into a clean dress, she decided to surprise Helen, hoping she'd offer a slice of bread or some oatmeal. She was regretting not finishing her supper from the night before. She looked at Snowball, telling him to stay as she closed the door behind her. Somehow, she'd have to find food for him, too.

"Land's sake," Helen's mother said while frying bacon and eggs for Grace. Helen and her family already had their breakfast, but the twins were still in their highchairs scooping scrambled eggs from their trays and shoving them in their mouths. "How's a child like you going to make it on her own?" Helen's mother asked as she flipped two eggs and some bacon onto a plate next to a slice of toast.

Grace didn't consider herself a child. She said, "I'm gonna look for a job."

"A job!" Helen exclaimed. "What about school?"

Helen's mother raised an eyebrow, placing the plate in front of Grace. "You can't stop going to school, sweetie."

Grace wasn't sure how she'd manage but school was suddenly no longer a priority. Survival was. But since it was summer and there was no school to consider, she wasn't going to worry about it just then.

"Dad just said a couple days ago," Helen said, "that the town is growing because of the railroad station."

Grace couldn't imagine any sort of job she could do at the railroad station and said as much.

"Well, eat up," Helen's mother said. "Things'll work out, I'm sure."

"So can I go with Grace today while she looks for a job?"

"No. You have your brothers to watch while I help your father in the field."

"Not fair!" Helen said.

"Maybe not," Helen's mother said, taking a wet washcloth to the twins' faces and then pulling them from their highchairs. "But at least you have a roof over your head." She turned to Grace, asking, "What sort of supplies do you have at the cabin?"

Grace swallowed a bite of her toast, then said, "Not much. But I did bring Snowball with me. He's my cat."

"Well, once I get back from helping in the field, I'll send Helen over with some things to get you started." She stopped and eyed Grace's appearance. "Helen, why don't you loan Grace one of your dresses?" She then went over to the sink and began pumping water into a pan, then put it on the stove top, warming the water. "And go get the shampoo."

Helen looked wide-eyed at her mother, who turned to Grace. "We're gonna give those beautiful locks a nice wash."

Before long, Grace was leaning over the sink while Helen's mother poured liquid from a brown bottle onto her scalp and scrubbed her hair. Grace had never used liquid soap on her hair before and this one had a nice aroma, unlike the powerful disagreeable scent from the soap her aunt made for scrubbing the body from top to bottom. Once Helen's mother stopped scrubbing, she rinsed the soap out with cold water right from the pump. She then took a towel and rubbed as much water out as she could before grabbing a brush and running it through the long locks. "You really have pretty hair," Helen's mother said. "Just remember to wash it at least once a week."

Once a week? Grace's aunt never followed any such protocol for herself or demanded it from her.

"Here," Helen said, "you can wear this one." She handed Grace a dress sprinkled with tiny flowers.

"That's too nice," Grace said. "What if I ruin it?"

"You won't ruin it," Helen's mother said. "You can keep it, as long as Helen is okay with it. Besides, I promised Helen a new dress once the school year begins."

"You did?" Helen said.

Her tone stern, Helen's mother said, "Yes, I did."

"That's so nice of you," Grace said, unaccustomed to such generosity. She wondered if that's what all mothers were like, if that's what her mother had been like.

"Just being a good neighbor," Helen's mother said, putting the brush down on the sink and going over to Helen, giving her a kiss on the top of her head. "Your father's probably wondering where I am. Don't let your brothers get into trouble." She bent down to where the twins were crawling on the floor and kissed them as well, saying, "I'll be back soon. Be good boys."

Once she was out the door, Grace said, "She's so nice. I can't believe she wants to help me."

Helen shrugged. "She's always felt bad for you. Said it wasn't fair that you had to go live up in the hills with your aunt. And I told her about your creepy uncle. She didn't like that one bit."

As unsettling as her future seemed, Grace was relieved to get away from Uncle Henry. She said, "And it sounds like you'll be able to come over now. Maybe we could have sleepovers!"

"That'd be fun," Helen said, watching as the twins crawled under the kitchen table giggling. "You can change in the catch-all." She pointed to a room off the kitchen. Grace went into the room where there were scattered boots and winter coats, some tools and other miscellaneous items. She quickly changed into the dress, liking the clean feel against her skin. When she walked out, she wondered what to do with the dress she'd been wearing.

"Just leave it," Helen said. "I'll bring it over to you later."

"Thanks," Grace said, getting her plate from the table and bringing it over to the sink to wash it.

"You don't have to do that," Helen said. "You're a guest."

"It's okay. I'm just dragging my feet before I go looking for a job." Truth was, she had no idea how to go about any such thing and wished Helen could go with her for support. At least she felt like she looked more presentable than she had before the shampoo and change of clothes.

Later, riding her bike into the town square, Grace thought Humphrey's Grocery Store might be a good place to work. She walked in, greeted by a variety of aromas from coffee beans to fresh baked bread. Taking a deep breath, she approached the counter with as much courage as she could where a middle-aged man stood. He looked her up and down, a twinkle coming to his eye.

Grace uttered, "I'm wondering if you could use some help."

"Help?"

Grace nodded. "I'm looking for a job."

"That right?" The man appeared to be considering it and said, "Well, the wife was just saying we could use help stocking those shelves."

Grace turned to look where he was pointing, her heart skipping a beat. Could getting a job be that easy?

A woman came from the back room, looking from Grace to the man, then back to Grace.

"Beatrice," the man said, "this young girl . . ." He stopped and said, "What'd you say your name was?"

"Grace," she said.

"Grace here is asking if we're hiring."

"Don't recognize you," Beatrice said. "Who do you belong to?"

"Belong to?"

The woman took a step further into the store, grimacing. "Who's your father?"

Grace's mouth went dry. "He died a long time ago."

"Then your mother?"

Grace lowered her voice. "She's dead, too."

With a note of arrogance, Beatrice said, "I had a feeling. You're that Dormand child, aren't you?"

"Beatrice," the man said, "you were just saying how we could use more help."

Beatrice didn't respond but looked to be waiting for Grace to answer her question.

"I'm . . . I'm Grace Cooke."

"You were born a Dormand."

The man said, "How old are you?"

"She'd be about thirteen," Beatrice snapped. "Been about that long ago when the unthinkable happened."

"I'm fourteen," Grace replied. "Well, just about. And I work real hard."

Just then, a man with white hair and a pot belly walked in. He nodded at the man behind the counter and headed down one of the aisles.

"Doesn't matter," Beatrice said. "We're not hiring."

"You sure?" the man said to his wife. "You were just saying—"

"I said we're not hiring," Beatrice snapped.

Using all her strength not to cry, Grace mumbled a thank you. As she walked out the door, she heard Beatrice scold the man for even thinking about hiring *that girl*.

She picked up her bike and began peddling down the single square block.

"Grace! Grace!"

She turned to see Claire running after her. "I thought you were coming to see me."

Grace looked back, realizing she'd passed Claire's house. She stopped pedaling and hopped off the bike. "Oh, no. I'm looking for a job."

Claire's eyes widened. "A job? Why?"

"I need one." Grace began to push her bike, not wanting to waste time in her efforts.

Claire started walking alongside her, patting the bike. "It's holdin' up real good, ain't it?" A reminder that it had been a gift and something was owed in return.

Grace nodded, spotting the post office just ahead. When she was in third grade, her teacher took the class on a field trip down the road to the post office so that they could learn about how mail was delivered. At the time it seemed like a fun place to work. She jumped on her bike and said, "Well, I gotta go."

As she pedaled away, Claire called to her, "When can you come over to play?"

"Not sure," she called over her shoulder. "Depends."

"On what?"

Grace pretended not to have heard the question and dropped her bike on the ground, running up to the door of the post office. Moments later, though, she was back outside, having been told she wasn't old enough to work there. Across the street, on the corner, she saw LeClair's Diner. Sometimes the older students who didn't have to rush home would go there after school for an ice cream sundae. She watched as two men opened the door and heard a mishmash of voices and the rattling of dishes flowing outside. She made her way down the road, reaching the diner. She leaned the bike against the clapboard building and walked in to find the two men taking stools at a counter where several other men were already sitting and drinking coffee; a number of other men were seated at tables. Everyone seemed to be yammering at once.

A woman rushing by, carrying plates of food, called to Grace, "Don't think there's any open seating just now, sweetie."

"Oh no," Grace called after the woman, whose face was flushed, her pace quick, "I'm not here to eat."

Soon three more men came in through the door, one of them muttering something about never getting a table. Another man said, "Told you we need to get here earlier." While they talked, they all studied Grace, one saying, "Ain't you a pretty little thing."

Grace took a step back, automatically crossing her arms in an attempt to hide what her aunt called her womanly parts. Just then she watched as the woman returned from some backroom, balancing plates piled high with food. Just as the woman dashed by her, telling the men that she'd have a table for them in a few minutes, Grace called out, "I'm wondering if you need help."

The woman stopped and gave her a look, replying, "Is that a joke?"

The men nearby chuckled but Grace, watching the woman go back into what had to be the kitchen, called out, "No!"

Across the room, a group of men got up from their table cluttered with dirty dishes. One of the men waiting said, "Let's grab it." The others followed as they passed the ones leaving and sat down.

Grace wasn't sure if what she was about to do would get her in trouble, but she dashed over and began clearing the dishes, stacking them up and carrying them in her wobbly arms. She headed back to where the woman kept going, passing her on the way.

"What're you doing?" the woman shouted, carrying plates filled with pancakes and bacon.

"Helping," Grace called over her shoulder.

The woman started to say something, but then made her way over to another table.

Grace went into the kitchen where a man was at a stove, breaking eggs on a griddle, wiping the sweat from his brow. Grace spotted a sink that was filled with dirty dishes. She went back to the table to clear the rest, then returned to the kitchen, taking it upon herself to start washing the dishes, the man at the stove watching her with a curious expression. He had a thick head of dark blonde hair and a drawn friendly face. He called over to her, "I'm Tim. What's your name?"

"Grace," she said, purposely not adding her last name.

"Rachel never told me she hired anyone."

Grace figured Rachel was the woman who'd passed her. She said, "She didn't. Just saw you needed help."

Tim nodded with a smile and went back to the business of breaking eggs and pouring pancake batter on a griddle while dashing over to toast the thick slices of bread. Sometime later, clean dishes were dried and stacked on a shelf while the dining room had quieted to a few stragglers left sipping the last of their coffee.

The woman appeared with another pile of dirty dishes, putting them in the sink while giving Grace a smile and wink. She gave an approving nod at the clean dishes on the shelf, and said, "Tim, let's feed this young girl something." She patted Grace on the back. "Once those are done, meet me at the counter."

A short time later, Grace went to where she'd been instructed to go. The woman, who was solidly built with an open face, had a hamburger and fries in front of her and there was another plate of the same next to her. The woman patted the stool motioning for Grace to sit.

"Hope you're hungry. Looks like Tim wasn't shy with the fries."

Hesitantly, Grace took the seat. "I . . . I can't pay for this."

The woman smiled. "No need. You deserve it." She reached into her pocket and put three quarters in front of Grace. "Tips. I'm happy to share 'em with you today."

Grace stared at the coins but didn't touch them.

"Well, eat up, then we can talk business. My name's Rachel, by the way. And you are . . . ?

"Grace," she replied, putting a fry in her mouth.

"You got a last name, Grace?"

Grace's throat closed up. Would she ever be able to escape the shame her family caused? She muttered, "Cooke."

"Cooke?" Rachel said. "Where do you live?"

That was a question Grace wasn't sure how to answer. After she took an especially long time chewing, she replied, "I just moved to the area and really need a job."

Rachel studied her for a minute. "Ever work in a diner before?"

Grace shook her head. "But I learn real fast."

"What hours can you do?"

She shrugged. "Any hours."

"You didn't graduate from school yet, did you?"

"No," Grace said, "but I'm off for the summer."

"What about when you have to go back?"

Grace shrugged. School didn't seem that important anymore while finding work was suddenly necessary.

"Well, I could use the help. The workers from the highway and train station keep us busy. This is my place. Well, my husband's and mine. He's the cook." She then called out, "Tim!"

When Tim appeared, Rachel said, "This girl's looking for a job. What do ya think?"

Tim took a moment, looking from Rachel to Grace then back to Rachel. "Well, if you're lookin' to lighten the load, it could backfire. Every hound dog in the North Country'll come here more for the view than the food."

Rachel laughed. "Ain't that the truth."

"But she did a hell of a job with those dishes."

Rachel turned to Grace. "You'll work for tips. We open at five in the morning and close at four in the afternoon weekdays. On Saturdays, we're open from nine to seven. Most of the men don't work in town on Saturdays so we don't open early. And we don't work on the Lord's Day. Think you can manage those hours?"

Even though she didn't have a choice if she wanted the job, Grace nodded.

"Well, finish up your burger. The lunch crowd will be comin' in shortly. Can you stay to help?"

"Yes!" Grace exclaimed.

Rachel looked down at Grace's feet. "Those shoes comfortable?"

Grace shrugged.

"Today, we'll keep you in the kitchen doing dishes. Tomorrow we'll start you with serving."

Grace wanted to scream with delight. She had a job! Now she wouldn't have to go crawling back to her aunt's, proving her uncle wrong.

After a long, rewarding day, Grace returned to the cabin. She'd asked Rachel if she could bring home the scraps of bacon and hamburger that was going to be tossed out anyway. When Rachel heard about Snowball, she poured some milk in a glass jar and gave that to Grace, too, saying, "See you bright and early!"

Grace had to guess the approximate time when she got back to the cabin so she could set and wind up the alarm clock, not wanting to oversleep. After she let Snowball outside to do his business, he came back in and took his place next to her in bed. She kept checking the clock, throughout the night, though, just to be sure while the tick, tick, tick told her it was working. Now, the following morning, the alarm having jangled her out of bed, Grace stood outside the diner at four thirty. The diner's door was locked and only a sliver of light came from the back window she was peering through. Mosquitoes went about their business, biting her legs and keeping her prancing and swatting them away. She wondered if she should knock, or maybe she'd miscalculated the time on her clock.

Just then, headlights approached from down the road and a rickety flatbed truck stopped near the entrance. Two men jumped out, giving her the once over, one of them emitting a low whistle while the other, a burly man, asked, "Who are you?"

"Grace," she replied. "I work here."

"That right?" the other man said. "Can't do much on this side of the door." He then made a fist and pounded.

Moments later, Rachel, calling from the other side, shouted, "We aren't opened yet!"

"Well, you gotta pretty young'un out here says she works here," the burly man called through the door.

Rachel opened the door a crack. "How long you been out here."

Grace shrugged. "A while."

"Next time go 'round the back. We could've used your help with the biscuits."

"I'm sorry . . . I didn't . . ."

"Not your fault. Can't do what you weren't told." She opened the door wider so Grace could slip in but refusing entrance to the men, saying, "Hold your britches, Ken. Give us a few more minutes."

It wasn't long before Grace was pouring coffee for the growing crowd and taking breakfast orders. *Quickly* was the key word, Rachel telling her it was important to get 'em in and out as quickly as possible to make room for more customers. "Besides," she said, "they need to get on the job so they don't lose it."

Grace soon learned that some of the men worked at the train station, while others helped pave Smith Street, which seemed to be the talk of the diner. Some men razzed others, asking why they'd need such a foolish thing as a paved road. "What're we, New York City?" Other men seemed surprised at the sight of her approaching their table. There were a couple of complaints because they didn't like having to tell her their orders, orders that Rachel knew by heart. "You're nice to look at, though," one of the complainers had said.

"She'll pick it up soon enough." Rachel placed a plate of scrambled eggs and ham in front of the man in question.

Grace wasn't as certain. When she brought a man named Lester bacon with his order, instead of sausages, he shoved the plate back at her, telling her to get it right. "I don't have all day to get good service."

By eight o'clock, there were only a couple of men still hanging at the counter, taking their time sipping their coffees and tapping their cups, which Grace soon learned meant they wanted a refill. Rachel told her that the refills were on the house. She had to ask what "on the house" meant. Overall though, she was ready to learn as much as she could, and jingled the change in her pocket from the tips she made. She was eager to get back to the cabin to count the money, almost feeling like the richest person in the world.

"Here you go," Rachel said, placing a plate of hash browns, eggs, and toast on the counter.

Grace gave Rachel an odd look. "I . . . I . . . ." Her stomach growled, but she didn't want to have to spend her tips on food even though there was no food at the cabin.

"Aren't you hungry?"

Grace couldn't argue that she wasn't and reached into her pocket, pulling out some coins.

"No, no, no," Rachel said. "You keep your tips. If we can't afford to feed a young girl like you, then we have no right to be in business. And don't forget to take some scraps home for Snowball."

Grace slipped the coins back into her pocket and sat down, doing all she could not to devour the breakfast in one fast gulp. She picked up the fork and stabbed into the potatoes, bringing them to her mouth. She couldn't be sure she ever tasted anything so delicious.

Rachel watched her for a moment or two before saying, "Take your time, but once you're done, finish washing up the dishes then see what help Tim needs. I'll be back down in a bit."

That's when Grace realized that Tim and Rachel lived upstairs from the diner.

Before she knew it, men began pouring in again and she and Rachel were rushing lunch orders out, clearing tables and filling them up again. Once two o'clock came, things slowed down where some stragglers who were on their break came in for coffee and a slice of apple pie. By four o'clock, Rachel walked over to the door and turned the open sign around. She said, "You did good, sweetie. I think you'll work out just fine."

Exhausted but thrilled, Grace pedaled her way back to the cabin, relieved that Claire didn't see her as she passed by. When she got to the cabin, she found a big cardboard box outside her door with a note on it: *Mom said you can have this stuff. Hope you found a job! Your friend, Helen.*

Grace leaned the bike against the cabin, went around the back and let herself in with Snowball greeting her. After she put the scraps on a tin plate for the cat, she went to the front, pushed open the door, and dragged the box inside. When she opened it, she found a blanket, some cups, a teakettle and a container of kerosene. Odd, too, there was a bra included in the box with a note pinned to it. "Mom wanted you to have this." She studied it, uncertain how it would go on, but suddenly felt like the luckiest girl in the world. Then she remembered her change. She rushed over to the rickety kitchen table and counted out two dollars and fifteen cents. It was more money than she'd ever seen in her life. Feeling overwhelming thanks, she dropped to her knees.

"Thank you, Jesus, for my new home and my job. Please help me make enough money to buy a guitar. I promise the first song I learn to play will be 'Jesus Loves Me.'"

"I know that song!"

Through tired, aged eyes, Grace, suddenly back in the nursing home in her bed, squinted to see the young girl scribbling on her notepad.

"My grandma sang that song to me all the time," Adele said.

"What song?" Grace said.

"The one you were just singing. *Jesus loves me, this I know . . .*"

"Who are you?" Grace leaned over to get a better look at the girl.

"You don't remember? I'm Adele," she said with some hesitation. "You're telling me about your life. I'm interviewing you."

Grace clutched onto her blanket, her mouth going dry. Had she been talking this whole time? She muttered, "They caught up to me?"

Adele studied the old woman. "Who?"

"S'pose it doesn't matter now. Simone's gotta be long gone by now."

Adele tapped her notepad. "So, did you keep that promise?" When Grace gave her a quizzical look, she added, "Learned to play 'Jesus Loves Me' on the guitar?" She nodded toward the scratched-up instrument in the corner.

After a moment with Grace staring off, she said, "Don't remember. Doesn't matter since he never really did much for me." She glanced down, her gaze on her thin-skinned veiny hands.

"Well, I can't wait till you get to the part of how you got the guitar," Adele said.

"Neither can I!" a voice from across the room piped up.

Grace and Adele looked over to see Mary sitting on the edge of her bed, holding a ball of yarn and knitting needles.

"She's been here over two years and barely said a word, now she doesn't keep quiet," Mary said. "Even at night, she mutters and mumbles. Talks about herself as if she were someone else and not herself. Keeps me entertained though."

Adele leafed through her notes. "Well, it does seem that some people were willing to help you. Helen's mother. And Rachel and . . ." She looked down at her paper. ". . . Tim."

Rachel and Tim? Grace hadn't thought of them or that diner in years. "Rachel and Tim," she muttered, taking the edge of her blanket and wiping her teary eyes. "They were good to me. Didn't pry too much. They didn't have kids." She sniffed with the memory. "They worried about me once they found out I was living on my own. Rachel would give me clothes, telling me her niece outgrew them. And made sure I ate, as well as Snowball."

"Did she ever find out who your parents were?" Mary asked from across the room.

Once again, Grace was back in that diner, standing near the kitchen. After she brought Beatrice and her husband, the couple from the grocery store, their chicken dinners with biscuits, Beatrice jumped up, going directly to Rachel. While she kept looking at Grace, she whispered loudly, warning Rachel about hiring *that girl*. Grace had a sinking sensation, certain she'd be fired on the spot.

Moments later, Rachel went over to Grace, "I'll take care of their table. You handle the others. But I'll need to talk to you once things calm down."

Grace nodded, trying to hold back her tears.

Later, as Rachel promised, she brought Grace into the kitchen where Tim was wiping down the griddle.

"You told me your last name was Cooke. Why'd you lie to me?"

Barely audible, Grace said, "Because that's what my aunt taught me to say."

"Your aunt? Up in the mountains?"

She nodded.

"Goodness, you ride your bike here every day from there and back?"

"No. I moved to where it happened."

Tim took a step closer. "You mean the murders?"

Again, Grace nodded, still looking down.

"They were your parents, right?"

"Yes."

"And you live back at that cabin?"

"Yes."

"With who?"

Grace looked up. "Snowball."

Rachel and Tim exchanged looks. "Just the cat?" Tim said.

"How on earth?" Rachel said. "I mean, to be living by yourself. That's just not safe, sweetie."

"I'm doing okay," she said, but knowing it was all going to come to an end when she got fired. "Well, I was."

"Why did you leave the mountains?" Tim said.

Grace hesitated before saying, "I had a fight with my uncle."

"A fight?"

Grace remained silent.

Rachel sighed. "Honey, I'd have you move in with us, but there's just no room up there."

"No, I'm fine," Grace said. "Really.

"I'm just not comfortable knowing you are in that cabin all by yourself. It's just not safe."

"Are you going to fire me?" she said.

"I don't want to, but I worry." Rachel reached over and brushed Grace's long blonde strands of hair from her face. "Listen, we'll keep things the way they are for now, but if I even think you're not safe living there on your own, you're going to have to go back and live with your aunt. You understand?"

"Okay," Grace said, feeling a sense of relief.

"Shame on Bea, though, for blaming you for what happened." Rachel pulled Grace into a hug. "Some people are just sad." Grace wasn't sure if she meant her or Beatrice, but welcomed the unfamiliar feeling of being embraced.

Eventually, Grace opened up to Rachel when she'd asked what she was doing with all her money from the tips. "I want to buy a guitar." She then took a sip of her root beer, something she'd only started drinking recently. "Someone told me that they sold them at some store a couple of towns over but I'm not sure how I'd get there. I don't even know where it is."

"He probably meant that five and ten in Chateaugay. Next time Tim and I go for some supplies, why don't you catch a ride with us?"

The kind suggestion added an extra thump to Grace's heartbeat, even though she said, "I don't want to be a problem."

"A problem? Not at all. You actually are bringing in more customers with that cute little figure of yours. We got customers coming here from all over, even if Bea chooses not to come back."

Grace felt her face go warm and couldn't believe her good luck when she'd walked through the diner's door those few weeks ago.

"I might even need to hire someone else with how busy we are! Besides, we're gonna miss you."

"Miss me?" Grace's throat closed up. "Why?"

"School'll be startin' soon."

Grace had been giving that a lot of consideration. If Jack wasn't part of the equation, she would quit school altogether and continue to work fulltime at the diner. But not seeing Jack was unacceptable to her. She said, "Well, if it's okay with you, I could come in for the breakfast shift, go to school, then come back for the lunch crowd."

Rachel scrunched up her face. "I don't know, honey. That's a lot of work and I'm not sure the school will let you leave in the middle of the day. I think Tim and I can take care of the lunch crowd, if you still wanna work in the morning and on Saturdays.

It would mean missing out on some of those tips, but Grace wasn't sure she had any other option and so she agreed.

"You're gonna be one busy girl," Rachel said.

"I like being busy," Grace replied.

Adele sat in the room listening to Grace's shallow breathing. She'd stopped talking, as if she ran out of steam. She studied the old woman who seemed nothing like the child she'd been. The old woman was damaged somehow and Adele needed to dig deeper to find out why she was so alone, never having any visitors, unlike so many others in the nursing home.

When she was in class earlier that day, Mr. Wilson gave her some suggestions, telling her to see if she could visit Churubusco, see if anyone remembered Grace. "Maybe you could even find that cabin. Take some photos to go with your article."

It was a good idea, but Adele didn't have access to a car, always depending on her parents to drive her to school and to the nursing home. They never complained, but Adele didn't like taking advantage of them. They'd had her later in life and sometimes strangers would assume they were her grandparents, not her parents. She had her permit, but she'd still need an adult to ride with her.

It was a warm day, the sun bright, so she decided to wait outside in front of the nursing home for her dad, even though he wasn't scheduled to pick her up for about a half hour. While waiting, she read through her notes, wishing she were home so that she could continue working on the article on her computer. So much time was wasted waiting to be driven here or there. Finally, when her father pulled up she ran around to his side asking if she could drive. He slid over, letting her behind the wheel.

"Dad," she said, "I want to sign up for my driver's test. Do you think I'm ready?"

Her father nodded and said, "Let's find out."

CHAPTER 10

Every once in a while, Grace would see Claire waiting on her front lawn as she rode by, Claire calling after her, asking if she could stop and hang out. Each time Grace had to turn her down, telling her she needed to get to work. She was grateful for the excuse, but she didn't even have much time to spend with Helen. Occasionally, Helen was allowed to come over to the cabin on Sundays after Mass and she and Grace would talk about boys. Well, Helen talked about boys while Grace talked about only one boy. She was looking forward to seeing Jack once school started so that she could invite him back to the cabin to listen to some music; turns out, though, she saw him sooner than expected.

Grace was not only waiting on two men who were on their break from the Summit Railroad Station, but dodging their rude comments and pinches to her backside when Jack walked in. He was with an older man and woman. She figured they had to be his parents. He gave Grace a nod and a smile. She began to perspire and said that she'd be right with them.

"Hey, sweetheart, how about a fill up?" one of the men said, reaching over and patting her on the behind.

She backed away, asking that he not do that, before dashing away to get the coffee pot.

Rachel appeared and brought the Finley family to an empty table, telling them that Grace would be right with them.

After Grace refilled the men's cups, purposely standing as far away from them as possible without spilling any coffee, she brought the pot back to the burner, and then went to Jack's table with her notepad and pen.

"I heard you worked here," Jack said.

Grace felt herself go warm, wondering who had told him. She wanted to ask when he could come back to the cabin, but glanced at the people with him and said, "So, did you get a chance to look at the menus?"

"Can't look at what we don't have," the woman snapped.

"Oh!" Grace said, realizing Rachel had forgotten to bring them over. She ran to the counter and grabbed three menus, bringing them back to the table, apologizing.

"This is my mom and dad," Jack said. "It's my dad's birthday so we're treating him to dinner."

"Waste to me," Jack's mother said. "I could've cooked anything better than what we'll find here."

"Mom," Jack intoned.

"Simone," his father said, "Jack wanted to do something special for me. Let's enjoy ourselves, okay?"

"I'll give you a few minutes then be back to take your order," Grace said.

The men at the other table whistled her over, telling her they needed their bill. When she went to put it on the table, one of the men grabbed her by the arm. "How about we go out dancin' sometime?"

She struggled to free herself from his grasp, trying to laugh it off. "No time for dancing for me," she said.

CHAPTER 10

"Ah, I don't believe that," he said. He turned to his buddy, adding, "Snotty little thing, ain't she?"

Out of the corner of her eye, Grace saw the Finleys watching. She just about wanted to die.

Jack's father called over to her. "We're ready to order." As soon as she got to the table, he asked, "Those fellas bothering you?"

Grace shook her head, forcing a smile. She must've been several shades of red with how embarrassed she felt.

"Why is a young girl like you workin' anyway?" Jack's mom interjected.

Grace blurted the first reply that came to her head. "I'm saving up to buy a guitar."

"A guitar! Whatever for?"

"Grace can sing real good," Jack said. He then quickly added, "Uh, I heard her in school."

Grace didn't think she could be any more embarrassed and changed the subject. Holding her pen aloft with the notepad, she said, "So, what can I get you?"

All three ordered the roast beef dinners but not without Simone first asking how it was cooked and if it was salty, the meat fatty. Once the order was finally in, Grace told Rachel that it was Jack's father's birthday. She said, "Is it okay if I give him a slice of cake for dessert? I'll pay for it."

Rachel said, "It's Gerald's birthday? That man deserves more than a slice of cake." She snorted, adding, "He's one of the nicest men around far as I'm concerned."

"Hey!" Tim shouted in protest while he was slicing the roast beef.

"Well, after my husband," Rachel said with a laugh.

Tim nodded with a grin. "I'll load up his plate with extra of everything."

"Be sure to give that one to Gerald," Rachel said to Grace. "And you don't need to buy him a slice of cake. It'll be on the house."

Once Grace returned to the table with their dinners, she couldn't help but notice the way Jack's mother picked through her food, inspecting the roast beef and making a face with each bite she took, leading Grace to ask if everything was okay.

Simone started to comment, but it was Gerald who interjected. "Couldn't be better. Thank you, honey."

Grace decided that was good enough for her. She then realized that the two men were gone and dashed over to the table, gathering the dishes. She noticed that they hadn't left a tip and knew why. But it was the fact that she felt Jack's eyes on her that distracted her. She overheard Simone snap at him, "What you staring at? Eat your meal so we can get out of here."

Not much later, with Rachel behind her, Grace hurried over to their table with a huge portion of chocolate cake, a lit candle stuck in it. When Rachel started singing *Happy Birthday*, Grace hesitantly joined in.

With the plate in front of him, Gerald sat there wearing a big grin.

"You're s'posed to make a wish then blow out the candle, Gerald," Rachel said, giving him a gentle nudge.

"Oh!" Gerald blew out the candle, not looking as though he'd made any sort of wish.

Rachel placed three forks and two more dessert plates on the table. "In case you want to share."

"We didn't order any cake," Simone said, giving Grace an accusatory look.

"I know!" Rachel put up a hand. "Don't you worry, Simone. It won't be on the bill. And I hope the roast beef was to your liking." She then shot a wink at Grace.

Simone shrugged, reaching over and taking the first bite of cake while Gerald and Jack were effusive in complimenting the meal. Gerald then added, "You made this day really special. We'll take the bill when you're ready."

Grace gathered up their dinner dishes and headed toward the kitchen, giving them time to enjoy their dessert before she returned. She wasn't quite sure who to hand the bill to, so she put it in the middle of the table.

Making eye contact with her, Jack said, "Everything was real good."

"Glad you liked it!" Rachel called from nearby.

"Sure did!" Gerald said, reaching for the bill. "Great idea Jack had coming here. Least Simone won't have dishes to clean."

Simone rolled her eyes, pushing away from the table. "Well, enough of all this celebratin'."

To Grace, Jack said, "Will you be coming back to school?"

Before she could answer, Rachel came over and replied, "She absolutely will. Tim and I insisted on it."

Jack nodded with a grin. "Did you hear they're starting a wrestling team? I'm gonna try out for it."

Grace said, "Really? That's—"

"Plain foolishness," Simone replied, heaving herself up from the chair. "I told you if it interferes with your chores, you can get that out of your head."

Jack didn't say anything, but Grace caught a look of understanding of some sort exchanged between him and his father. She told them to have a good night, and as she grabbed their empty dessert plates, Gerald handed her some cash, saying, "This should do it." She took the money over to the register and realized he'd given her an extra dollar. She ran after them just as they were walking out the door. Gerald hustled Simone outside, then turned and barely above a whisper, said, "That's yours. To help pay for that guitar." He then shut the door behind him in a rush.

Grace gazed at the dollar bill. Usually, tips consisted of nickel and dimes, and the occasional quarter, but this was the first dollar she'd ever gotten.

Rachel went to the door, locking it and turning the "open" sign around to "closed." Then she said, "Seems to me that young one has a thing for you."

Grace took a deep breath. Not knowing what to say, she headed to the back to wash the dishes.

"Couldn't take his eyes off you," Rachel called in a sing-song voice, following Grace into the kitchen.

"I don't think his mother was too happy with that," Grace replied.

"She's not happy with much. I've never seen that woman smile." She sighed. "Guess it could have something to do with her brother gone missing all these years."

"What do you mean?"

"Oh, he just vanished," Rachel said. "Lots of rumors about him running off from the law." She scrunched her face as she looked to be thinking. "Guess it's been well over ten years now. Maybe something like that can make someone bitter."

The comment reminded Grace of her Aunt Gladys who rarely smiled, who always seemed to carry such a burden. Maybe having a sister murdered and then forced to care for Grace did that to her, making Grace suddenly feel guilty for not going back to let her know that she was fine. Maybe she'd bring her some cookies she'd bake when she was off on Sunday. She'd have to do it soon before winter set in, making her bike useless in the snow.

Usually, by the end of the day, she was exhausted and had to force herself to keep going, but this day she felt buoyant, as if she could float. Without a doubt it was thanks to Jack showing up. She placed the dishes in the sink and turned on the faucet, which still amazed her when water poured out. All she'd ever known was using a pump that teased out only a small stream.

Tim appeared next to her. "Grace," he said, "Rachel and I think you're doing a great job."

"Thank you," she said, scrubbing gravy from a plate and rinsing it before placing it in a dishrack.

"I'll be heading to Chateaugay in the morning to pick up some supplies. Was wondering if you want to take a ride with me. Maybe you could check out Alix's for that guitar. Has all sorts of items, including a couple of guitars," Tim said.

Grace's heart began to pound. The very idea of possibly getting her own guitar seemed like a dream, but then she had a thought. "What about Rachel?" she said. "Won't she need me here?"

"It's Saturday, remember?"

Saturdays the diner opened later since a lot of the men didn't work on the weekend at the railroad, which carried coal, grain and lumber, as well as a few passengers; rarely, did the passengers disembark at Churubusco, though, but were headed to Montreal, Burlington, and other destinations.

Rachel walked into the back. "I'll stay here and get things ready for the day, but you go on ahead with Tim in the morning and see about that guitar."

Tears came to Grace's eyes. She mumbled a thank you, even though she wasn't sure if she had enough money yet to make such a purchase, but would find out the next day. She'd been scrimping and saving her tips, only buying kerosene for the lamps and flour and yeast to bake bread. Helen's mother would send Helen over with eggs every once in a while, and Tim and Rachel often sent her home with leftovers, for both her and Snowball, so she was managing quite nicely. She couldn't believe how fortunate she was, almost forgetting the dreary life she'd had up in the mountains, reminding her that a visit to her aunt's might be the right thing to do.

"Okay," Tim said, "meet me here at eight in the morning and we'll head out. We'll have to get back here by eleven at the latest."

Having finished the dishes, Grace dried her hands and dashed out to her bike. She raced home, eager to count out her tips once again. The last she recalled, she was up to twelve dollars and fifteen cents. She reached the cabin, dropping her bike on the ground and ran inside. Snowball dashed out the door, but she knew he'd be back in to eat his dinner after he did his business. She left the door open for him while she pulled the tin can down from the shelf and dumped the money on the table. She pulled the dollar bill she got from Jack's father and the change from her pocket, cradling the money in her hand.

"Well, look at that, you greedy little bitch!"

Startled, she looked up to see Uncle Henry standing in the doorway.

"What do you want?" she stammered, remaining in place, wondering how he found her.

"After all we done for you and here you are living the high life." He ambled around, inspecting every corner of the small home Grace had made for herself. A blanket covered the holes and exposed springs in the couch that had been there when she first discovered the cabin. A woven rug was in the middle of the room in an attempt to make it look cozy. Wood was stacked near the stove, wood she'd been chopping during her time off from the diner in preparation for the cold weather. She supposed compared to the shack she'd lived in with her aunt, this was the high life.

He took a step closer to her, his eyes on the money. Grace shouted for him to leave, wishing she could scream loud enough for Helen's father to hear.

"How'd you make all that money? Whoring around?" He rushed at her, grabbing her by the arm, the money falling from her hand.

"No, I work at the diner!" she said, attempting to push him away.

CHAPTER 10

"Never occurred to you to give some to your aunt for all she's done for you?" He pushed Grace out of the way and began scooping up the change, shoving it into his pants pocket. "Well, I'll see she gets her share."

With balled up fists, Grace began swinging and pounding his body. He took a free arm and swung it, knocking her to the floor. Her dress hiked up to her thighs, he stopped, gazing at her. She tried to scramble away, but he dropped down and landed on top of her, smothering her with angry kisses while calling her all sorts of names.

"Stop it!" she shrieked, trying to get out from under him.

He grabbed her breasts, groaning, his body bucking, his pants sliding down. Using his leg, he attempted to spread her legs, but she clamped down on his arm, biting him with all her might causing him to yowl. The next she remembered was his fist coming at her, blood spurting from her nose before everything went dark.

CHAPTER 11

What happened?" Rachel said when Grace shuffled into the diner the following morning. "Tim waited long as he could for you."

Grace made sure her hair hung over her bruised and swollen face. She also wore a long-sleeved dress, even though the thermometer was nearing ninety degrees; riding her bike had been painful, her entire body feeling battered. She mumbled an apology, saying she had some stomach bug.

"Goodness," Rachel said, "then you shouldn't be working, if you're sick."

"No, no!" Grace said. "I'm feeling better now."

"Well, Tim'll be heading to town again soon enough, though."

Truth was, she didn't want to lose a day's pay since it would take weeks to save what she'd had stolen from her. When she'd come to the night before, having been awakened by Snowball's meowing outside the door, her uncle was gone, but so was all her money. She found her underwear down to her ankles while feeling stickiness between her legs. She managed to let the cat back in, wash herself and make her way to the couch where she remained throughout the restless night. She knew, without any money, there'd be no reason to go with Tim to town in the morning.

She grabbed her apron from the hook and tied it around her waist, trying not to grimace. The front door opened with a tinkle of the bell. Their first morning customer was Phil, owner of the gas station down the road. He took a seat at the counter, asking for coffee. Grace felt Rachel studying her as she poured the brew, her movements slow and stiff.

Rachel said, "Grace, could I see you in the back for a minute?" As soon as Grace got to the kitchen, Rachel said, "What happened to you, sweetie?" She reached over, pushing back Grace's hair from her face. Gently, she touched the bruise.

Grace did everything in her power to hold back the tears. She didn't want to say what really had happened, afraid Rachel would keep her word and say she'd have to go back living with her aunt . . . and uncle . . . if she wasn't safe living on her own. Her mind raced as she said, "I ran into a branch. Got me pretty good. Knocked me to the ground."

Rachel started to say something but was interrupted by Tim as he appeared from the back door, carrying a huge sack of flour. "There you are!"

"Says she had a run-in with a branch," Rachel said, before turning back to Grace. "But didn't you say you had a stomach bug?"

Grace raced to think of a reply that made sense, and eventually managed to say, "Yes, yes, but, um, then I was in a rush to get here and that happened."

"Hell!" Tim said, dropping the sack on the counter. "You okay?"

She nodded.

"Enough to work?" he added.

She nodded again. "Just a bit slower today."

"That was some branch," Rachel said skeptically.

Grace was grateful for the tinkle of the bell from the front door. She said, "I'll get it," heading into the dining room. She hesitated, though, upon seeing that the customer was Jack. He pointed toward the counter as if asking for permission to sit. Grace motioned for him to take a seat but turned and went back to the kitchen in an attempt to find something to keep her busy. She didn't want Jack to see how damaged she was.

Just as she went to the sink to wash the single cup sitting in it, Tim said, "Didn't somebody come in?"

"Uh, oh, yes," Grace said, seeing that Rachel was busy preparing the specials for the day, so she tried her best to cover her face and went out to take care of Jack.

"Was hopin' you'd be here," Jack said.

Phil, who was also seated at the counter, clanked his empty cup. His way of telling her he wanted a refill. She made her way to the coffee pot and brought it to him, filling up his cup. She then turned to see what Jack wanted.

Scowling, he leaned over to get a closer look at her. "What happened to you?"

She stuck to her story and said that the branch got her.

"Got you pretty good," he said. He then hesitated before asking, "So, do you stay there now all the time? At the cabin?"

She nodded.

"With who?"

"Just me," she replied.

"Really?" he said, an expression of surprise coming to his face. "I mean, how?"

She motioned around the diner. "This job helps and I've been fixing it up when I can."

He shook his head in astonishment. "Wow, living on your own."

Not wanting to think about what living on her own meant the night before, she said, "So what can I get you?"

"Got any more of that cake? And I'll take a glass of milk with it, if you do."

"I think so," she said. When she returned with the cake and glass of milk, he put his money on the counter before taking a single bite. She rang him up and then started to go back to the kitchen when he said, "What time you done today?"

"I'm here till closing."

Jack looked disappointed. "I was hoping I could come over to listen to some more of those records."

Grace would have loved to have him come over. If her uncle came back and was waiting for her, he wouldn't dare try anything with Jack around. Jack wasn't big, but she couldn't help notice his muscular arms.

"Thanks for the coffee," Phil said, standing and tossing a nickel on the counter before walking out.

Rachel called Grace back into the kitchen. "Listen, we won't be that much busier today. Why don't you go home and rest? And maybe listen to some music with that nice young man." She then winked and smiled.

As much as she needed to make tips, Grace didn't want to lose the opportunity to spend time with Jack. "You sure?"

"Sure," Rachel said, putting out her hand. "Now give me your apron an' get outta here." She hesitated, then added, "And drink some tea for that stomach bug you said you have."

Grace went over to Jack and told him the good news. He grinned and said, "My bike's right outside."

"Mine, too."

The bike ride to the cabin was a struggle, but Grace made every effort not to let it show. Once they got there, she opened the back door with some trepidation but sighed in relief to see that there was no sign of her uncle.

"Hey, who's this?" Jack said, greeted by the cat.

"Snowball," she said.

He bent down and began petting the cat for a few minutes before heading over to the Victrola and going through the records. He picked out *San Antonio Rose* and put it on the turntable, asking Grace if she knew the words. When she shook her head, he added, "'Cuz you sing real pretty. Like Kitty Wells."

She looked down, unable to respond.

"Maybe you could join the school chorus."

She knew that the chorus met after school hours, which was when she needed to head directly to the diner for the supper hour since Rachel and Tim had extended their weekday hours to seven o'clock.

"I'm gonna take wrestling," he reminded her.

"Will your mom let you?"

He shrugged. "Dad said it wouldn't be a problem."

Soon she and Jack were sitting on the floor, listening to one record after the next, until he paused after taking a record off and giving her a long look before reaching over, pushing strands of hair from her face. "That's quite a shiner, Grace. You sure you're okay?"

She looked over at the door, remembering her uncle standing there, but said she was fine. "But, um, I wonder if maybe you could help me with something."

"Sure, what?"

"Well, livin' here alone can be kinda scary. I need locks, real locks, put on my doors somehow. Don't have any idea how. I . . . I just don't want anyone comin' here and stealing my records or anything while I'm at work."

"Or worse," Jack said. "My pa and I didn't like the way those fellas were grabbin' at you. If they followed you here sometime, I'd kill 'em."

"You would?" She wished he'd been with her last night.

"Yup," he said. "I like you, Grace. I don't care what any-body says. I was hopin' you'd be my girl."

"You would?" *Jack's girl?* Something she'd fantasized about for years. It was like a dream.

"If you'd like. You're the prettiest girl at school. I'm just a farmer, but . . ."

"What changed your mind?"

"What do you mean?"

"Well," she hesitated, "you didn't even know I existed for the longest time."

"That's not true. It's just the guys were being idiots and kept saying stuff to me about you and it made me angry."

"Like what?"

He shrugged. "Doesn't matter." He paused before continu-ing. "But I always thought you were different from the other girls. I mean, in a good way." He reached over and held her hand.

Grace suddenly felt safe. Before she had a chance to know what was happening, Jack leaned in and kissed her quickly on the cheek. She winced in pain causing him to back away.

"I'm sorry. Did I hurt you?"

She shook her head. She couldn't imagine him ever hurt-ing her.

"I hope that was okay. The kiss I mean."

She felt herself go warm all over. "Jack Finley, I've liked you for the longest time," she said barely above a whisper.

"You have?" he exclaimed. "Whoo-wee!"

She laughed, ignoring how her ribs hurt when she did.

Jack got up and went to the back door. "I could get a latch for this and put it on for you probably tomorrow. Would that be okay?"

"How much do they cost?"

"Nothing. Dad has all sorts of things in the garage. I know he'll have something for this door." He then went over to the front door. "All anyone really needs to do is push this real hard. I'll get a better lock for this one, too. But I should get back home now. Cows need milkin'."

Grace didn't want him to leave, but couldn't bring herself to say as much. He walked over and this time kissed her lightly on the lips. "I'll be back tomorrow, after Mass. Will you be around?"

Sunday was her day off. She remembered how she'd planned to go see her aunt, but after her uncle's unwelcome visit, she had no intention of doing so.

"Yes," she said. "I'll be here."

"Okay, I'll see you then," he said, walking out, grabbing his bike and pedaling away. She couldn't believe it. Jack Finley liked her! She then dragged a chair over to the door, and tried to wedge it beneath the doorknob so no one could get in. She didn't have any money to steal but couldn't shake off the memory of her uncle's body on top of hers, and doing what she'd seen him do to her aunt, even though her aunt didn't seem to mind.

"Did you end up telling anyone?"

Grace looked across the room to see Mary lying in bed facing her. "Did I what?"

"Well, I'm guessing that horrible man had his way with you."

Once again, she couldn't believe she had been talking this whole time. She looked around the room. The young girl was nowhere in sight, but over the past few days she'd certainly stirred Grace's memories, memories she had buried long ago. She'd learned, though, that what has been buried can sometimes resurrect and stir trouble.

"Why don't you mind your business?" she said to Mary. Then she turned on her side with her back facing the nosy body, her mind refusing to stay quiet.

CHAPTER 12

Adele didn't have much time left before her article was due but she knew there was so much more to cover and doubted she'd be able to get to Coyote Hill to take photos as Mr. Wilson suggested. Grace had yet to reveal why she walked out on her family. Adele suspected a couple of possibilities but knew as a reporter she had to keep those out of the article. When Grace was outside the solarium having a cigarette, Mary motioned for Adele to come over to her bedside. Barely above a whisper, Mary said that Grace muttered something quite disturbing and told Adele the revelation about what the uncle had done. The very idea kept Adele awake at night, trying to see Grace as the young girl she had been. Adele's life was so uncomplicated in her small town. And charmed, comparatively. That was apparent the day before when, having passed her driver's test, her parents surprised her with a new car. Well, new to her anyway. The Honda Accord was three years old but didn't have a lot of miles on it.

"This way you'll get your feet wet," her father had said.

"My feet wet?" Adele said, gazing at the silver vehicle as she circled around it. There was barely a scratch on it.

"Well, chances are you'll ding it up so it's better it's not brand new."

"Adele," her mother said, standing nearby, "just be careful. Don't drive too fast." She reached over, pulling Adele in a tight hug as if not wanting her to get into the driver seat. Adele did so anyway, eager to drive to the lake and show her friends. Instead, though, she ended up going to the nursing home, which was when she found Mary alone and was filled in with what she'd missed. She went out to the solarium to find Grace slumped in her wheelchair, a cigarette down to its nub. Adele gently reached over, taking it from her, causing Grace to jerk awake with a snort. She looked down at her hand to see that the cigarette was gone before she turned her sights on to Adele.

"You ain't sick of me yet?" Grace said.

Adele pulled out a nearby chair, the metal hot from the beating sun, and sat cautiously on the vinyl seat, opening her notebook. "So, how old were you when you and Jack started dating?"

Grace squinted, looked to be thinking. "Guess around fourteen," she said, the question opening the floodgates.

By the time school was in session, her black eye and bruises were colored a slight yellow, but her classmates didn't seem to notice; they were more intrigued that Jack didn't hide the fact that Grace was his girl. Helen wasn't sure what to make of it, exclaiming, "Wow, you're dating a tenth grader!"

Grace showed up for ninth grade but wondered if it was worth staying in school. Before classes, she did the morning shift when it was the busiest and tips were better. But the hours were long and focusing on her studies was a struggle. Being in high school meant that she had a different teacher for every required subject and was failing in just about all of them. She wasn't sure she could keep up with her grades *and* working at the diner with how exhausted she always felt. And there was no time to go with Tim to Alix's to look at any guitar. At least she used that as an excuse, not wanting Rachel and Tim to know that her money had been stolen. Therefore, making money was more important than schooling. Besides, she wouldn't be the first to drop out, if she decided to do so. To her surprise, Claire hadn't returned for the fall session.

"Her mom's gonna have another baby, so Claire has to help around the house," Helen had said.

There was also Jack's wrestling matches that she kept missing, much to his disappointment, but it interfered with her afternoon shift at the diner. The one bright spot was Sundays, her day off. Jack would come over to listen to music and they'd make out on the couch, the springs poking them in their backsides. Sometimes Helen would come over, too, and they'd all hang out, talking about how happy they were that the war was long over and local boys had returned home—at least most of them, and the world around them seemed to be free of worry.

"Dad says," Helen began one afternoon, "that we can all breathe easier now."

Still, breathing easier had been a challenge for Grace. By the time she headed back to the cabin after work, it was dark. As she pedaled as fast as she could, she tried to see behind the bushes, hoping her uncle wasn't skulking in them, ready to rob her again. Just in case her uncle did show up, Grace had money hidden under the floorboards in the kitchen beneath a throw rug that Rachel had given her. Yet, there was still the concern that he would physically harm her again, money or not. However, once she got inside the cabin, thanks to Jack's handiwork, the back and front doors now with their new locks, she felt relatively safe.

Each time she returned home, she had the skeleton key ready and hastily put it in the chamber, listening for the release, and then rushed inside, immediately locking the door behind her. Once she felt safe, she'd let Snowball out and wouldn't open the door until she heard him yowling to come back in. Jack had also brought nails and wood to replace the slats on the front steps and fixed the screen door, telling Grace on warm days she could leave the front door open to let in a nice breeze. She didn't say as much, but Grace never felt safe enough to do any such thing, unless he was there with her. Besides, the weather was getting too cold to do that now that autumn was upon them.

It was the end of October when Rachel and Tim asked to talk to Grace after Rachel turned the opened sign around to closed. She reached into her pocket and pulled out a wad of bills, saying, "Tim and I discussed it a while back and wanted to start paying you. We're giving you fifty cents an hour plus you can still keep your tips."

Grace's mouth dropped open. "Are . . . are you sure?"

"We are," Rachel said, pressing the money in Grace's hand. "We've been saving it for you for a couple months now."

"You have?" she said, looking down at the cash in her hands, wondering why they were only telling her now. Certainly, it would be enough to buy her guitar.

"The thing is, sweetie," Rachel said, "you're gonna need supplies for the winter."

"Supplies?"

"A good winter coat and boots," Tim said. "And canned goods."

Rachel rested a hand on Grace's shoulder. "You're gonna find living on your own in that cabin in the winter will have its challenges and you need to be prepared." She hesitated. "We hope you'll be able to get that guitar, but we think you need to get the provisions first. Tim'll help you."

"I'll be going in the morning," he said. "You come with me and we'll get you what you need."

The following morning, as they rumbled along the main street in Chateaugay, Tim pointed to a store, saying, "That's Alix's. We'll go there after we get your necessities."

Grace strained to see through the store's window as they drove by, hoping to see a guitar in it, but couldn't make out much. Moments later, they pulled up in front of the IGA with Tim explaining that the grocery store offered much more than Humphrey's in 'busco did. Soon they were going up and down the several aisles and filling up their baskets with canned goods. Tim always gave Grace a block of ice every few days to put in her icebox to keep the few food items that needed refrigeration, but her icebox wasn't that big so she kept the items that would need to be kept cold to a minimum. Besides, Rachel and Tim always made sure she had something to eat when she was working but said that there'd be days they'd have to be closed due to inclement weather and didn't want her trapped without any sustenance. Unlike when she lived with her Aunt Gladys, who had set traps to catch rabbits and used a shotgun to kill deer or wild turkeys, Grace had no means to do any such thing. However, Tim promised that he'd give her some of the beef from the cow he planned to butcher within the next week.

Once they were finished in the IGA, Tim took Grace's bags from her, saying, "I'll put these in the truck and you go over to Pearl's."

"Pearl's?"

"We can't go back to 'busco without you getting boots. And a good coat."

Rachel had implored her to buy new boots for the winter. "What you're wearing won't do," she had said, and insisted Tim make sure Grace understood the necessity.

Slowly, Grace wandered across the street, seeing that Alix's was next door to Pearl's. She peered through the window at Alix's and sure enough spotted a guitar leaning on a stand. She glanced over her shoulder making sure that Tim wasn't watching and went inside Alix's. She hurried over to where the guitar was displayed, a tag attached to the neck.

A man came from around the counter. "Could I help you?"

"I was just wondering . . . how much does this cost?" Grace said.

"It's right there on the tag," the man said.

Hesitantly, Grace reached over to get a look: $24.95. Her heart sank. She'd come to town with twenty-five dollars and already spent about seven at the grocery store.

"It's a Gibson," the man said.

She wasn't sure if that was good or bad but couldn't consider it anyway. Grace nodded and walked out, going to Pearl's next door as Tim instructed. If she didn't care what he and Rachel thought, she would have found a way to buy the guitar and forfeit dressing for the winter. The moment she opened the door to Pearl's, she was stunned by the racks of clothes, the aroma of perfume greeting her. She stood in the doorway, not knowing how to proceed when a woman approached her, asking what she was looking for. Soon, she was trying on boots when Tim came in. He and the saleswoman talked her into buying a pair that was pricier than what she was initially looking at. "They'll hold up better," the saleswoman insisted.

"Where are your coats?" Tim asked. "For her." He motioned to Grace.

"Someone as pretty as her needs to be in the latest style," the woman said.

CHAPTER 12

"Should be practical, though," Tim called out.

After Grace had boots, coat, and mittens picked out, she lowered her voice so Tim couldn't hear and said, "I need . . . undergarments." The brassiere that Helen's mother had given her was all stretched out and the underwear only stayed up if she used a safety pin.

The saleswoman motioned for Tim to stay where he was and brought Grace over to the lingerie section.

Before long Grace was at the counter, counting out her money while the woman bagged the items, including the under-garments, saying, "You're such a pretty girl. Be sure to come back for Christmas. We'll have so much more in stock then."

Not caring a bit about getting new clothes, Grace just hoped by then the guitar would still be for sale.

Tim met Grace at the door. "Well, look at you!" he exclaimed, seeing her cradling the bag. "That should keep you warm enough. Now let's go check out that guitar."

Grace shook her head, saying she had nowhere near enough while trying not to cry. She said, "I think I'd rather get back home and put away everything before work."

"You sure?" Tim said.

Unable to speak, she nodded.

"Well, least you can feel good that you're pretty much set up for the winter now. Rachel'll be pleased to see those new boots and coat."

When they reached her path to the cabin, Tim parked the truck alongside the road and helped her carry her supplies to the cabin. He said, "You won't be able to use your bike when it snows, Grace."

"I know. It's not that far, though. I'll just leave earlier and walk."

Tim had a look of concern, shaking his head, but didn't say anything more. While he held the screen door open, she let them in with her trusty key. Tim followed her inside, traipsing through the small living room into the kitchen where he placed her bags on the table.

"Don't worry, hon," he said. "You'll get that guitar soon enough. You made a smart choice getting these things." He pointed to the purchased items. "You'll be glad you have 'em when the thermometer dips below freezin'." He paused, then said, "Need help puttin' anything away?"

"No, thank you."

He then left with her promising to be in to work for the lunch shift. The moment she locked the door behind him, instead of putting the items away, she went upstairs and curled up on her bed, in her mind's eye learning how to play the guitar.

Later, she woke with a start. That's when she realized Snowball hadn't greeted them when they came back from the stores. She got up and called him but he didn't come. She then went downstairs. "Snowball. Here Snowball."

And there he was, lying on the floor next to the couch.

"Snowball?"

He didn't budge.

She went over to him, reaching for him and immediately knowing. She slumped down and scooped him up, cradling his lifeless body. "Snowball. My Snowball." She rocked him for several minutes before taking him outside. She found the shovel and dug a deep hole in the back. She and Aunt Gladys had to bury lots of animals over the years, her aunt telling her it was the way things were, and she'd accepted it. But this time it was like saying goodbye to a family member and she cried with each pile of dirt she tossed in over the one who had been her sole companion for months.

That afternoon, she rushed into the diner, spewing apologies for being late without saying why. It was too painful to talk about just then.

"Don't worry about it," Rachel said. "Heard you're all set for the winter. Good girl." She handed Grace an apron. "Didn't get a chance to wash a few dishes. Would you mind?"

Grace was greeted by the strong smell of trout frying, reminding her of the fish her aunt fried, which was always Snowball's favorite. The memory caused her stomach to churn and she rushed to the bathroom where she heaved. Once she collected herself, wiping her sweaty brow, she made her way to the kitchen. Once the dishes were washed, she went to the dining room to see what needed to be done.

"Yup, they're gonna be bringin' more 'lectricity down the Gagnier Road in the spring," said one of the men sitting at the counter.

"Things changing pretty fast around here," Rachel replied.

Grace was too shy to ask, but wondered if electricity could reach her cabin in the woods. Helen's family had electricity *and* a telephone. Grace couldn't imagine having such luxuries.

Just then, a local family of five walked in. Grace was grateful for the distraction, keeping her from being too sad. She hurried over and led them to a table. She decided then and there to keep herself focused, work hard for tips and push aside all sadness and exhaustion that had taken a hold of her. She needed to do well so she would receive good tips. Then she would go back to Alix's and see about getting that guitar.

But keeping her mind off how sad she was turned out to be difficult since at closing time, Rachel reminded Grace to take the scraps they'd saved for Snowball. That's when Grace told them the news.

"Oh, sweetheart," Tim said. "I'm so sorry. But he had a long life, didn't he?"

"And you gave him a good life, especially the last few months," Rachel said. "It would've been a rough winter for him, with how old he was."

Grace nodded, then headed back to the cabin where there'd be no one to greet her. If Jack wasn't in her life, she'd feel hopeless.

CHAPTER 13

One early Sunday afternoon in November, when they were keeping warm near Grace's wood-burning stove and listening to records, Jack said, "What're you doing for Thanksgiving?"

Grace shrugged. Her aunt had never made a big deal out of the day and it wasn't until she was in school that Grace discovered that families feasted that day on turkey and pumpkin pie.

"Wanna come to my house for Thanksgiving?"

Grace hesitated before saying, "I don't think your mom would like that."

"Dad told her she had to be neighborly, no matter what. We don't ever have anyone special over so this would make it a fun day. Besides, once she gets to know you, she's going to see how nice you are." When Grace didn't say anything right away, Jack continued. "We always have mashed potatoes, gravy, pumpkin pie and all kinds of vegetables. Oh, and the turkey."

The diner would be closed on Thanksgiving, which meant she'd have to fend for herself since Rachel and Tim went to his sister's home in Plattsburgh. And what Jack just listed sounded too delicious to pass up. "Okay," she finally said, causing Jack to plant a big kiss on her lips.

The next morning, she told Rachel about the invitation.

"Well, then, you'll need to bring something."

"Like what?"

"A pie, I suppose." She must've seen Grace's expression because Rachel added, "Don't worry. We'll bake one here and you can bring it."

Thanksgiving morning Grace trudged from the cabin out to the road through three inches of snow, grateful for the warm boots, coat and mittens. She carefully cradled an apple pie in her arms. Jack told her he'd be by to pick her up around eleven. "We eat dinner at noon," he'd said.

She stood trembling in the cold, not wanting to be late. The dress she wore was too thin for the weather, but she wanted to look her best—more for Jack's mother than for Jack himself. About twenty minutes later, a truck headed in her direction and pulled up alongside her, kicking up some snow. But Jack wasn't driving. Instead, it was his father.

Jack jumped out of the passenger side and held the door open for her. He took the pie from her so she could climb up onto the seat, her body shivering.

"Well, there's the beautiful singer!" Jack's father exclaimed. Then, "Let me crank this up." He reached over, turning a knob. Grace was thankful to feel heat suddenly blasting in her direction.

"So, what's this?" Jack said, motioning to the pie.

"It's an apple pie. I baked it myself." She felt proud of how it came out, having followed Rachel's directions while insisting she was to do all the mixing of apples and rolling of dough herself.

Jack cleared his throat as Grace caught him giving his father an odd look. She said, "I hope that's okay."

"Well, Ma made an apple pie, too."

Grace distinctly recalled Jack saying that his mother always made pumpkin pie, which is why she and Rachel decided an apple pie was a safer bet. She said, "I should've made a pumpkin pie then," feeling like the day wasn't starting out the way she'd hoped.

"Oh, she made that, too," Jack said.

"Never can have too much pie, I say," Jack's father piped up. "We're gonna have a real fine meal."

Soon they were walking into the farmhouse, all stomping snow from their boots. Jack's mother was at the stove, peering into a large pot, without acknowledging Grace.

"Look what our young guest brought us," Gerald said.

Simone looked over at Grace who was holding the pie.

"I should've brought something else," Grace said. "It's apple."

"Well, you can take it back home with you. I made plenty."

She left Grace holding the pie, until Jack hurried over and took it from her. He brought it to the counter, placing it next to his mother's pies.

"Come in, come in!" Gerald said. "Jack, take her coat."

Even though the stove had a roaring fire and steam poured from some pots on the burners, Grace felt a chill in the room. She supposed it was from Jack's mother and wished she hadn't agreed to come.

After Jack took her coat, hat, and mittens, he put everything in the corner with a pile of other coats. Then he said, "I'll show you around." He led her from the roomy kitchen into the living room. There was a wood stove roaring with fire in the corner, a stack of wood piled nearby.

"My parents' bedroom is off the kitchen and mine is upstairs. But someday, I might move into the little house across the field."

Grace was having a hard time paying attention to what he was saying. She lowered her voice. "Should I ask your mother if I can help her with anything?"

Jack shrugged. "I guess. That would be nice."

Grace went into the kitchen, Simone's back to her. She looked to be mashing potatoes. "Mrs. Finley," she said, barely above a whisper, her voice shaking, "can I help with something?"

Simone turned and glared at her. "I've been cooking for years. Lot longer than you've been at that diner. I don't need no help."

"She was just being polite, Simone," Gerald said. He looked at Grace. "How about you and Jack stay in the living room and Simone will call you when everything's ready?"

Grace nodded. As she left the kitchen, she heard Simone sputter, "She's a *Dormand*. She has no right being in my home."

Gerald snapped, "Will you stop that? None of that was any fault of her own."

Grace walked into the living room to see Jack putting more wood in the stove. She said, "I should leave. Your mom doesn't want me here."

Jack looked over at her, closing the door to the stove. "Don't let her bother you. Most times we just ignore her."

Jack's father walked in the room, pointing to the couch while he sat in a rocking chair. "Sit down, you two." Jack took Grace by the hand and had her sit down with him.

"So, Grace, did you get that guitar yet?" Jack's father said.

Grace's stomach began to churn, wishing she was back home in her cabin. "No," she replied.

"Well, soon I bet. Sometimes we sing around here without the benefit of any guitar," he said. "Maybe after we eat we can do some singing."

Grace had a difficult time imagining Simone singing.

Jack said, "Grace sings 'Red River Valley' real good, Dad."

"That so?"

"It's one of his favorites," Jack said, looking at Grace.

"Come eat!" Simone called from the kitchen.

They all got up and shuffled into the kitchen. Grace gazed at the variety of food on the table. Gerald said, "You really outdid yourself this year, Simone. We should have company more often."

"What're you talkin' about? I didn't do anything special for anyone." Simone dropped down on her chair with a thump, scowling at her husband. Once they were all seated, Simone, Gerald, and Jack all made the sign of the cross and said in rushed unison: "Bless us, O Lord, and these Thy gifts, which we are about to receive from Thy bounty. Through Christ, our Lord. Amen."

Simone picked up a bowl of mashed potatoes, scooping them onto her plate, saying, "I noticed you didn't pray. Aren't you Catholic?"

Grace didn't know what to say but she nodded. If having gone to the church with her aunt at Christmas and Easter meant she was a Catholic, then she was. Besides, she had the baptismal certificate as proof.

"It's just that I never see you in church."

Gerald interjected, "Do you like white or dark meat, Grace?"

Grace had no stomach for much of anything, but said, "Whatever you can spare."

He laughed. "With a bird this size, why don't I give you some of both?" He then carved too many slices and put them on her plate.

The meal was filled with forks and knives clanking against plates and loud smacking, intermingled with requests for more of this and more of that. Grace didn't ask for seconds of anything, struggling enough with what was already on her plate. The conversation starters were strained and didn't go very far. She was relieved when everyone seemed to have had their fill.

Simone got up and brought over her pies, placing them on the table, leaving Grace's pie on the counter. "So, who wants pumpkin?"

"I'll take a slice of each," Gerald said. "But why don't we serve our guest first?"

Simone looked at Grace. "What'll you have?"

Grace hesitated then said, "Pumpkin's fine," not knowing how she'd manage a single bite.

"Let's hope you like it better than the meal. You didn't seem to like my cookin'." She put a plate filled with a big slice of pie in front of Grace.

"It was delicious," Grace said. And she supposed it was, but her nerves had her so unsettled she found it difficult to enjoy the spread. "And the pie looks good, too."

Simone muttered something under her breath, placing large slices from both pies on Gerald and Jack's plates, then sliced some for herself. Grace watched the three of them dig in, shoving large portions in their mouths, her stomach roiling, afraid she'd vomit right then and there. Still, she took a bite, forcing it down her throat, all the while feeling Simone study her.

As soon as Jack scraped the last bits from his plate, Grace said she should probably be getting back to her place.

Jack looked surprised while Simone reached over, grabbing Grace's plate from her. "This is a waste. You shouldn't have asked for it, if you weren't going to eat it."

"Ma," Jack said, "she's just nervous."

"I'm sorry," Grace said. "I feel out of sorts, I guess. I should get home."

"Suit yourself," Simone said. "No need to worry 'bout this mess." She pointed to the dirty pile of plates, pots and pans.

"Oh," Grace said, pushing herself away from the table. "Let me help before I go."

"You don't need to do any such thing," Gerald said.

"No, that's fine," Grace said. "I always wash the dishes at the diner."

"The soap's under there." Simone pointed underneath to where the sink was.

Jack and his father stayed seated while Simone put away leftovers, adding more dirty dishes to the pile.

"How about we sing that song Jack mentioned earlier?" Gerald said.

A strong twinge in her belly caused Grace to grip the side of the sink for support. The last thing she felt like doing was singing. She began scraping dried up food from the bottom of a pan while Gerald broke into song.

"*From this valley they say you are goin'* . . ." He stopped and said, "Come on, honey. I'd love to hear you sing."

"Don't be shy, Grace," Jack said.

She leaned into the sink, feeling flushed.

"*I will miss your bright eyes and sweet smile,*" Gerald prodded.

A powerful spasm seemed to pull from her insides and she dropped to her knees.

"You okay?" Jack rushed over to her.

Gasping, she said, "I don't feel so good. I . . . I should go home."

"Maybe she's not used to such good food," Simone said. "Maybe it's too rich for her."

She tried to stand up but couldn't. Something was wrong. The cramps were worse than she'd ever experienced before.

"What on earth?" Simone said.

Grace used all her strength to push herself up, blood streaming down her legs. She'd never had her monthly so bad before. *Her monthly?* She'd been too busy to pay attention, but she couldn't remember the last time she'd had it. She began to shake uncontrollably.

Gerald scooped her up and carried her to the bedroom off the kitchen, telling Simone to call the doctor.

"You can't put her on our bed!" Simone shouted. "She'll get it all bloody!"

"For crying out loud," Gerald said, "then put something down first."

Grace's breathing was labored, and she was whimpering, wanting to be anywhere but there. Once Simone tossed an old blanket on the bed, Gerald lay Grace down on it.

Jack poked his head in the bedroom. "I called the doctor. He's on his way." He stared at Grace. "What's wrong with her?"

"Looks like she's hemorrhaging," Simone said.

Grace was sure she was dying and wished she would if it meant the pain would stop. She didn't know how much time had passed lying in the bedroom alone while Jack and his parents were in the kitchen bickering until the doctor appeared.

"Sorry, little lady," the doctor said after examining her, "but you lost it."

She looked up at him, the cramping having lessened. "Lost what?"

"The baby. How far along were you?" He wrapped whatever came out of her in a cloth.

"How far . . ." she muttered.

He sighed. "When was your last menstruation?"

She wasn't sure, but if she thought about it, it had to have been sometime during the summer. When she didn't reply, he said, "Well, let's get you cleaned up so you can rest some."

"I have no clothes here," she whimpered. "I have to get home."

The doctor went to the bedroom door and opened it. "Simone, you got something this girl can change into?" He then walked out, closing the door behind him. She heard bits and pieces of conversation, followed by hysteria with Simone accusing Jack of something and Jack yelling in protest. *Was he crying?*

The doctor returned, examined her again, and said, "The bleeding seems to have let up some for now."

Simone rushed in and went to her dresser where she pulled out a worn, wrinkled dress, tossing it on the bed. "Change into this, then Gerald'll bring you home."

"I . . . I don't know what happened," Grace said, her voice quavering. "But I'm so sorry I ruined your Thanksgiving." Tears streamed down her face,

"You're not foolin' anybody, 'specially me. I know you're a Dormand. Just 'cuz you changed your name to Cooke don't change nothin'." She went back to her dresser and pulled out a sanitary pad and belt to hold it. "Use this for now." She tossed them on the bed. "But let me say one thing. What you did to my boy, you ought to be ashamed."

"What I did . . .? Mrs. Finley," Grace stammered, "I don't know what you're talking about."

"Typical Dormand, playing stupid." Simone went to the door. "Change and get out of my house."

A little while later, Grace tottered out of the bedroom, her bloody clothes rolled up in a ball in her arms, the worn dress hanging loosely on her hunched and shaking body. Jack stared at her as if he didn't recognize her.

"I'll walk home," she said, not wanting to cause any more trouble.

"No," Gerald said. "I'll be driving you." He guided her out to the truck, Jack staying behind, his eyes red-rimmed.

She trembled as Gerald helped her onto the passenger seat then hurried around to the driver side. The truck was so cold it felt like the walk-in storage room at the diner. Grace couldn't stop shaking during the entire drive back to her place, Gerald not speaking a word. He pulled the truck to the side of the road, shut the engine, and then went to her side as she attempted to get out. He reached her first and scooped her up, carrying her along the narrow path while she tried to tell him he didn't need to do any such thing. Once they reached the cabin, he set her down on her unsteady feet.

It took her a few moments before she'd managed to get the skeleton key out of her coat pocket. She hadn't put on her mittens and her hands were numb and shaking. Gerald took the key from her and unlocked the door. Then he followed her inside where she collapsed on the couch, all the strength drained from her. He went over to her stove that still had some embers glowing, put in some wood that was stacked nearby, and got a fire going.

While he was poking at the wood, he said, "Jack swears you and him haven't done anything to have gotten you in that situation. I believe him." He turned, looking at her. "I also remember him telling me that you were pretty bruised up a while back. You said it was a branch or something like that, but then you wanted to be sure there were locks on your doors."

Grace remained quiet.

"I'm not the smartest, but I tend to put two and two together and recall the way those fellows were grabbin' at you at the diner. I ever see 'em again, you can bet they won't ever do it again." He looked around her cabin, walked to the back and checked the door. When he returned, he said, "If someone wants to get in, they will. You own a gun?"

She hesitated and shook her head.

"I'll see you get one." He walked over and wiped her tears with his calloused hand. "You've had a rough go of it already." He turned and checked the stove, appearing satisfied that it was beginning to warm up the room.

"Jack'll be coming tomorrow to check on you. Doc says you'll be fine with some rest. Now get some but be sure to lock the door behind me."

Unable to speak, Grace shuffled behind Gerald and locked the door the minute he walked out. She didn't have the strength to go upstairs to her bed, so she curled up onto the couch, not caring that there was a spring poking into her back. Eventually, she fell into a deep, fretful sleep.

CHAPTER 14

Once Adele's friends discovered she had a car, they were hoping she'd pick them up and drive them to the lake, Dairy Queen, or most anywhere, reminding her that summer would be over before she knew it. They implored her. "You got a car! Take advantage of it."

"*Not once*," Nicole texted, "*not once have you spent any time with us!*" She then used a sad emoji.

Adele, sitting cross-legged on her bed, texted back. "*Can't. Need to get this assignment done.*"

"*You suck.*"

The truth was, Adele was shocked by Grace's latest revelation and there had to be so much more to her story. She'd approached Mr. Wilson earlier that day, requesting an extension.

"Adele," he'd said, "you have to respect deadlines if you want to be in the business of journalism."

"I go almost every day!" Adele said. "And when I get home I take all my notes and try to put them in some kind of order. I . . . I want to do some more research. *Please*."

Mr. Wilson hesitated, but then told her he'd give her an extra week, even though the session would have concluded. "You can get the article to me then. But not a day later or you will have failed."

Getting a good grade was no longer the issue for Adele; it was her strong desire to find out more about Grace Finley that was keeping her going. Obviously, she and Jack got married and she somehow got a guitar and learned how to play. *But when did that all transpire?*

Adele looked at her watch. It was almost three in the afternoon. Now that she wasn't dependent on her parents to drive her anywhere, she decided to go back to the nursing home and get Grace to continue her story.

Grace woke trembling and drenched in blood. It must've been well past the time she was expected to be at the diner but she was too out of it to worry. She realized that the stove had only a few embers left, which explained why she was so cold. She pushed herself off the couch, seeing blood on the cushion before going over and tossing some kindling and then larger pieces of wood into the stove, moving them around with the poker. She then scuffed over to the kitchen, pumped some water into a pan, then scuffed back to the stove and put the pan on the burner to heat up the water before making her way upstairs to get a change of clothes and some rags. The pad and belt to hold it that Simone had given her was something she'd never seen before and wondered if next time she went to Chateaugay she'd be able to find them for herself. It certainly beat using rags.

She trudged downstairs carrying a clean pair of dungarees, shirt and some undergarments. The fire was roaring but the water was barely lukewarm. Grace didn't care since she was eager to get out of Simone's dress and clean herself up. Still weak, it took her some time to strip down. Once she was clean and changed, she took one of the rags, wet it and tried to scrub the blood off the couch cushion. After several minutes, she gave up and flipped the cushion over. A sudden knock at the door caused her to shriek.

"Grace, it's just me, Tim! Are you okay?"

Grace shoved the pile of bloody clothes into a corner and went over to open the door.

Tim said, "We were worried about you. Rachel sent me to check on you."

"I'm so sorry," Grace said, opening the door wide enough to let Tim in.

"You look kind of peaked," Tim said, shutting the door behind him. "You feelin' okay?"

"I'm trying," she said. "I'll be ready in a minute or so and can—"

"No, no. You stay home today. We weren't that busy anyway. Everybody must be home eatin' leftovers." He hesitated, then added, "Rachel was chomping at the bit, though. Wanted to know how everything went yesterday."

Grace's mouth went dry, not knowing how to reply.

"I mean, did Simone like the apple pie?"

Grace remembered her pie she'd left on the counter. "Well, she made her own, so served that."

Tim frowned. "That right?" He looked over at the small stack of wood. "Got enough wood there? I could get some more for you, if you'd like."

She wanted more than anything to take him up on the offer, but said, "No, thank you." He had done enough for her. Besides, she didn't want to look helpless or they'd make her move back to the mountains.

He looked around. "You made this place real nice, sweetie."

She shrugged. "I guess."

He cleared his throat. "Well, if you're up to it, come in tomorrow morning."

"I'll be up to it," she said, grateful it was going to be a later start since it would be a Saturday.

After Tim left, Grace locked the door, then took the pan of hot water off the stove and carried it over to the kitchen counter. She grabbed a bar of soap and the pile of clothes she'd tossed in the corner and began washing Simone's dress. While she scrubbed the blood away, the water turning pinkish, she tried to make sense of what had happened to her. Helen had told her how babies came to be, but she and Jack hadn't done anything of the sort.

After she scrubbed as much of the blood from the dress as she could, she went to the back door, opening it before taking the dirty water and dumping it outside. She then closed and locked the door and went back to the sink, pumping clean cold water into the pan and rinsing the soapy dress. She wanted to give it back to Simone without a trace of blood on it. While wringing clean water from the dress, images of her uncle on top of her before she'd blacked out came to mind. Then there was the memory of seeing him on top of her aunt followed by the mewing sounds having come from the bundle he'd brought outside. He'd refused to tell her what it was, but then there was her aunt, who was bedridden and bloody. The very idea caused Grace to feel nauseous. Prior to the Thanksgiving night-mare, she'd pushed out of her mind what he'd done to her, only thinking of the money he'd stolen. Now it seemed he'd stolen so much more.

She squeezed as much water as she could from the dress and brought it upstairs, tossing it over the banister to dry. *Had she really had a baby growing inside her?* With that thought, she couldn't imagine Jack ever wanting to come near her again. She recalled his expression from the day before as she staggered out the door, his father leading the way. He'd looked appalled.

While sorting it all out, there was a knock at her door. She quietly went down the steps and listened. Another knock.

"Who is it?" she said, barely above a whisper.

"Grace! It's me, Jack."

She took a deep breath, trying to gather herself, before she opened the door. He rushed in, slamming the door behind him.

"Damn, it's cold out there." He held a gun and burlap bag. His voice quavered when he said, "How you feelin'?"

"Okay." She avoided looking directly at him.

He walked into the kitchen and put a sack on the table. "I brought back your pie and some leftovers."

She mumbled, "You didn't need to do that."

"And this." He placed the rifle on the table next to the sack. "Dad wants you to be safe."

Grace stared at the gun. "I didn't even know, Jack. I . . . I . . ."

"I can't stay. Ma wants me to come right back home. I can't see you anymore."

It was as though her heart stopped. *But what else could she have expected?* She said, "I washed her dress. It's not dry yet, though."

"That's okay. I gotta show you how to use the gun. Dad told me to show you." He pulled bullets from his pocket.

Thing was, Grace knew how to use a gun. Her aunt had shown her when they went hunting for game or when a coyote tried to get to the chickens. Still, she acted as though she didn't know, wanting a reason for Jack to stay longer. He went through the motions of showing her how to load, cock and aim the gun.

"I'd keep it where you can get to it right away," Jack said. "Those guys come around, just point it in their direction. That'll get them to leave. But if it was me, I'd shoot every last one of 'em."

She wanted to tell him what had really happened, but her throat closed up and she couldn't speak.

"Well," he said, walking over to the door, "I best be going. Ma said if I don't get back in fifteen minutes, she'll have my hide."

Grace did everything in her power not to cry. She stood at the door, yearning for him to turn around and hug her. He started to, but then just patted her on the arm before dashing out the door and running down the path.

She spent the afternoon lying on the couch sobbing. She didn't know how she could possibly see Jack every day at school without it being uncomfortable, without Helen and the others asking what happened. That's when she made a decision. She would quit school. That way she would be able to work weekdays, all day, and make money, even though the idea of buying a guitar no longer seemed so important. She'd try and make enough money so that she could move someplace else, far from Simone and the gossip that had always seemed to trail her.

"That's just not fair," Adele said.

Grace was sitting in her bed, seemingly more alert as she'd told her story. "What's not fair?"

"That you paid a price when it wasn't even your fault!"

"That's what being a woman in our generation meant," Mary said from her side of the room.

"So, did people find out what happened to you?"

Grace gazed off. "I know Jack didn't tell anybody. But his mother found a way to let anyone she ran into know."

Grace slid down under her covers and said, "No more today. I can't take anymore today."

Adele looked over at Mary in a panic. Mary said, "Let her rest. She seems to be able to talk more once she's rested."

Adele didn't have a choice and gathered her things to head home.

CHAPTER 15

The next couple of weeks Grace kept busy. Rachel tried to talk her into going back to school, but she refused without giving a reason. Rachel prodded, "So, how's Jack?" Grace would mumble that he was fine, as far as she knew.

Finally, when Grace showed up for work early one morning, Rachel asked her to come upstairs to the apartment with her. "There's something I want to talk to you about," she'd said. Grace had never been upstairs before but followed Rachel toward the back of the diner and up the stairs. The space was small but felt cozy. Rachel pointed to some of the boxes near a couch. "Christmas decorations," she explained. "It's coming fast."

Grace hadn't thought much about the holiday, her mind too distracted to care.

"Come, sit down," Rachel said, walking into the kitchen area, pulling out a metal chair from the table for two. The moment they were both seated, Rachel sighed before saying, "So, Simone came to see me the other day."

Grace hung her head down, using her hair to cover her face. "Are you going to fire me?"

"Fire you? No!" She hesitated, before continuing. "I know that you and Jack are young and without any adult guiding you, well, you made a mistake. Simone insists that Jack can't see you again and I'm sorry about that but maybe it's for the best. Like Simone said, unfortunately, boys will be boys. Well, she didn't exactly say boys. Tended to accuse you."

Barely above a whisper, Grace said, "He didn't do anything. He's not like that." Sure, they would kiss and a couple times Jack placed his hand on her breast, but then would stop himself before they went any further.

Rachel studied her for a moment. "Well, between you and me, it's a blessing how it ended. I don't know how you would've been able to care for a baby under the circumstances."

Just as Grace was about to tell Rachel that it wasn't Jack but her uncle, Tim called up, "Rachel! We're running late."

"Be right down," she called back, standing up. "Let's just put this all behind you and start fresh, okay?" She leaned down brushing Grace's forehead with a kiss. "Now, let's get to work."

The opportunity to reveal the truth was lost so Grace nodded and wiped at the tears streaming down her face. She got up and followed Rachel downstairs and went about making the coffee and preparing the biscuits. She wanted more than anything to put what happened behind her, but that meant not having Jack in her life.

The following Sunday, Helen showed up at her door. It was a blustery, chilly day. When Grace invited her into the warmth of the cabin, she came in but remained standing by the door with her coat on.

"I can't stay," Helen said. "I was just wonderin' why you weren't in school. Jack won't tell me."

Grace gazed at Helen. "He didn't say anything?"

"No, but, um . . ."

"What?"

"Well, I heard you had a baby."

"Jack said that?"

"No. My mom said she saw Mrs. Finley at Humphrey's and she told her that you had a baby at her house on Thanksgiving."

Grace's heart began to pound. "Why would she say that?" she snapped. "Do you see a baby?"

"She said you lost it."

Grace sputtered, "Jack and I never did anything to cause that."

"So you did? Have a baby?"

In reality, she wasn't quite sure what she had since she hadn't any proof, but Grace needed people to know that Jack was not responsible. She began, "Oh, Helen, it was awful," but Helen interrupted, saying, "Mom said I had to get back home right away."

"Please stay," Grace said. "I just need to tell somebody what really happened."

Helen shook her head, her expression alarmed. "I can't."

"Let me warm up some milk, if you want and we could—"

"I said no!" Helen shouted, turning around and rushing out, leaving Grace standing there in silence.

When Grace wasn't putting in long hours at the diner, she was shoveling snow to maintain a path from the cabin to the road or cutting wood to keep the cabin warm. Fortunately, she was surrounded by trees, many with large limbs that had fallen. She focused on clearing one particular spot so that when spring came she could start a garden. It wasn't too overgrown, and she could tell that someone had already done most of the clearing years earlier. She imagined it had been her father and mother, recalling the couple of canned jars on the shelves when Helen first brought her to the cabin.

The Victrola sat in the corner, songs no longer pouring out from it. She didn't feel like singing anymore. However, she couldn't get away from music because Tim and Rachel had recently purchased a jukebox and loaded it up with records, saying that it would be another way to bring in some money. And it did. In fact, some families would come into the diner just so they could play Gene Autry's "Rudolph the Red-Nosed Reindeer" for their children. The fact that it was Gene Autry made listening to the song difficult for Grace. Rachel streamed gold garland around the windows and taped a Christmas tree cutout to the front door. It seemed everyone in town was filled with joy. Well, almost everyone. Grace forced a smile while taking and bringing food orders, collecting dirty dishes and washing them, all the while trying to do what Rachel had suggested and put the nightmare behind her. But that didn't mean she stopped thinking about Jack.

Rachel had told Grace that they would be closed the week from Christmas Eve to January 2nd. "Tim and I will be going to his family," Rachel said. "He has a pretty big one. They live in Canton."

Grace didn't know where Canton was.

"If we were staying here, I'd invite you, but . . ."

"That's okay," Grace said.

"What will you do?" Rachel said.

Grace shrugged. She remembered how she and her aunt bundled up to take the trek to church for midnight Mass. She said, "I'll catch up on things, I s'pose."

"Well, here," Rachel said the day before Christmas Eve, bringing out a basket filled with home baked bread, cookies and ham slices. "Merry Christmas, sweetie."

Tim appeared and said, "We'll see you next year." He smiled and winked.

Christmas Eve, while snow spit from the sky, Grace picked her way down the slippery path toward the main road, bundled in a coat and boots, a swinging lantern in her hand lighting the way. Once she got to the main road, she turned down the wick and put the lantern beneath some bushes. It was almost midnight. As she got closer, she spotted people climbing out of their vehicles, wishing each other a Merry Christmas. She purposely lagged behind, waiting for the small group to go in through the side door. She tried to recall all that her aunt had instructed her to do when they entered St. Philomena Catholic Church and made sure that her scarf kept her head covered before walking in through the door. Her stomach sank when it looked as though most of the pews were already filled and all eyes seemed to turn in her direction. She was ready to turn and run out when she spotted Claire who waved Grace over. She shuffled down the aisle, certain she heard some tsks and hisses before reaching Claire and cramming in next to her.

"You didn't genuflect or make the sign of the cross," Claire whispered, her eyes wide.

Oh! Grace suddenly recalled more instructions from her aunt and hurriedly went back into the aisle, doing a quick curtsy and one, two, three with her hand, hearing some snickers from those around her before she squeezed back in next to Claire. Then she remembered how she was to drop to her knees, clasp her hands, bow her head and pray. Well, she dropped to her knees and clasped her hands, but instead of praying, she took a surreptitious look around the church, hoping to see her aunt. Instead, a few pews over, she spotted Simone's stern glare fastened on her. Immediately, she put her head back into her folded arms that were resting on the back of the pew.

Claire tugged on her sleeve and said. "Aren't you done praying, yet?"

Grace nodded and sat back in her seat. While waiting for the priest to appear, as guardedly as she could she allowed herself to look around, again for her aunt, but this time she noticed Jack, who was kneeling, but with his head turned and secretly gazing at her. She thought he was smiling at her, but couldn't be sure. But then the priest and altar boys came out from a back room and everyone stood, providing her another opportunity while standing, sitting, and kneeling repeatedly to look for her aunt, but saw no sign of her.

Just as it had been when she attended with her aunt, she didn't understand what the priest was saying. The Latin sounded like gibberish to her, but she found the hymns a joy to sing. "O Holy Night" was her favorite and she allowed herself to sing it loud and clear. Once everyone stood and nodded to each other as they began pacing outside, she knew Mass was over. She followed the shuffling feet with Claire telling her that she liked how she sang. "You have a pretty voice," she said.

"Thanks," Grace replied, spotting Helen an aisle over. She waved but Helen turned and said something to her mother, who looked directly at Grace with pursed lips.

Claire leaned in. "I heard you . . ." she lowered her voice, "had a baby."

A little boy with snot dripping from his nose, pushed the girls apart, saying, "Come on! I wanna see if Santa Claus came yet."

Grace was grateful for the interruption so she wouldn't have to reply to Claire and made her way outside. She put some distance between herself and the people pouring out of the church before she turned to look for her aunt. She noticed Jack walking out with his parents, but he didn't look in her direction, his mother gripping his arm, pulling him along.

Disappointed, she headed back to the cabin, first finding the lantern in the bushes near the side of the road where she'd left it. She took matches from her pocket and lit it, heading down the path. It had stopped snowing, the moon and stars bright in the sky.

When she reached the cabin, she had her key ready and let herself in, immediately locking the door behind her. As she always did when she got home, she went to the stove and loaded it with more wood. As late as it was, she didn't feel tired. Something about singing at church had inspired her, so she went to the Victrola and decided to put on a record and began singing with Gene Autry while recalling what she was sure was a smile from Jack when he'd gazed at her in church. The memory would have to suffice. After singing with a few records, she decided it was time to go to bed.

The following morning she was awakened by a light knock on her door. She'd fallen asleep on the couch to be near the wood-burning stove. She got up and looked out the window. *Jack!* It was Jack, but he was running down the path toward the main road. She ran and unlocked the door, calling his name, but he didn't stop. She started to run after him, but she was barefoot and he was no longer in sight. She shouted his name again, waiting, hoping he'd heard her and come back. Just then, she spotted something next to the door. She gasped to see that it was a shiny guitar, just like the one she'd seen in Alix's.

She grabbed it, noticing a note attached that read, *Merry Christmas! Love, Jack.* There was also a booklet strapped around the neck of the guitar titled *Teach Yourself to Play the Guitar.* She looked down the path again, but he was gone. She trembled from the cold, going back inside, gingerly carrying the guitar and locking the door behind her. Without drying her feet from the snow, she rushed over to the couch, dropping down, grazing the body of the guitar, plucking the strings. She had planned on making breakfast with the bread and ham Rachel had given her but now she had no desire to eat. Jack brought her a guitar! *Did that mean he still loved her?* She looked at the note he signed, *Love,*

Jack. She began strumming and humming, not having a clue how to make the strings sound like music. She flipped open the book. Now she knew what she would be doing the following week. Suddenly, she understood the meaning of Christmas.

Adele realized Grace, who was huddled in her bed and lightly snoring, was done for the day. She took out her cell phone and went over to the corner of the room where the guitar was leaning and snapped a couple of photos, certain it would complement the article. She then left, but planned to be back again bright and early to try to get Grace to share more of her story. The deadline was looming.

CHAPTER 16

By the time leaves started budding on the trees and grass emerged from what had been snow-covered ground, Grace could play several songs on her guitar. Not only was she able to follow the directions from the booklet, she could pick out tunes from records she'd play repeatedly on the Victrola. She wanted Jack to know his gift hadn't been a waste, but he hadn't returned since Christmas day. That's when she decided to bring back the dress his mother had let her borrow as an excuse in hopes of seeing him.

Her hand shook as she knocked on the front porch door. She tried to keep as steady as possible once she heard the latch turn. She hoped it would be Jack on the other side since it was a Sunday afternoon and there was a better chance he'd be around. Instead, to her disappointment, it was Simone, her eyes wide and expression grim, once she realized who was standing in front of her.

Without giving Simone a chance to shut the door in her face, she held the dress out to her. "Sorry it took me so long to get this back to you."

Simone scowled. "What makes you think I want that back after you ruined it?"

Barely above a whisper, Grace said, "I don't know. I . . . I . . ." She desperately wanted to ask if Jack was home but before she had a chance, Simone said, "You keep it," and then slammed the door.

"When are you goin' to bring that guitar here and show us what you know?" Rachel said one afternoon between the lunch and supper crowds.

Grace blushed. "You wanna hear me play?"

"Would love to."

Tim appeared in the doorway from the kitchen. "Maybe you could play 'Waitin' for a Train' so Rachel isn't always feeding the jukebox coins to hear it.

Rachel rolled her eyes, but said, "That would be something."

"Okay," Grace said, looking hesitantly at Tim, "but I'd like to hear it a couple more times if that's all right."

Rachel laughed and practically skipped over to the jukebox, putting in a coin, punching the letter and number she knew by heart. Moments later, Jimmie Rodgers' voice filled up the diner:

All around the water tank
  waiting for a train
A thousand miles away from home
  sleeping in the rain
I walked up to a brakeman
Gave him a line of talk
He said if you've got money boy
I'll see that you don't walk
I haven't got a nickel

Not a penny can I show

Get off get off you railroad bum

And he slammed the boxcar door

   He put me off in Texas

A state I dearly love

The wide open spaces all around me,

The moon and stars up above

Nobody seems to want me

Or to lend me a helping hand

I'm on my way from Frisco

Going back to Dixie Land

Though my pocketbook is empty

And my heart is full of pain

I'm a thousand miles away from home

Just a waiting for a train

She'd heard the song dozens of times, but now Grace, who edged closer to the jukebox, paid close attention to the chords and words. She'd go home after work and practice only that song for about a week. Finally, early one morning, she walked into the back of the diner carrying her guitar. Even though the path from the cabin to the main road had no snow, it was still muddy and rutted, so instead of trying to bike it, she walked to the diner, not wanting anything to damage her prized possession. Tim was at the stove, preparing for the day. Rachel must have been in the front. Tim shot Grace a wink and whispered, "You gonna play that song she likes?"

Grace nodded, feeling accomplished. "I don't know all the words, but most." More importantly, she knew the chords. Music seemed to be second nature to her.

He grinned. "Go ahead."

It wasn't yet five in the morning. "Right now?"

"Surprise her."

Sucking up some nerve, Grace situated the guitar, placed her fingers on the right strings and began strumming. She then sang, "All around the water tank waiting for a train . . ."

Rachel suddenly appeared with her mouth wide open. There were a few phrases Grace had forgotten, but Rachel guided her to the finish. Grace didn't have to wait for a reaction. Immediately, Rachel and Tim burst into exuberant applause.

"You've sure got an ear for music," Tim said.

"You sure do!" Rachel wiped a tear that escaped from her eye. "I'm so proud of you, sweetie. You're really making somethin' of yourself."

Their praise gave Grace a warm feeling, but she wasn't sure just what she could do with singing and playing the guitar. However, as the morning went on and patrons started coming in, Rachel encouraged Grace to perform for them. Soon, the men were calling out songs they'd like to hear. She didn't know many of them, but the ones she did, she was happy to oblige more than once. Eventually, though, she put the guitar away and went back to waitressing. After all, she thought, she wasn't making any money singing.

As time went on, when she wasn't working at the diner, she was learning new chords. When she was getting the garden ready for seeds, cleaning the cabin or chopping wood, she sang enthusiastically without the benefit of the guitar. At night, however, the instrument was her companion and she practiced, practiced, practiced, her calloused fingers seemingly improving her sound. Her confidence was growing and there were times Rachel encouraged her to show what she'd learned, which always led to playing for the patrons.

One day a man with graying hair and wearing a suit, which wasn't common for Churubusco unless it was for a funeral, walked into the diner. Grace had never seen him before and could tell by the way he was dressed that he wasn't one of the laborers. She headed in his direction to seat him.

"Not here for the food," he said. "I heard there's a pretty gal who works here and can sing and play guitar."

Rachel came from the back, calling over, "What you want, Sam?"

"Your waitress. I hear she can sing." He looked at Grace. "That you?" Before Grace could reply, Rachel said, "News travels fast. Grace, that's Sam Cole. He owns Summit Hotel."

"And the tavern," Sam said. "In the hotel. Would you be interested in performing there this Saturday night?"

Grace gasped. She'd gone by the hotel on occasion but never went inside, since there'd been no need. Rarely was Churubusco a destination, but people often stayed at the hotel when the railroad couldn't get through due to inclement weather. However, on the weekends the tavern was filled with locals who took advantage of the pool table and bar, especially since prohibition was long over.

Rachel stepped further into the dining room. "They get pretty rowdy there, Sam. She's just a kid."

Sam looked Grace up and down, his expression pleased. "Kid? She don't look like any kid to me. I'd like to try her out."

Grace glanced at Rachel but couldn't read what she was thinking.

Sam said, "You'd play from seven to ten, a dollar an hour, plus tips."

It was as though her heart stopped. The money would be welcomed but she knew she didn't have enough songs to fill up the three hours and said as much.

"Don't matter," Sam said. "I just want live music for my customers. And don't think the fellas'll mind if you repeat a song or two. Besides, you got four days to learn more tunes. So, are you interested?"

Was she? Singing always made her happy and making money at it would be a bonus. In a word, she said, "Yes."

Tim came out from the kitchen, strolled over, shaking Sam's hand. "Can you promise us she'll be safe? No monkey business?"

"Ya got my word, Tim."

Tim hesitated then looked over at Rachel. "Wanna go out Saturday night?"

Rachel expelled her breath. "That's a good idea."

That Saturday night, at a quarter to seven, carrying her guitar, Grace walked into the Summit Hotel to find Sam waiting in the small vestibule. He looked her over and asked if she was ready.

She nodded. For the remainder of the past week, Rachel and Tim made sure she was as prepared as possible, encouraging her to practice even when there were customers. They also played certain songs repeatedly on the jukebox so she could strum along and memorize them. That morning, they drove her into Chateaugay, bringing her to Pearl's, telling her to pick out something pretty. "It'll be a gift from Tim and me," Rachel had said.

Even as she was demurring at their kindness, Grace had spotted a red polka-dotted dress, cinched at the waist. She ambled over to try and find the price tag, but Rachel intercepted her.

"That would look real cute on you. Why don't you try it on?"

The saleswoman nearby said, "It's perfect for this time of year, now that summer has officially begun. And with your little figure . . . well . . ."

"Oh," Grace said, "I just couldn't. It's so pretty."

"So are you," Rachel said, looking through the sizes. She pulled one out. "Here, try this on. No arguing."

CHAPTER 16

Turned out the dress was a perfect fit and by Sam's expression, he thought so, too. He said, "Follow me," bringing her through a door into a big room. Across the way was a long L-shaped bar, surrounded by people, mostly men, some she recognized from patronizing the diner. Sam led her to the corner of the room. "The mic is already set up for you."

"What?"

"The microphone. So people can hear you."

She gulped, never having sung into a microphone before. "Will I really need it?"

"Gets pretty loud 'round here on Saturday nights. You'll need it."

Just then, Tim and Rachel walked in. She wanted to run over and embrace them out of relief but they came over to her first and gave her an encouraging hug.

"You all set?" Tim said.

"I guess." She whispered to Rachel. "He wants me to sing into that." She pointed to the microphone.

Rachel reached over and brushed a strand of Grace's blond hair from her face. "You'll get used to it. And you look real pretty."

Grace couldn't help but smile because for the first time in her life she felt pretty. She touched the fabric of the dress. "Thank you again."

"Got the cup?" Tim said.

"Oh!" Rachel pulled one of the diner's large ceramic coffee cups from her purse. "Here."

Grace was confused. "What's that for?"

"We knew you'd forget," Tim said, giving her a wink. "Remember, Sam said you'd get tips. You need somethin' to put 'em in."

Rachel set the cup on the floor in front of the mic. "It just might not be big enough."

Sam looked at his watch. "You can start now."

"You going to introduce her?" Tim said.

"Hadn't planned on it," Sam replied.

"Plan on it," Rachel said.

"She always this pushy?" Sam said to Tim with a chuckle while grabbing the stand, pushing a button on the mic. He started to speak before he turned and said, "What's your name again?"

"Grace."

"Got a last name?"

She hesitated. Her last name seemed to always cause her problems. "Just Grace."

He shrugged, cleared his throat, then said, "Ladies and gentlemen," interrupted by a screech that made Grace jump. Sam backed up slightly. "We have a special treat for you tonight. This here young thing is going to sing for us."

Hoots came from the bar and pool table while Tim and Rachel applauded, having taken seats at a nearby table.

"Please give a fine hand for Grace!"

Grace stared as everyone began clapping. She didn't want Sam to leave her side and looked over at Rachel who gave her a nod of encouragement. She stepped toward the mic and mumbled, "Hi," the screech making her jump again. She did what Sam had done and stepped a few inches back. She situated her guitar and, without saying much else, began to sing a bluegrass song she'd been playing repeatedly on the Victrola to learn. She hoped it wasn't too old for this crowd.

> If you go down in Black Bottom
> Put your money in your shoes,
> Got them Black Bottom Blues.

Sam turned and looked at her, his expression pleased.

Oh, good mama, your daddy's got them black bottom blues.

If you go down in Black Bottom

Just to have a little fun,

Have your sixteen dollars ready

When that police wagon comes.

People at the bar spun around on their stools, facing her, tapping their toes.

Well, I had a good little woman

And I taken her to the fair,

She would have won the premium

But she had bad hair.

Well, I went down to Black Bottom

Just to get a little booze,

And now I'm on the chain gang

Wearing them brogan shoes.

If you've got a good little woman,

Better keep her by your side,

Take your baby and ride.

After a moment, when it was obvious the song was over, applause filled the room, along with shouts for more. Tim and Rachel were beaming. When a waitress went to their table, they each ordered a beer. Tim also told the waitress to bring Grace a Coke and to put it on his tab. Meanwhile, more people wandered in, taking seats at tables instead of heading directly to the bar and turning their chairs in Grace's direction.

Grace sang for over an hour without needing to repeat any song before Sam told her she could take a ten-minute break. "I think you're gonna work out just fine," he added.

Glowing, Grace rushed over to Tim and Rachel's table.

"You're a natural," Tim said, pulling a chair out for Grace just as the waitress came over and handed Grace another Coke.

"Oh, I still have one," Grace said. "Thank—"

"It's from him," the waitress said, pointing toward one of the young men standing at the pool table, holding a stick but watching Grace.

"Oh." Grace looked over. He was tall and sporting a mustache. When she nodded a thank you in his direction, he replied with a wink.

Tim said, "Rachel and I'll get you home when you're done."

"That's okay," Grace said. "You must be tired." She knew from their conversations that they rarely stayed up past eight o'clock.

"We wouldn't sleep anyway, until we knew you got home okay," Tim replied with Rachel nodding in agreement.

At ten o'clock, Sam appeared, handing Grace three singles. The bar was still buzzing with activity and the guy who'd winked at her strolled over while she was scooping out the tips from the cup Rachel had brought for her.

"You're not leaving already?" he said, putting an arm around her waist.

She nodded, seeing Tim and Rachel hurrying toward her.

Sam said, "Maybe we can get her to stay next time till eleven. I'd like you to come back next Saturday. That a problem?"

"No," Grace said, stunned at her good luck.

"Well, how 'bout staying for a drink now?" the guy said.

Tim pulled Grace away from the guy. "Nope, she's too young to be drinkin'." The guy stood about a head taller than Tim, but that didn't stop Tim from staring him down.

The guy sniffed, shrugged, and said, "Then I'll see you next week, Grace," before strolling back toward his buddies.

"Next week?" Tim said, looking at Sam.

"She's a hit already," Sam said. "I'd like her to come back and she's agreed."

Tim looked from a smiling Grace to Sam. "Listen, we can't be here every week so we're dependin' on you, Sam, to make sure she's safe."

"She'll be safe," Sam said.

On the way home, being jostled between Rachel and Tim in their Chevy pickup, Grace couldn't stop grinning, the guitar laying across her and Rachel's laps.

Tim glanced over at her, cleared his throat, and said, "Rachel and I don't go out too often, ya know. We can't be there for you next week."

"That's okay," Grace said, even though their presence had been a comfort to her.

"Keep an eye on those young men," Rachel said. "A drink often comes with expectations."

Tim pulled the truck up to the edge of the road where the path to her place was. Rachel let her out, giving her a hug. "You really are somethin' else, sweetie. You sing real good."

"Thanks."

Tim had climbed out and was standing next to her. "Pretty dark this time a night. We need to getch you a flashlight."

"Wait," she said, handing him the guitar, going over to the bushes and pulling the lantern out. She then pulled some matches from her pocketbook and lit it. "I always keep this here."

He nodded approval and started walking with her.

"You don't have to come with me," she said.

"Yes, he does!" Rachel called. "I'll wait right here."

Still carrying the guitar while Grace lit the path, he said, "I wish we had more room for you. We'd have you stay with us."

They reached the cabin and she pulled the trusty key from her pocketbook and unlocked her door, thanking Tim.

He handed her the guitar. "Grace, we never had kids of our own. You're the closest we could claim."

Grace reached over and gave him a quick hug of appreciation.

"Please be careful." He then turned and rushed back down the path without the benefit of the lantern, calling back, "See you on Monday!"

Grace shut and locked the door. In the corner rested the rifle during the day, but at night she brought it upstairs with her. Next to Tim and Rachel, it was the only other thing that made her feel safe.

"Whatever happened to them?" Adele said.

She and Grace were sitting off in a corner of the solarium. Adele brought chocolate chip cookies as a gift for Grace who was nibbling on one.

"Can't be sure. Every once in a while they said that once they retired, they planned to move to Plattsburgh to be near Tim's sister."

"But you don't know?"

Grace's content expression turned sad, her bottom lip quivering. "Wish I did. But I had to get out of there and real fast."

"Out of the diner?" Adele said, jotting notes in her book.

Grace shook her head. "'busco. I had to get as far away from 'busco as I could. But that was years later."

Adele scribbled, "Research LeClair's Diner," then said, "It sounds like things were starting to go well for you. How about you tell me how Jack came back into your life."

Grace took a final bite of her cookie and brushed the crumbs from her nightdress. There was a distant look that came to her eye and, once again, she went down yesterday's path to happier times.

CHAPTER 17

There was a crispness in the air and the leaves were beginning to turn a deep orange. Summer was over. The sound of buses rumbling informed Grace that school was back in session. But school was still a thing of the past for her.

Grace had been performing every Saturday evening from seven to midnight during the summer months since the crowds didn't want to leave and Sam didn't want to lose the revenue. Grace, too, liked the money, making more in one night than she did waitressing at the diner for a week. But she had no intention of leaving Rachel and Tim, since it was obvious they were also benefiting from her presence. By the way the men gawped at her, she knew she wasn't hard on the eyes. It didn't escape her attention, though, that her reason for learning to play the guitar was to get Jack's attention and she only wished that he could hear her play, especially since he was the one to have given her such an opportunity.

Her only day off was Sunday, which meant working in the garden. She'd taken advantage of the ground that had been prepped years earlier by her parents, even though it had over-grown, but she could tell where they'd hoed and planted, and she did the same, after digging up roots and planting rows of green beans, cucumbers, carrots, and potatoes. Soon she would be canning them, as well, just as her aunt had taught her. The reminder of her aunt made Grace want to go visit her, but the idea of going anywhere near her uncle frightened her. She was just grateful he'd never come back and hoped it would stay that way. Other than that, life was good; her only regret was losing Jack.

She thought maybe if she attended church, she'd see him, so one Sunday she went to Mass. Sure enough, on the other side of the church, there was Jack. But there also were his parents, his mother not looking at all pleased. Once Mass was over, Simone ushered Jack out the back door in a rush. Grace found it too painful to see Jack and not be able to talk to him, so she didn't go back. Yet, a couple of times, after working in the garden, she'd taken a bike ride, bravely going past Jack's farm, hoping he'd be outside in the field. But he never was so she went back to the cabin, took out her guitar and practiced playing, building up quite a repertoire. Yet, there were times she felt so alone, wishing she and Helen were still friends.

Then, one Sunday afternoon, she decided it was time to surprise Claire with a visit; however, Grace was the one given a surprise since Claire stood at the door, leaving it barely cracked open while nervously looking over her shoulder. She whispered, "I can't hang out with you."

"Oh," Grace said, "maybe next Sun—"

"No!" Claire replied. "My mom calls you Jezebel."

"Jezebel?" Grace had no idea why anyone would call her such a name.

"She heard about you, you know . . ." Claire pointed to Grace's belly.

"But that wasn't my fault," Grace said.

"And that you're playing at the tavern."

Grace frowned, wondering what was wrong with that.

"She thinks nothing good can come out of being a Dormand. I know you say your name is Cooke, but everybody knows who you really are. She even wanted me to go get the bike back from you."

Grace glanced back at where she'd dropped it on the lawn.

"You'd better just leave before she sees you," Claire said, "*and* the bike."

Without waiting, Grace ran and got on her bike, pedaling away.

Once again it was Saturday night and she was on her first break of the evening. Initially, Grace hung out by herself between sets, keeping Rachel and Tim's warnings in mind, even though she was always encouraged to go over to the bar by the imbibing flirty patrons, most of them men, some even boys not much older than she was. They'd always try to get her to join them in a shot or a beer, even though she wasn't of age, but she guessed half of the boys who were getting sloshed weren't of age either. There wasn't a time that one of them didn't try to sneak a kiss from her or place a hand on her bottom. Some even implying they'd heard rumors about her being a good time. Using good humor, she'd push them away, making some back off with a laugh while others expressed the rejection with nasty responses, which was when Sam, keeping his promise to Tim, would step in and tell them they'd have to leave if they didn't behave.

That September night while on break at the bar and gulping down a Coke she spotted a familiar face standing off in the corner. She pushed her way through the sweaty, noisy crowd but managed to get by and walk unsteadily over toward Jack. He appeared to be alone.

As she reached him, he said, "You seem to be pretty popular here." He looked over at the bar with a grim expression.

"Thanks to you," she said, needing to raise her voice over the crowd's noise.

"To me?" He frowned.

"You got me the guitar that started all this."

"What?" he said, leaning in to hear her better. She repeated herself but the comment didn't make him smile as she'd hoped it would.

"Which one's your boyfriend?" he said loudly.

She stared at him for a moment. "None of them. I . . . I . . . I'm glad *you're* here."

He looked to have caught his breath. "You are?"

She took a step closer so she wouldn't have to shout. "Jack, I miss you so much." Tears came to her eyes. "I know we can't . . ."

He looked down. "I should've never stopped seeing you. I know none of *that* was your fault."

"Grace," Sam called out as he walked by, studying Jack, "breaks 'bout over."

She nodded then turned back to Jack. "Can you stay a while?"

"I guess," he said. "I wasn't sure how I'd find things when I got here."

"What do you mean?"

He shrugged. "Like maybe you had a fella."

As bravely as she could, she said, "You're the only one I ever wanted."

"Really?" He looked pleasantly surprised.

"Jack, you bought me the guitar for Christmas. I figured you couldn't hate me as much as I thought you did."

"Hate you?" he exclaimed. "I haven't stopped thinking about you." He hesitated, then added, "I want to see you again."

"Me too," she said. "But . . . what about your mother? I know *she* hates me."

"Grace," Sam called over, pointing to his watch.

"Listen," Jack said, "I'll be over there." He motioned toward a corner in the room. "I can't wait to hear you sing," he yelled.

Grace went to the microphone, putting the guitar strap over her head and situating herself. She didn't know if she'd ever felt happier.

One of the guys shouted from the pool table, "Hey, sweet thing, sing a song just for me!"

She looked directly at the guy and said, "This is for him," nodding toward Jack. She began singing.

Have I told you lately that I love you?

Could I tell you once again somehow?

Suddenly, Grace was no longer that young girl singing alone at the Summit Hotel. She gazed at her surroundings, at herself sitting in a wheelchair parked at the foot of her bed. She looked over and saw two women across the room changing the sheets on Mary's bed. They were singing, "*Have I said with all my heart and soul how I adore you? Well, darling, I'm telling you now.*"

And there was that writer girl sitting on a chair across from her.

One of the women, tucking the sheet in, stopped crooning and said, "Don't know all the words, but my daddy used to sing that to me all the time."

"Grace," the young writer said, "I'm guessing you and Jack got back together that night."

"How long you been here?" Grace said, trying to remember just where she was.

"A while. It's a shame you quit school."

Grace waved a feeble hand. "Not much I could do about it."

One of the women patted the girl on the shoulder. "Adele, you miss a lot 'cause she doesn't stop talking, even when you're not here." She then shook her head. "Poor Mary, can't get a moment's peace." She then gathered up the bundle of sheets, saying to the other woman, "We can tell Mary her bed's ready." Then as she walked out of the room, she continued, "*Have I told you lately how I miss you, when the stars are shining in the sky? Have I told you why the nights are long when you're not with me?*"

"*Well, darling, I'm telling you now,*" Grace sang, once again back at the Summit Hotel, seeing Jack's wide smile of approval.

Finally, when midnight came, Grace collected her tips, no longer using a coffee cup but a mason jar, and the five dollars Sam gave her. She walked outside with Jack, greeted by an autumn chill in the air.

"Where's your bike?"

"Oh, it's too hard to pedal and make sure nothing happens to this," she said, cradling the guitar.

"So you walk home?" Jack looked back at the hotel where the jukebox was blasting, and rowdy patrons were still drinking. "I don't like that. I got the truck. Let me take you home."

"Won't your mother wonder where you are?"

He shrugged. "I'm almost eighteen. She doesn't get too much of a say anymore."

Grace looked over at him. *Jack Finley was a man.* Did that make her a woman at almost seventeen?

Jack dashed over to open the passenger door for her. He stopped and gave her a steady look before helping her climb in. She put the guitar on the seat next to her. "You sure are beautiful, Grace."

Just then, two regulars stumbled by, and one said, "You should be leavin' with me, Grace. Not that drip."

Jack turned. "What'd you say?"

"Nothin' important. Just wonderin' why she's going with you?"

"Because I'm her boyfriend, that's why." He then shut her door and went to the driver's side, ignoring the drunks as they stood and watched. He climbed in, his face red, his expression angry. "I don't like this."

"What?"

"All those guys trying . . . trying . . ." He stopped, then blurted, "I don't want to lose you again, Grace. I love you."

At that moment, she thought life couldn't get any better. She didn't hesitate when she said, "I love you, too, Jack Finley."

He shook his head. "I figured you'd never want to talk to me again," he said. "I should've been there for you. I was a stinkin' coward, letting my mother boss me around." He stared out the window. "She just can't get over that you're a *Dormand*. After what your father . . ." He stopped himself before finishing the sentence. "Doesn't matter. You're about the sweetest girl I ever knew." He pounded the steering wheel. "And I'm mad as blazes that I wasn't able to protect you from what happened. You didn't deserve that."

She couldn't speak, too choked up, but then the next thing he said, stunned her.

"I don't care that some people think I got you in that situation. Let 'em think it. My mom still thinks we lied about it. Well, let *her* think it!" He then leaned over, bringing his lips to hers for a moment before settling himself in front of the steering wheel and starting up the truck. When they reached the path to the cabin, he climbed out, carrying her guitar for her. She found the lantern, lit it, and they made their way to the cabin. That night she didn't feel a need to be on alert for another visit from her uncle. She hoped Jack would come inside when they reached the door, and he did.

"I can't stay long," he said. "Gotta be up early to milk the cows."

She nodded in understanding, seeing him spot the gun he'd given her in the corner. She said, "Came in handy the other day when a raccoon kept trying to help itself to my garden."

Jack grinned. "You got a garden?"

"In the back."

He kissed her some more before saying, "Maybe we could do something tomorrow."

"Well, I have to can some of those vegetables before any more raccoons try to claim them."

He smiled. "I could help you, if you'd like. I could come after Mass, unless you want to come with me."

"To Mass?" She paused, then said, "I . . . I . . ."

"Or I'll just come here after."

"That would be good."

He pulled her close to him. "All I could think about was you."

"Me, too," she said.

He leaned in and gave her a long kiss, one that she didn't want to end, before he gently squeezed her and said goodbye.

"Oh!" she called to him as he started down the dark path. "Do you want the lantern?"

"Nah, I can make my way back. Not that far." He stopped and turned to look at her, she barely making him out. "I love you, Grace!"

Just above a whisper, she said, "I love you, too, Jack Finley." She then shut and locked the door all the while smiling.

CHAPTER 18

The next morning, Grace was up early, already in the garden harvesting beans and carrots when she heard the church bells. About two hours later, when she had a basket filled and water boiling on the stove for canning, Jack showed up.

"Wow," he said, "you've been busy!" He walked over and gave her a quick kiss on the lips. "What can I do?"

While she showed him how to pack the vegetables in the Mason jars, he talked about school and the wrestling team he was on. "I wish you could come and watch me some time," he said.

"Do you ever get hurt?"

"Nah. There's rules and stuff." He wiped the sweat from his brow, the room hot from the roaring stove that she needed for the canning. He walked over to her front door, opening it. "This should help cool things down a bit," he said. He then went to the back door and opened that one, too. "Least you get a nice cross breeze."

She never dared keep her doors open like that when she was there alone; she just dealt with the oppressive heat, but with Jack there, she wasn't worried about her uncle barging in.

"You know," Jack said, "you fixed this place up real nice. Too bad there's no 'lectricity, though."

By mid-afternoon, while they were eating chicken sandwiches, waiting to hear the pop of the canning jars to know they'd sealed properly, their conversation seemed strained until Jack said, "Grace, I don't want anyone havin' an opportunity to steal you away."

"No one's gonna steal me from you, Jack." True, there were many guys always trying to get her to go out with them, but none tempted her in the least. It was Jack who was always on her mind.

"The way those guys look at you when you're singing—"

"Do you want me to quit?" She wasn't sure how she felt about that, but if he said yes, she would do so.

"No! I was so proud seeing you at that microphone and all those people admiring you, but I want them to know you're spoken for. Grace, I wanna marry you."

She stared at him. Even though she wasn't speaking it sounded like the room was filled with noise, so many questions running through her mind.

"I graduate next spring," he said. "Then we could get married."

"Next spring?" It felt like a lifetime away. *Pop*! It was the sixth jar to seal. There would be four more to go.

"I guess I should ask you. Properly." He got down on one knee. "Grace Cooke, will you marry me?"

Without hesitation, she nodded, and threw her arms around his neck. "But what will your parents say?"

"My dad'll be happy for us. He likes you."

"But your mom doesn't."

He hesitated, then said, "I s'pose I won't tell her right away. She'll know I'm coming over here and won't like it. And I don't want to hear it from her all the time."

"Where'd you tell her you are?"

"Hanging with my buddies. Wrestling practice. That kind of thing."

"So it'll be our secret for now?" Grace said, eager to tell someone. If only Helen were still her friend.

Pop! Pop! Pop!

"Well, I wouldn't mind those fellas knowing at the tavern," he said. "But I plan to be there on Saturday nights anyway."

She laughed.

"Thing is," Jack said, "Dad always said it's only proper to ask a girl's father for her hand in marriage before he asks the girl, but . . ."

"We could tell my aunt. I'm not looking for her blessing or anything, but I should let her know." Just then the last pop sounded. "Maybe I could bring her a jar of green beans." She wasn't sure why she really wanted to go back. Maybe it was because she wanted to prove that she had made something of herself, recalling how her uncle had told her aunt she'd be back.

"She lives in the mountains, right?" Jack said.

"Coyote Hill. You'll come with me, right?"

"Sure. I'll ask my dad if I can borrow the truck. When you want to go?"

"Well, Sundays are the only days I'm free really. Maybe once I get done with all the canning, we could go." She had cucumbers and tomatoes that still needed to be harvested. She figured by the end of the month, she'd be finished and said as much.

"Okay," Jack said. "We'll go the first Sunday in October."

"You weren't kidding about your aunt being up in the hills," Jack said, as they rumbled along the narrow path while Grace guided him, telling him what turns to make.

"You should try riding a bike up here," she said.

BEFORE SHE WAS A FINLEY

Jack glanced at her, shaking his head and reaching over, giving her a comforting squeeze on her leg. His touch always made her go warm without understanding the feelings she was having. She could only describe it as love.

True to his word, Jack had come to the Summit Hotel every Saturday night, much to the dismay of the male patrons; the womenfolk, always cool toward her, didn't seem to mind at all. He'd take his place at a small table in the corner, order a soda, and, with a sense of pride, watch his bride-to-be entertain the crowd for the night. He'd told Grace that by the way the men looked at her, he knew he'd made the right choice of claiming her before anyone else did, even if they couldn't let everyone know; otherwise, it might get back to Simone and there'd be hell to pay.

Even so, on Sundays, more often than not, he came to the cabin with schoolbooks to study, while Grace cleaned or tried to learn new songs on her guitar, the vegetables canned, and the garden having gotten one final weeding before the snow came. The young couple tried to keep busy so that they didn't end up on her couch or bed, determined to wait until they were married.

Just then, Grace said, "Right here!"

"Here?" he said with surprise.

Grace saw the shanty through his eyes and what she saw was horrifying. She certainly didn't remember it looking so pathetic. The small building was leaning to the right, as if ready to collapse. The grass was about knee-length with a rusty wheelbarrow nearby. A post once holding the clothesline was on the ground. Compared to where she was living now, it looked to be nothing more than an overgrown, lifeless dump.

Jack parked on the side of the road, turning off the engine. They climbed out and lingered near the truck, Grace holding a jar of green beans and basket of cookies she and Rachel had baked the day before. Rachel and Tim knew that Jack was back in Grace's life and that they were going to visit Grace's aunt, but Grace hadn't told them about the marriage proposal.

As they headed toward the shanty, the front door creaked open. Uncle Henry stood there, squinting, trying to make out who was in the yard before he said, "Whatch you want?"

Suddenly trembling. Grace said as forcefully as she could, "I came to see Aunt Gladys."

Uncle Henry sputtered, stumbling down off the step onto the ground, his t-shirt filthy and ripped. "'bout what?"

"None of your business," Grace snapped, glancing back at Jack for support.

Uncle Henry scowled. "Well, I'm making it my business." He studied Jack for a minute before saying, "Don't think we been introduced, boy."

"I'm Jack. Jack Finley."

"We're going to get married," Grace said with certainty.

"Married? You in the family way?"

"No, sir!" Jack said while Grace shouted for her aunt.

"Stop your caterwauling. I doubt she's up for any visitors."

As bravely as she could, Grace walked toward the shanty, passing by her uncle and going inside. "Aunt Gladys?" she called. She wasn't in the kitchen, so Grace headed to the back where her aunt's bed was. She stopped at the sight. Her aunt was lying there with a blanket over her. She looked so much older than Grace recalled and there seemed to be a gray tone to her skin.

"What's wrong?" Grace said, walking closer.

Her aunt stared at Grace with a haunted expression without speaking.

"I brought you some beans and cookies. I grew the beans in my garden and canned them. She hesitated, then said, "Just a minute." She went into the kitchen and put what she'd brought on the table and then went to the door and asked Jack to come in. He walked by Uncle Henry, who trailed behind him.

In a whisper, she said, "I want you to meet my aunt, but she seems to be under the weather." She led the way, finding her aunt trying to sit up, and introduced Jack.

"Said they gonna get married," Uncle Henry said, poking his head in the room.

Aunt Gladys squeezed her eyes closed, as if in pain, while straightening herself. "Where you been this whole time?"

"I . . . I got my own place. I'm doing really good."

Jack interjected, "She even learned to play guitar and sings every Saturday night in town."

"And I waitress," Grace added. "So things—"

"Rollin' in the dough, are you?" Uncle Henry said. "Bring any of it with ya?"

Grace ignored her uncle and took a step closer to her aunt. "You got the bug or something?"

Her aunt slowly shook her head. "Got the cancer."

Grace gasped. "Are you . . . are you sure?"

"Shouldn't be surprised," she said. "God's way of punishin' me." Aunt Gladys's gaze turned toward Uncle Henry. He waved her off and walked back into the kitchen.

"Punishing you?"

"Glad you stopped by, Grace," she said. "Been real quiet 'round here since you left. You all growed up." She looked over at Jack. "You gonna take good care of her?"

"Yes, ma'am."

She nodded. "I have some good days and some bad ones, but maybe I'll make it to your wedding."

Grace and Jack hadn't discussed when they'd be getting married, but Jack said, "That'd be real nice."

She swung her legs around to climb out of the bed. "If you excuse me, I gotta do my business." She pointed to a metal can off in the corner.

"Well, we should get going, anyway," Grace said. "It was real good seeing you." She walked over, kissing her aunt on the forehead, an action that felt foreign to her. "Take care."

She and Jack walked out to find Uncle Henry in the rocking chair, eating one of the cookies Grace had brought. "Braggin' how good you're doin and all that money you're makin'. Least you could do is hand over some."

She stopped and glared at him. Quivering, she said, "After what you did to me?"

"Just like her father," Uncle Henry said. "Won't even help family." He looked over at Jack. "If I were you, boy, I'd run from this one. And fast."

Grace ran out the front door with Jack following her. After she climbed in the truck, she looked out the window to see her uncle standing in the doorway, staring her down.

Jack turned the truck around and as they drove off, she saw her uncle shoving another cookie in his mouth.

"You okay?" Jack said, reaching over and taking Grace's hand. She nodded but wasn't sure she was.

"What you said to him, what did you mean?"

Without going into detail, then and there she decided no longer to think about what her uncle had to done to her. As far as she was concerned, it was the past and would stay there. No one, including Jack, would ever know. "He's despicable," she said. "That's all."

"You really lived there, huh?"

When they got back to the cabin, Jack was pacing from the living room to the kitchen and back while Grace was putting together ingredients for stew. It occurred to her that maybe he was trying to find a way to break up with her after having seen where she'd lived and hearing her uncle's warnings. Maybe Jack was questioning marrying a Dormand. She finally dared to ask him if everything was okay.

He gazed at her and said, "No, no it's not." He walked over to her. "I wanted us to come back here feeling good about visiting your aunt. I never expected to find what we did."

Grace stopped cutting up the potato, her heart pounding. He *was* going to break up with her and who could blame him?

179

He'd seen a part of her that she'd managed to keep hidden until now.

He stuck his hand in his pants' pocket. "I should've given you this a while ago." He held out a little square box. "I want people to know you're spoken for."

Grace's mouth dropped open. "You're not breaking up with me?"

"Breaking up with you? Grace, I love you." He placed the box in her hand. She opened it to see a tiny diamond set in a gold ring.

"Sorry, the diamond isn't too big. I've been saving for this for a while now."

Grace's bottom lip quivered. "It's an engagement ring?"

He smiled and slipped the ring on her finger. "It fits!"

She stared at it in awe. "But . . . but . . . can I wear it to work?"

"I don't want you ever taking it off. I want it to be official."

She threw her arms around his neck, feeling love, real love for the first time. It was official. She was going to be Mrs. Jack Finley and had a ring to show for it.

CHAPTER 19

Grace walked into the school hesitantly. It felt foreign to her, but she welcomed the warmth. Autumn was long over, and winter had proven especially cold with lots of snow, so walking was her only means of getting anywhere. She stomped the snow from her boots and went down the hallway toward the gym where she heard clapping along with the intermittent sounds of a whistle and cheers. Jack had told her he was in the wrestling tournament for his weight class, having lost only one meet, and hoped that she would be able to come watch. He'd been asking her to come watch him ever since school began and, now that it was January, she finally asked Rachel if she could have the afternoon off to do so.

"Not a problem," Rachel had said. "You should be there." She winked, happy when Grace and Jack told them that they were engaged.

"We kinda expected as much," Rachel said, "and kinda knew why you didn't want it to get out yet."

"We're just telling a few people," Jack replied. "Since Grace wanted you to know, though, we knew we could trust you to keep it a secret from, well, you know."

Rachel gave Jack a hug, saying, "Don't you worry. It's safe with us."

Grace pushed open the gymnasium door, immediately greeted with the scent of boys' hot sweat. The bleachers were filled with students and adults, all riveted to what was happening on the mats. Grace looked for Jack but couldn't find him. She decided to look for a place to sit first. When she scanned the bleachers, she spotted Helen staring directly at her. Grace gave her an exuberant wave and big smile only to have it ignored with Helen leaning toward Jean, who was sitting next to her, and whispering something in her ear. Jean then looked in Grace's direction with a horrified expression.

"Grace!"

She looked up toward the top of the bleachers to see Gerald, Jack's father, motioning for her to join him. It would be a feat to navigate through the noisy crowd, some people sitting on the steps, but she managed to reach where he'd shifted over and made room for her.

"How are you?"

"Good," she replied, looking for Jack's mother. "I don't want to take Mrs. Finley's place."

Gerald laughed. "She wouldn't be caught dead here. She thinks all this is foolishness and a waste of time." He pointed toward the center of the gym where two boys were grappling with each other. With what Grace saw so far, she had to agree with Simone.

"Jack should be coming up shortly," Gerald said.

Grace nodded, glad she hadn't missed his bout.

"So, Jack says you learned to play the guitar real good."

"It was so nice of him getting it for me."

Gerald smiled. "He's a good guy and was determined to get it to you by Christmas. I'd love to come hear you play sometime, but . . . Simone . . ." He ended the sentence without finishing it, but he took her hand, holding it for a second, and saying, "Looks real pretty on you," nodding toward the ring.

Grace didn't know what to say. What she knew, though, having Simone as a mother-in-law would be a challenge but Gerald seemed determined to make up for his wife's sullenness. The recent Thanksgiving and Christmas holidays meant Grace had to be alone since she and Jack were certain his mother would not welcome her after what had happened the previous Thanksgiving, and he couldn't leave his house on a holiday without a valid reason. Yet, somehow, they also knew Simone would eventually have to accept Grace into the family, even begrudgingly. Meanwhile, they preferred keeping the peace for as long as they could; so the fact that they were engaged was still kept among only a few people, in hopes it wouldn't get back to his mother just yet.

"There he is!" Gerald waved toward the floor and then pointed toward Grace. Jack looked up. The moment he saw Grace, he grinned and waved back.

Grace blushed to see how Jack was dressed. It looked like he was only in his undergarments. And in front of so many people!

He shook hands with a guy who looked to be about his size and then they began grabbing each other and trying to get each other down on the mat. Gerald called, "Come on, Jack! You got 'em!" He then stopped and explained to Grace what was happening.

"Who's that man with the whistle?"

"He's the umpire."

"So, how do they know who's the winner?" Grace said.

"To be honest, sweetie," Gerald said, "I'm not sure. All I know is whoever has the highest score at the end of the rounds is the winner." He pointed. "There's the scoreboard." He scowled. "Looks like Jack is behind by two points."

At that, Grace shouted, "Come on, Jack! You can do it!"

A smile played on Gerald's lips. After several minutes, and change in the score, the umpire raised Jack's hand, and the crowd applauded, none harder than Jack's dad.

"Well," Gerald said, "we'll have to celebrate."

A little while later, Gerald, Jack, and Grace were sitting at a table in the diner. Rachel came over with slices of cherry pie for everyone, patting Jack on the back. "You're quite the winner," she said. "But how can you not be when you have this gal in your life?" She gave a gentle tug on a lock of Grace's blond hair.

"True," Jack said, gazing at Grace.

Rachel didn't stop there. "Gerald, I hope you know how special this girl is. And a hard worker, too."

Grace felt her face getting hot, wishing Rachel would stop.

"Oh, I'm embarrassing you," Rachel said. "I'll let you all enjoy your pie."

Gerald leaned in toward Jack. "We'd better not fill up or your mother'll know we were here."

Jack laughed, then studied his father before saying, "Pops, can I ask you something?"

Gerald hesitated but then shrugged and said, "Sure."

"Why is mom always so angry?"

Grace didn't say a word but wondered the same thing.

"She never learned how to be happy, son. Not since her brother went missing," Gerald said.

"Oh my goodness," Grace said. "What happened?"

Gerald cocked his head. "Not really sure. Just one day he vanished."

"And she won't ever talk about it," Jack said. "We can't even mention his name, which doesn't make any sense, if you ask me."

"I agree," Gerald said. "Anyway, I've been determined to be happy for the both of us."

Grace thought about how her Aunt Gladys had never been happy, either. Or maybe she had been before her sister was murdered and she was saddled with taking care of a baby. Grace had wanted to go back to visit her aunt, but the winter weather kept her from doing so, the road up to the shanty deep with snow. Jack's truck would never make it.

"The thing is, son, I don't really like keeping secrets from your mother. You two need to consider telling her your plans soon."

Jack and Grace exchanged a look, Grace uneasy at the prospect.

"Well, we should get going so she's not worried 'bout us." Gerald ate the last of the pie on his plate, threw some money on the table even though Rachel had said the pie was on the house, and then stood to leave.

Grace stayed behind to help Rachel clean up their mess. Jack gave her a kiss on the cheek and then left with his father.

While Grace was washing the dishes, Rachel went over to her. "Sorry if I embarrassed you earlier. I said what I said so that maybe Gerald would let Simone know Jack has someone right for him." She rested a hand on Grace's back. "Now why don't you get going before it gets too dark?"

A short time later, with her lantern lighting the way, Grace was trudging through the snow on the path to her cabin, noticing human foot tracks that weren't hers. She paused, then decided to turn the flame off. As quietly as she could, she slogged along, finally reaching the cabin. Foot tracks looked to have circled her home. She held her breath. What if he'd gotten inside and was waiting for her? The front door didn't look to have been broken into, so she went around to the back door. That, too, was locked. She returned to the front, pulled out her key and let herself in, immediately slamming the door behind her and locking it. She lit the lantern, standing at the entranceway, ready to run if she had to. Even though nothing seemed to be amiss, her heart was pounding so loud she could almost hear it. She went to the corner, grabbed her gun, and cautiously went up the steps, wishing the stairs didn't creak so loudly. Keeping the gun pointed, she went from the hallway to both rooms. No one was there and nothing seemed to have been touched. She then went to the kitchen, shifted the rug and picked up the floorboard where she'd kept a tin filled with the money she'd been saving. She expelled a sigh when she saw it was untouched. She then replaced the floorboard and covered it with the rug.

Once the fire was roaring in the stove, and the cabin warm, Grace had calmed down some. It could have been just about anyone being nosy because, she figured, if it had been Uncle Henry, he wouldn't have just left without finding a way in. She did wonder, though, how her aunt was doing and decided that once spring came and the road was accessible, she and Jack would pay her a visit. After all, Rachel had consoled her, saying that sometimes people can last for months with cancer. "Besides, did a doctor tell her that's what she had or was she just making her own prognosis?" Rachel asked.

"Not sure," Grace had said, since she never recalled her aunt, or herself for that matter, ever going to the doctor. Maybe her aunt believed she deserved cancer and said that's what she had. By now, she was probably back up and about.

That night Grace decided to sleep downstairs on the couch, as uncomfortable as it was, with the gun at her side, just to be on the safe side and try to put her uncle out of mind. Instead, she thought of what her life would be like as Mrs. Jack Finley. She fell asleep with a sense of satisfaction.

CHAPTER 20

April arrived, bringing with it weather so warm it melted the piles of snow that had been lingering for most of the winter. Grace was excited to start her vegetable garden that spring, knowing this time she'd be canning vegetables for both her *and* Jack. She planned to grow a row of corn since Jack said it was his favorite.

The first Sunday after Easter, Grace used her hoe to begin digging and figuring out what would be planted where. It was going to be an impressive garden, as far as she was concerned. Just as she was pulling some stubborn weeds, she heard the church bells chime and knew where Jack was right then. They didn't talk about religion, but he often mentioned that their wedding would be taking place at St. Philomena. Grace promised him after they were married she would go with him to Mass every Sunday as a couple, and then, hopefully, as a growing family. It was fun to imagine the life the two of them would have together while keeping thoughts of Simone out of it.

When Jack showed up later that morning, he joined in helping, asking her to sing while they hoed and pulled weeds.

"Without the guitar?" she said.

"Sure, it's your voice I love."

"Didn't you get enough of it last night?"

"Never. And you'd be singing just for me."

She laughed and broke into song but then stopped herself, looking up from her digging and said, "Jack, I'd like to go and see my aunt next Sunday. Would you come with me?"

"Next Sunday?" Jack shrugged. "Sure."

"I want to bring her a pot of soup."

"Let's hope your uncle doesn't eat it all," Jack said.

Once they finished for the day, the rows organized, Grace went upstairs with her bucket of water and wash rag to clean up. Jack tried to follow her and was annoyed when she said an adamant no.

"But we're practically married," he whined.

She shook her head, insisting they wait until they took their wedding vows. Jack would be graduating high school in a couple of months and then they were going to begin making plans to get married, no matter what Simone thought of it. "She can't stop us," he'd said more than once. "Besides, Dad'll make sure of that."

Eventually, instead of begging, he relented and said that he'd be going home to wash up, as well, and help with milking the cows. He gave her a close hug and long kiss, even though she yearned for more, before she encouraged him to leave.

A little while later, after she'd washed and changed, she happened to glance outside the window from her bedroom and saw a figure crouched by a tree and then rushing toward the back of the cabin. She stumbled down the stairs, racing to the corner and grabbed the gun. It was already loaded. In one quick move, she unlocked the back door and yanked it open to see her uncle standing only a few feet away. Without hesitation, she aimed the gun directly at him, believing it would be enough to chase him away.

"Whoa, whoa, little lady!" he said, lurching back. "Put that thing down."

Without putting the gun down, she said, "What do you want?"

He lifted his hands as if resigned. "Just thought I should come by and let you know that your aunt went to be with the Lord."

Grace lowered the gun. "She . . . she died?"

"That's what I'm tellin' ya."

"When?"

He teetered on unsure footing. "A few months ago. She didn't want no fuss. Just wanted to be buried on Coyote Hill." He paused and said with a chuckle, "Just like she was one of the livestock."

"Oh my God," Grace muttered, trying to sort her emotions out.

"So how 'bout you let me come inside so we can commiserate together?" He took a step closer to her.

"No!" she said, raising the gun again. "You told me what you came to tell me. Now leave."

"You think I came all this way just to deliver that news and leave?"

Keeping the gun on him, her hand shaking, Grace said, "Yes, I want you to leave."

"That ain't being very hospitable." He reached down, groping himself. "You still a pretty little thing. A tease I'd say."

"You'd better go. My boyfriend's here."

"That so? Unless you got another one hidden in there, I saw your boyfriend leave a while ago."

Her mouth went dry with the thought of her uncle watching her.

"I said leave!"

"Uh, uh," he said, taking a step closer. "We both know you don't have it in you to harm a fly, let alone your own flesh and blood."

She cocked the gun. "I said stop!"

But he didn't. He took another step toward her and without debating, she pulled the trigger, the force keeling her off her footing. Immediately, her uncle tumbled back, dropping to the ground. His eyes widened as he gaped at her in shock before he slumped over.

"Go home!" she yelled at him, hoping he'd get up and scamper away. But he didn't.

She had no idea how long she was standing there, staring at him, his body motionless. Had she really killed him? The idea was incomprehensible. The gun still propped in her hand; the breathing was deafening. He was still alive! But then she realized it was her own breathing, actually gasping, that she heard. She didn't budge, expecting him to leap up, tell her she'd missed. But how could that be with blood coming from his chest, gurgling from his mouth, his eyes open but looking at nothing?

Eventually, she collapsed in the doorway, the gun dropped at her side, the reality sinking in. He was dead. She had killed him. She was a murderer. She pushed herself up from the floor. *Jack.* She needed Jack. And tell him what happened. She stumbled to the front of the cabin, going out the door, and running down the path. She never bothered with the rusty bike anymore but hoofed it wherever she needed to go. About halfway to the main road, Simone's image came to mind causing Grace to stop cold. The Dormand name was synonymous with murderer and Grace would always be a Dormand, no matter what.

She started to question herself. Maybe she should have given her uncle more of a warning instead of shooting right away. Why couldn't he just have given her the sad news and be on his way? But she knew why.

She turned around and headed back to the cabin, weighing her options, which didn't feel like options at all. She'd go to prison, never see Jack again; never be his wife. He loved her despite knowing another man already had his way with her, but would he still love her if he knew she was a murderer? How much forgiveness could Jack have in him? In reality, though, it wasn't Jack in her mind's eye but his mother, who would prove she was right all along about just who Grace was.

As it was when she was a baby on the floor grasping bloody strands of her mother's hair, it still is that the sound of guns going off in the woods is no cause for alarm. It wasn't until Helen's father had heard her squealing, the infant that she was, did he investigate. Quite likely, had anyone heard her gun going off, there'd be no reason for concern, usually meaning hunters were shooting game.

Once she got closer to the cabin, it no longer looked like the cozy home she'd created but something much darker. It was where her father had killed her mother and then himself. And now there was her uncle. Slowly, she made her way to the back. Seeing his body lay there motionless, she saw all her joy and dreams vanish. It wasn't fair. Her life was just about to begin, and he destroyed it.

Or tried to.

She looked over at the freshly dug up garden. The sun would be setting in a couple of hours, but she had to get busy, if she were to hang on to her future. Without another moment's consideration, she grabbed the shovel and went to work, digging up the soft ground, sobbing and shaking, admonishing the body for making her do what she had done, what she now had to do.

By the time the hole was big enough to fit her uncle's corpse, it was dark, the evening cool. She knew the grave had to be deep and she'd kept at it until about two in the morning. She'd be expected at the diner in a couple of hours. Forcing herself not to vomit, she struggled as she dragged the body by the arms toward the hole. It was much heavier than she expected. At one point the hand flopped on her foot and she screamed and scrambled away. *He was alive!* She sat frozen for several moments watching, waiting but realizing he was as dead as dead can be. She made her way back to his body and with a powerful push, she shoved it into the hole. She prayed it was deep enough to keep the animals away and began heaping the dirt on top of the corpse. Eventually, she was leveling the ground, still sobbing, trying to keep the bile down.

As dawn approached, she realized all the gardening and organizing rows for specific vegetables that she and Jack had done the day before was now destroyed. She would have to come up with a lie as to why. The truth, even to her, no longer made sense.

There was no sleep to be had. She scoured her sweaty, dirty body, her skin raw before putting on clean clothes. She could barely keep her eyes open as she stumbled to the main road, her mind racing to come up with a story to tell Jack about the garden. Certainly, he'd notice how the rows they'd carefully organized were now just flat without any definition. Then a thought began to unfold. Maybe it would work. When she got to the diner, she figured she'd try the story out on Rachel first.

"So you were digging all night to find that ring?" Rachel pointed to Grace's finger.

Grace nodded.

"I can't believe you found it!"

"I . . . I was so upset when I realized it was missing and I wasn't going to give up." She avoided making eye contact.

Tim replied, "I'll say. Like finding a needle in a haystack."

"But you found it!" Rachel said. "And you look exhausted."

"Took me all night."

"Well," Rachel said, looking at Tim, who was stirring a large batch of pancake mix. "Mondays aren't always that busy. Why don't you go home and get some sleep?"

As much as she wanted to sleep, she wasn't eager to get back to the cabin where the body was buried yet haunted her. "I'll be okay," she said.

"Grace," Tim said, "I gotta say, you look pretty rough. You need to get some sleep."

Rachel put out her hand. "Give me your apron and go get some rest. We'll see you later for the supper crowd, if you're up to it."

Not feeling she had a choice, Grace handed Rachel the apron and walked out the back door.

"And be sure to hang on to that ring!" Tim called.

When she got back to the cabin, the sun was just beginning to rise. She still couldn't believe that her uncle was not only dead but buried in what was to be rows of vegetables. How could it be? Hesitantly, she entered through the front and walked to the back door, opening it and looking out at the garden. That's when she noticed blood on the ground from where her uncle dropped. She immediately got the bucket and filled it with water, pouring it on the ground until there was no hint of red. Then she clambered up the stairs to try and sleep away the anxiety, wanting to believe it was all over and life could go on the way she'd planned.

However, anxiety went up the stairs with her and she kept seeing her uncle fall to the ground, over and over again, blood gushing from him. In another dream, he was knocking, pounding on her door, trying to break in, until she realized that there was someone really pounding on her door. She sprung up and listened, her body trembling.

"Grace! Grace!" The voice was Jack's.

She stumbled down the stairs, ran to the front door, unlocking and opening it. "What time is it?" she mumbled.

"'bout one," he said. "I went to see you at the diner during recess, but Tim told me what happened." He pulled Grace into a hug. "I can't believe you were up all night looking for that ring."

She refused to let go of him and began sobbing into his chest.

"Honey, honey. It's okay."

Snot dripped from her nose, and she couldn't stop shaking. She wanted to tell him the truth but what that could mean stopped her.

"Did I wake you up?"

"I don't know."

"You don't know?" He laughed.

She had such frightening dreams that she couldn't call it sleep. She hesitated before saying, "Jack, could you come lay down with me for a while?"

His eyes widened. "Sure. I don't need to go back to school today."

He held her hand, leading her up to her bed. She rested her head against his shoulder while he caressed her, his lips finding hers. Then he began to undress her. She didn't stop him. Soon, they found a rhythm, their bodies merged, while she pushed away any thoughts of blood, death, and murder.

Breathless, they clung to each other, Grace determined not to let anything rob her of feeling safe and loved. Yet she was uncertain he'd ever forgive her had he known what she'd done. She drifted to sleep in his arms with that thought.

"Psst, Grace." Jack shook her gently. "I gotta go. Pops'll need help milking the cows."

She opened her eyes, reminded that she was naked under the covers, and so was he.

He whispered in her ear, "I love you. I know you wanted to wait, but it just felt right."

Without a doubt, something major had changed in their relationship, even though she realized that what they had done was risky. Barely above a whisper, she said, "I wasn't thinking clearly. I just wanted to be as close to you as possible."

He gave her a squeeze and then slid out from under the covers, slipping on his underwear and pants.

"Listen" he said, "don't worry about the garden. We can get it back into good shape soon enough."

She lunged up. "No, no, Jack!"

He zipped up his pants, while giving her an odd look.

"Let's forget about the garden."

He put on his shirt, buttoning it up. "But all those things you wanted to plant. Just take your ring off before you—"

"No!" she snapped, making him scowl. She had to think fast, and said, "I think we need to tell your mother. About us."

"What does that have to do with the garden?"

Think, Grace, think. "Well, here we are planning our lives together and it's not fair to keep it from your mother. I mean, your father asked us to tell her a while ago."

"True. He *has* been badgering me to tell her. Besides, I want to make us official." He leaned down, kissing her. "Guess we could tell her tonight."

"*We?*"

"I want you with me when I tell her. I'll come back and pick you up once I'm done with the milking."

"I'll be at the diner," she said.

"Oh, well you get done around what time?"

"Depends. Seven or eight."

"Okay, I'll swing by and pick you up there then."

She nodded. Going face to face with his mother was frightening but she believed there was no choice.

That night Jack walked into his house, holding Grace's hand. Simone and Gerald were sitting at the kitchen table with cups of coffee in front of them.

"What's she doing here?" Simone said, her eyes wide.

"Ma, we got something to tell ya." Without giving his mother a minute to absorb what was coming, Jack blurted, "I love Grace and we're gonna get married after I graduate."

Simone stared at her son, refusing to look at Grace. Her chest heaved up and down. "Just like that? You come in and say such a thing? How long you been seeing her?"

"A while now, Ma."

"After I told you to never see her again?"

"I love her," he said.

Grace stood behind Jack while he still had her hand in his.

"You don't know what love is." She looked at Gerald. "How could he do such a thing to me? Of all the girls, *she's* the one he wants?"

"Simone, Jack's not a boy anymore," Gerald said.

"I don't think he really knows what kind of stock she comes from," Simone said. "He cannot marry a Dormand!" She pushed her chair back, started to stand up, but then dropped back down onto the seat. "You have a reputation of being a wrestling champion, Jack, and all anyone will remember is that you married a Dormand!"

Jack let go of Grace's hand and took a step toward his mother, his jaw tight, his face a bright red. "That's the first time you ever said anything about my championship! The first time ever!"

Gerald stood up. "Calm down, son."

"Me?" Jack said. "She's the one—"

Simone stood and this time managed to stay standing. "Did you forget about what happened on Thanksgiving? We know she's not a—"

"That wasn't her fault, Simone," Gerald said. "And Rachel says the nicest things about Grace. She's a hard worker, reliable." He looked directly at Grace. "She's gonna make a good wife for Jack, I know."

Grace wanted to rush over and hug Gerald in appreciation, but felt it was too dangerous to make a move of any kind.

"I'm not gonna change my mind," Jack said.

Gerald asked Grace, "Do you love my son?"

Grace caught her breath before saying, "With all my heart."

"We're getting married, Mom," Jack said. "Whether you approve or not."

"Simone," Gerald said, "it's better if we just support this. Jack is determined to marry her. You don't want to lose a son over this, do you?"

No one spoke for a few minutes, until Simone uttered, "Well, where are they gonna live? How's he gonna support her? It's all foolishness." She tossed her hands in the air, as if resigned to the fact.

"You know that I've been fixing up the little house," Jack said.

Simone scowled. "I didn't know it was for this."

"Jack wants to keep farming," Gerald said.

"I plan to get more cows and—"

"And I can help," Grace said, barely above a whisper.

Simone looked at her for the first time since they got there, glaring at her. Then, to Jack: "So after graduation—"

"We're going to get married." He turned to Grace. "We'll have to go talk to Father Bernier."

"He won't even know who she is," Simone said. "I don't ever see her at Mass."

"Sundays are my only day to get things done, but I plan—"

"First thing you need to get done is go to church!" Simone snapped. "You told me you were a Catholic. Well, good Catholics go to Mass."

"We'll go see Father tomorrow," Jack said, taking Grace's hand in his again.

Simone huffed and pushed her way past Jack and Grace, going into her bedroom, slamming the door.

Gerald said, "Well, that went pretty well." He then forced a grin.

The nursing home was quiet, most of the so-called guests in their beds, as was Grace. Adele was seated next to the old woman whose face was gray, drawn. The staff let the young reporter stay after she pleaded with them, telling them that she needed more information to finish the article. She'd never guessed the dramatic turn it would take. She looked across the room to see that Mary, thankfully, was asleep. To find out she was sharing a room with a murderer might freak her out.

Adele studied the woman, who appeared drained, her expression regretful. *Grace Finley, or would it be Dormand, was a murderer.*

"Did you ever tell Jack?" Adele said, leaning on the bed. "I mean, not right away because you had kids and stuff." She hesitated, trying to get a handle on the timeline. "I guess what I want to know is why did you leave when you did? Did Jack kick you out?" She tapped her notebook, then said loudly, "Simone! Simone found out and you couldn't—"

Grace hunkered further down into her bed. "Why'd you come here and bring all this up? You got enough out of me."

Adele thought for a moment, then said, "But you told me that you did what many women didn't do back then: walked out on your family. That's what my article is about. I need to find out why."

Part Two

CHAPTER 21

He was born in 1949."

"Who was?"

Through blurry eyes, Grace barely made out Adele sitting nearby. She said, "Kevin."

"Your son?" the young writer confirmed.

What was her name again? Amy? Annette? Grace couldn't remember, so she asked.

"I'm Adele. I've been coming here for a few weeks now." She scribbled on her notepad.

"Oh, that's right," Grace said, shifting in her bed. "He was the sweetest little boy."

"So. No one knew what you did?"

"What I did?"

"To your uncle. You know—"

Grace saw Adele motion over to the other side of the room. Mary was sitting on the side of her bed, leaning closer to hear what was being discussed. "Someone should give her a bowl of popcorn the way she's sitting there listening like it's some movie or somethin'."

Mary looked startled and pushed herself back some.

"We could go out to the solarium, if you want," Adele said.

Grace shook her head. She didn't much like leaving her bed anymore. "Let her listen. Don't much matter anymore, I guess. What was I saying?"

"You said Kevin was a sweet little boy," Adele prodded.

"He was. Had the same disposition as his father and grandfather."

"So, what happened? To make you leave, I mean."

Grace hesitated, thinking before she began, "At first we lived in the little house. It was tight but we were happy. Right across the field from the big house. I couldn't help but think Simone was always looking out her window watching me, criticizing me. She liked to remind me how I always seemed to let her down. Kept saying I lied to her about being a Catholic."

"You weren't?" Adele said.

Grace shrugged. "Thought I was. I was baptized as a baby, but I never made my First Communion or had my confirmation. Didn't even know about those things, so if we were to get married in the church, I had to get those over with."

"Did you?" Adele said.

"Had to. His mother was angry enough without her son not marrying a Catholic. Held the wedding up, though, and by the time we went before the priest, I was pregnant." Grace snickered. "We hoped she'd think it was a premature baby."

"Did she?"

Grace grunted. "Then we were at least hoping the baby would soften her."

"And . . . ?"

Grace shook her head. "The minute he was put in my arms, I couldn't believe the joy I felt. And to see Jack's expression." She paused remembering the moment, before adding, "All she said was 'let's hope he's got more Finley blood than Dormand blood in him.'"

"Wow," Adele said. "But were you happy?"

"As happy as I could be with that cloud always hanging over me. Guess you'd call it guilt."

"Did you stop working after you got married?" The question came from Mary, who no longer hid the fact that she was eavesdropping.

Grace glanced across the room, then looked at Adele, who said, "Good question."

"When I began to show, I did. For a while anyway. A pregnant woman wasn't really seen in public. By then, Rachel and Tim hired Claire to help with the diner, so I no longer worked there. But after Kevin was born, Jack said he liked hearing me play and the money was good. So, one night a week, we'd head to the Summit Hotel where I'd sing and make money to help with our expenses while Gerald stayed home and watched Kevin."

Grace had a faraway expression in her eyes and started singing, "I was dancin' with my darlin' to the Tennessee waltz . . ." She stopped and said, "Kevin liked that one when he heard me practicing. I would sing it to him all the time."

"What about the cabin?" Adele said. "Did you ever go back to it?"

"I moved out right away. I convinced Jack that I wanted to help fix up the little house, so I lived there and he stayed with his parents until we were married. Only thing I brought with me from the cabin was the Victrola and the gun, but that was about it. I put the gun in Jack's gun rack and never touched it again."

"Then you had your daughter."

Grace rolled over, turning her back to Adele.

"Grace," Adele nudged. "I'll be leaving soon. I just have a few more questions . . . for now. You had your daughter then."

"Not right away. I had a miscarriage or two before I had Vicky. She was a pretty little thing. Jack always said she looked like me. Kevin just loved his little sister so much. Was always watching out for her."

"Did they ever ask about what happened to your parents?"

"Vicky was too young, but Simone told Kevin they'd been killed in a car accident. She believed he didn't need to know the truth about my side of the family." Grace turned back around, facing Adele. "S'pose she was right."

"I still don't understand. You and Jack were happy."

"We were, even though I couldn't ever really allow myself to be totally happy. Jack somehow knew that. He figured it was his mother causing me to be on edge all the time. It didn't help but it was more knowing what I'd done that ate at me. Still, I kept busy with my music and managed to have a much bigger garden than I would've had at the cabin. I would bring a lot of the vegetables to Rachel and Tim for the diner. They were real special people and would pretty much drop everything, making patrons wait, when I brought the kids in to have ice cream. They just loved my babies." Grace stared off before turning her gaze back to Adele. "I'd give Simone and Gerald dozens of canned vegetables so Simone wouldn't have to do all that work lifting the hot pot of boiling water out of the big kettle. I was still determined to show her I wasn't the person she thought I was. Maybe I was trying to prove it to myself. I'd invite them over for meals. Gerald loved playing with the kids while Simone felt discipline was more important. She was always pointing out what I was doing wrong. But I loved being Jack's wife and Kevin and Vicky's mother."

"So, I still don't understand," Adele said. "Why'd you leave?"

Grace pulled the covers over her head and rolled on to her side, longing for eternal sleep. After a few moments, she heard Adele packing up and shuffling out of the room, but it didn't stop her from reliving what happened.

CHAPTER 21

There was a knock on the front door. By then, due to their growing family, she and Jack took the larger house while Gerald and Simone moved into the little house. Grace kept telling Simone that they would be fine in the little house, knowing Simone was none too pleased to move, but Gerald insisted that they switch, saying, "I'm sure there'll be more grandkids to come."

Grace ran to the front door, hoping the knocking wouldn't wake up Vicky who was taking a nap. Kevin was at school. Jack was in the seven acres with his father, which was out of sight from the house. Grace opened the door to see an imposing figure in a uniform.

"May I help you?" she said.

"I'm Sheriff Clark," he said, tipping his hat. "You Grace Dormand?"

"No," she said, her heart starting to race.

"You're not Grace Dormand?"

"I'm Grace Finley." She'd hoped Simone hadn't seen the sheriff pull into her driveway from her window.

"Dormand is your maiden name then?" Sheriff Clark shifted from one foot to the other.

"What is this about?"

"Ma'am just answer the question."

"My aunt gave me the name of Cooke. My parents were Dormands."

He nodded. "Would you know anything about the property right off Route 189? I believe it had belonged to your parents."

She shook her head. "I lived with my aunt up on Coyote Hill, after my parents . . . died."

"After the murders, you mean."

"That was about twenty years ago," Grace said. She was grateful to hear Vicky crying and used the excuse, "I have to get my baby."

205

"This won't take long," he said. "I have a few more questions for you."

All she wanted to do was shut the door, tell him to leave. "Could you please tell me what this is all about?"

"There was a body found on the property. We're just trying to find out who it could be."

Vicky's cries were getting louder, more persistent. Grace steeled herself. "Listen, I wish I could help you, but my baby needs me."

"You don't seem shocked," he said.

"I . . . I . . . what kind of body? Somebody's cow or something?"

"A human body," he said.

She feigned surprise. "Oh my goodness. How awful." She motioned toward where the cries were coming from. "Really, I have to get her."

"Well, you give it some thought," Sheriff Clark said, "and I'll be back soon when you have more time to answer my questions."

Grace shut the door, leaning against it, trying to catch her breath. She ran to the bathroom and threw up, then hurried to get her crying daughter. She scooped Vicky up, holding her, squeezing her, trying to figure out what to do. She ran to the kitchen to look out the window to see if Simone was making her way across the field to ask why the sheriff had been there, but to Grace's relief she figured the squad car was far enough in the driveway that her mother-in-law couldn't see it from her vantage point.

That night, even though she tried to act like nothing was wrong, Jack kept asking if everything was okay. When supper was nothing more than egg salad sandwiches and pickles, he seemed concerned.

"Oh," she said, "Vicky's been fussy all afternoon and I couldn't seem to calm her down. I just didn't have time to make a hot meal."

Kevin took a bite of his sandwich, chewed and swallowed, before saying, "But it's really good, Mommy."

Later, after Kevin and Vicky were down for the night, while watching *Country Hoedown* on their small black and white television, Jack pressed Grace again about what was wrong. "I know you, sweetheart," he said. "Something's on your mind."

She almost told him, nearly said that they needed to pack up and leave Churubusco, and why, but then thought better of it. The Hames Sisters were singing, and she listened for a minute before saying, "I . . . I just want to do more for the family."

"More? What do you mean?"

"Well, I love singing and wish I could do more of it. I mean, look at them." She pointed to the TV. "And then there's Patti Page and Kitty Wells. Wouldn't it be something if I could be as famous as they are, make as much money as they do?"

She wasn't sure why she'd said that but realized she may have been laying the groundwork for escape, if need be. But how could she leave Jack? The kids? She loved them more than life itself. But how could she let them ever know that she was indeed a murderer, no matter what the circumstances had been? Simone was right: once a Dormand always a Dormand.

Jack pulled her into a hug. "Where would you go? I know there's bars in Chateaugay and even further in Malone, but, I mean, you draw a big crowd at the Summit."

She gave Jack a sad smile and said, "I suppose."

That night she lay in bed, trying to make sense of everything, trying to decide what to do. She thought maybe while Jack was working in the fields, she'd pack up the kids and leave a note, telling him she was leaving him and taking the kids with her. But she didn't give that much thought. Kevin adored his father, and his father adored him. And why should Jack be punished for her mistake?

She then thought about going to the sheriff and telling him it was self-defense, but after so much time had passed, even she started to question herself. Maybe if she had reasoned with her uncle, things would have turned out different. Maybe she could have given him some money to keep him happy. But, in her heart, she knew he'd shown up for more than money. It would be her word against a dead man's.

And, of course, there was Simone. She'd rather have her think she, Grace, was a selfish woman, instead of a killer. *Once a Dormand, always a Dormand*, played over and over in her head as she fell into a restless sleep.

The next day, Grace wanted to get out of the house, in case the sheriff returned. She decided to take Vicky to visit Rachel and Tim at the diner. Kevin was in school. The sky was clear and the air warm on that day in May so she put Vicky in the baby carriage and took the one-mile walk into town along Looby Road, the entire time looking over her shoulder whenever she heard a vehicle approach, fearing it would be Sheriff Clark.

"There's our angel!" Rachel squealed the minute Grace carried Vicky in through the door, leaving the carriage parked outside of the diner. She ran over and pulled the baby from Grace's arms and started cooing to her.

Tim came out from the back wearing a big grin, heading directly over to her and the baby.

"Looks like I'll be more than busy now that she's here," Claire said, rolling her eyes as she cleared a nearby table.

Grace mouthed an apology, but Claire didn't acknowledge it, carrying the dishes to the back.

"We still miss you," Tim said, looking over his shoulder. "She's good, but doesn't draw them in the way you did. Sure you don't wanna come back?"

"Why would she wanna come back when she's got this beauty to love up on?" Rachel said, bouncing a giggling Vicky in her arms.

A couple of workers from the railroad came in, forcing Tim to hurry into the kitchen and Rachel to hand the baby back to Grace. "Vanilla or chocolate?" she said.

Grace went to the counter, placing Vicky on her lap. "Vanilla. Much easier to clean."

After Rachel sat the two men down, she went behind the counter and scooped some ice cream into a bowl, bringing it and two spoons to Grace. She said, "Let me take care of those fellows and I'll be back to catch up with you."

While Grace was giving Vicky small tastes of the ice cream, Rachel took the men's orders and then went into the back.

"Who the hell knows," one of the men said. "Sounds like he's been rotting there for a long time."

Grace caught her breath.

"Far as I know, no one's been missin'," replied the other man. "They say it wasn't far from where that murder took place all those years ago. The sheriff's been going around seeing if anyone knows anything."

Rachel came over just as Grace stood up. "Where are you going?"

"I better go." She didn't bother trying to pay for the ice cream since past experience proved it to be an insult to Rachel and Tim.

"But you just got here."

Vicky stretched out her little hand toward the ice cream and started to cry when Grace backed away from the counter.

"She wants her ice cream," Rachel said. "Let her have some more." Rachel took a spoonful and brought it to Vicky's mouth.

"Okay, I really gotta go. I didn't intend to walk all the way here, but I have to get back before Kevin gets home from school."

Rachel had an odd expression but then said, "Well, let me give that sweetie a kiss goodbye then." She came around the counter and pressed her lips to Vicky's forehead.

"Tell Tim I said goodbye," Grace said, rushing out the door with Vicky howling in protest, her arm outstretched toward the bowl of barely touched ice cream.

She almost ran home, the carriage bouncing along the way with Vicky curled up beneath a light blanket. Grace's mind raced. Had the sheriff already talked to Simone and Gerald? If so, why hadn't they mentioned it to her? She felt trapped and afraid, unsure what to do next. When she got back home, Jack came out from the barn, which was several hundred feet from the house.

"Hey! Where you been?" He strutted across the yard, looking into the carriage to see that Vicky was asleep.

"Uh, went to see Rachel and Tim."

He laughed. "Surprised that they let you leave with her." He motioned to Vicky. He then looked at Grace. "You okay?"

She gave a quick nod. "I . . . I just keep thinking about my singing. I'm itching to do more. I mean, I want to put that guitar to good use."

Jack studied her. "I don't know what you mean." He shifted from one foot to the other.

She reached over, brushing hay from his hair and shirt. "You work so hard. I'd love it if I could make enough money so you wouldn't have to. You *and* your father. It would give you more time to putter on those old cars you like."

Presently, there was a 1935 Ford sedan in the garage Jack had bought from a junkyard dealer a few weeks ago to tinker on. It was a hobby he was starting to enjoy.

"Grace, we're getting along just fine. Is there something you want that I'm not getting for you? One of those new washing machines maybe?"

She shook her head. She was relieved he hadn't mentioned anything about the sheriff stopping by.

When Vicky whimpered, Grace said, "Well, she's probably hungry," picking the baby up.

Jack nodded but had an uneasy expression. "I'll see you later. Dad and I will be out in the field."

"Okay," she said, bringing Vicky inside the house.

The following afternoon, Vicky was in the playpen nearby in the yard while Grace was weeding and hoeing to get the garden ready for planting. Every year it seemed to expand more and more and became a sense of pride for her. Kevin would be home from school soon. Jack and Gerald were one field over, plowing. Every once in a while, from a distance, she and Jack would catch sight of each other and she'd return his friendly wave, or was it one of concern?

She looked up at the sound of tires on the gravel driveway and saw a blue car pull in. She didn't recognize it and stood, shielding the sun from her eyes, watching a woman climb from it and call over to her. "Grace? Hi!"

Grace dropped her hoe and hesitantly approached the woman.

"Don't you know who I am?"

Grace took a step closer. There was something familiar about the face, but the hair was bleached blond. Tentatively, she said, "Helen? Helen Poupore?"

"Yes!" Helen laughed. "But I'm Helen Miller now. I married Roy Miller."

Grace had no idea who Roy Miller was. She looked back to see that Vicky was content playing with her blocks. "So, um, what can I do for you?"

Helen became serious. "Is there some place we can talk?"

Grace didn't feel like being hospitable, still hurting from the way Helen had treated her, even though it had been years earlier. She motioned to her dirty pants and hands and said, "I'm really in the middle of something."

Helen took a step closer. "Sorry, but . . . well, I just thought you should know that my dad told me there was some sort of activity over on your property?"

Grace steeled herself, played stupid. "My property?"

"You know, the one that borders ours. Well, my parents' property. I moved to Chazy when I got married. Anyway, they found a body that had been dug up right near your cabin. The sheriff told dad it looked like wild dogs or wolves or something found it."

Grace recalled how the sheriff found her lack of surprise curious, so she muttered, "Oh my god, that's horrible."

"I know. So creepy." Helen looked over where Vicky was. "Is that your baby?"

Grace nodded, trying to keep herself steady.

Helen walked closer. "A girl? She's so cute! I don't have any kids, yet." She paused, then added, "Not for lack of trying, though."

"So, did your father say anything else? I mean about everything?"

Helen looked confused when she said, "He did. He said the sheriff told him he'd talked to you already and that you never said anything about living there. You told him you had lived with your aunt."

Grace looked down, brushing the dirt from her pant for distraction. "Yes, yes, the sheriff stopped by, but he caught me at a bad time. I . . . I wonder who it was."

"What do you mean?"

"The man they found."

"I don't think I said it was a man," Helen said.

"Oh, I just figured. I don't know. Maybe a hunter or something." She realized that lying was going to have to become second nature to her.

"Well, he also told my dad it looked like murder 'cuz there was a bullet wound in the chest."

Grace was barely listening now, mentally planning her escape.

"I wonder if it was there when you were living there. Or maybe it happened after you moved out. Dad says the sheriff said they have ways of figuring out about when it happened."

Grace gaped at her. "What?"

"You know, they have ways of figuring out about when he was shot."

Grace slumped onto the ground.

Helen ran over. "Are you okay?"

She tried to collect herself. "This is all just so . . . I mean, I haven't seen you in years and then you show up like this."

Helen tossed her arms up, stammering, before saying, "Okay. I've been wanting to come see you for a long time but didn't know what I'd say. I thought this news was a good reason to see you. And look how things worked out for you. You have a nice home and you married Jack! Can you believe it? All your dreams came true."

Grace looked over her shoulder, seeing Jack and his father in the distant field. They had to have seen there was someone in the driveway. She wondered if Simone had seen the car pull into the driveway.

Just then, the school bus pulled up and Kevin climbed down the steps and ran toward his mother, looking curiously at the car in the driveway as he passed it. There wasn't a day that he didn't run up to Grace and hug her. This time she held onto him longer than usual before she let him go.

"Who's this?" Helen said.

"This is my son," Grace said, ruffling his hair.

He ran over to Vicky, who was eagerly waiting for her brother. After he reached into the playpen and gave his sister a hug, he said, "Can I have a snack?"

Grace nodded. "Go inside and put away your things first." She turned toward Helen. "Well, thanks for dropping by."

Helen acted as though she weren't ready to leave. "Maybe I could come over another time or you could come to my place. Roy doesn't like company so it would have to be during the day."

"Maybe," Grace said, walking over and picking up Vicky from the playpen. "Take care."

Helen took her cue. She said, "If I hear anything else, I'll call you. What's your phone number?"

"You can find it in the phone book." With Vicky in her arms, she watched as Helen slowly got in her car and pulled out of the driveway. She then went into the house barely able to walk without shaking.

"Who was that lady?" Kevin said, waiting for Grace to give him his snack.

"Don't worry about that," she said, bringing Vicky to her crib and laying her down. She went back to the kitchen and took some oatmeal cookies from the bread box and put them on a plate. She then poured a cup of milk for Kevin before going to her bedroom and pulling a suitcase from under the bed. She knew what she had to do, as difficult as it would be.

"Who was that lady?" Jack said, walking into the house an hour or so later, covered in hayseed and smelling of sweat. Kevin was in the living room watching *The Mickey Mouse Club* on TV with Vicky nearby in her playpen.

"Remember Helen, Helen Poupore?"

He nodded, going to the sink and splashing water on his face. "What'd she want?"

Grace shrugged. "She told me she got married and is living in Chazy."

He grabbed a nearby towel and dried his face. "I don't remember her hair being that color. I could see it all the way across the field." He went over to the stove and lifted the lid to a big pot of beef stew. "Mmm."

She followed Jack into the bedroom so he could change into a clean shirt. He noticed the opened suitcase on the bed, her clothes stacked inside it.

"What's this?"

"Jack, don't be upset but I decided it's now or never. I'm going to try out for *Country Hoedown*."

"What do you mean?"

"I don't want to keep talking about it. There's a train leaving for Montreal later tonight and I'm going to take it."

He scowled and took a step closer to her. "Tonight? Just like that? What about the kids?"

"I know your mother'll watch them and Kevin is a real big help with Vicky." As if to herself, she said, "He's such a good big brother."

"Grace," Jack said, still in his sweaty shirt, "this isn't like you."

He had no idea how difficult this was for her, no idea that there was no intention of coming back. How could she? Once Helen told her there were ways of figuring out when her uncle was shot, she knew she would be arrested. Her mother-in-law would gloat, knowing she was right about Grace all along.

"Grace?" Jack said.

She went to her dresser drawer and pulled out some undergarments and put them in the suitcase.

"I'm talking to you."

"I know, Jack. I took some money from the safe."

He scowled. "How much?"

"Fifty dollars."

"Fifty!"

Most of it was money she'd saved from singing on Saturday nights, so she didn't feel guilty for taking it.

"We were saving that for a new car, a new car for *you*."

"Well, I'd rather use the money for this. Like an investment."

"An investment?"

"Don't you believe in me, Jack?" She choked when she added, "Let me do this for us."

He went over to her and pulled her into a hug. "Of course I believe in you, but why don't you wait? We'll go together. We never had a real honeymoon. We could make it real special."

"I have to leave now, tonight," she said.

He pulled away, studying her. "Why the rush?"

She hesitated, then said, "Because we'll say we'll go together, but we both know you can't leave everything to your father to do. Especially after you just got more cows."

"Mom?"

Grace and Jack turned to see Kevin standing in the doorway.

"I'm hungry. So is Vicky."

"Oh!" Grace looked at her wristwatch. It was suppertime. The train would be leaving the Summit Station in a couple of hours. She ran into the kitchen and put some beef stew in some bowls and got out a loaf of bread and sliced it. She put everything on the table then went and got Vicky and brought her to the kitchen and put her into the highchair.

"Jack! Supper."

He came out of the bedroom, still having not changed, looking shell shocked.

Grace nodded for Kevin to start eating and pulled a chair out next to Vicky's. She cut up the beef in tiny pieces and mashed the vegetables and began feeding her.

"Daddy," Kevin said, "aren't you gonna eat?"

Jack shook his head, saying, "Can't." He then went out to the garage.

Kevin had a concerned expression. "What's wrong with Daddy?"

Grace shifted in her chair. "Kevin, Mommy's going to tell you something, okay?"

"Okay," he said with some hesitation.

"I'll be going away and I need you to be a big brave boy and always take care of your sister, okay?"

Kevin put his fork down, his bottom lip quivering. "Away? Where you going, Mommy?"

"You never heard of it," she said. In reality, she had no idea where she'd end up.

"When will you be back?"

Lying to her child was more difficult than to her husband. She said, "I . . . I can't say, sweetheart." Tears filled her eyes. Seeing him look at her the way he did, broke her heart. She decided to give him something to hope for once she was gone. She said, "I'm going to see if I can sing."

"You can sing, Mommy!" Kevin said. "You're real good."

"But on TV."

His eyes widened. "Really?"

"I'm going to try," she said, even though she already knew she wasn't going to do any such thing.

The sound of Jack working on the jalopy came from the garage. Kevin said, "I'm not hungry anymore. Can I go help Daddy?"

Grace nodded, grateful that the inquisition was over. She finished feeding Vicky, wiped her face off, and then brought her to her crib, laying her down. Vicky started to cry in pro-test, reaching her arms out to Grace. Usually after supper meant playing with Daddy and Kevin while Grace cleaned up the kitchen. She hurriedly put away the beef stew and bread, washed the dishes, then went and got her suitcase and guitar. The walk into town wouldn't take long, but she wanted to be sure she had enough time to buy her ticket.

One last time, she went to give Vicky a kiss, wishing she could take her with her, but knew that couldn't be. She wiped her tears off of Vicky's downy-like hair and rushed out of the room, attempting to block out her daughter's cries.

She went into the garage, carrying her suitcase and guitar. Kevin screamed at Jack, who had his head under the hood of the jalopy, "Don't let her leave, Daddy!"

She found speaking impossible. She went to Kevin, giving him a kiss on the forehead. He squeezed her, not letting her go at first. She wanted to tell him she'd be back soon, but couldn't lie. Vicky's cries reached them.

"She needs her bottle," Grace said, looking at Kevin.

"Don't leave!" He stared at his mother, tears streaming down his face, before he rushed to take care of his sister.

Grace put down her suitcase and guitar and went to Jack, grazing him on the back with her fingertips. He stood, gazing at her, his eyes also filled with tears. He said, "Something's not right about this, Grace. But I love you and want you to do this, to get it out of your system." He pulled her into a hug, whispering, "I wish I never got you that damn guitar now." He kissed her then let her go.

She picked up her suitcase and guitar, hurried out of the garage and headed down Looby Road, hoping that the sheriff wouldn't be crossing her path before she reached the train station.

CHAPTER 22

Oh my gosh," Adele said, putting down her pen. "Was that the last time you saw your family?"

Grace had a faraway expression without responding.

Adele managed to get Grace to sit outside on the patio since warm cloudless days in Upstate New York were rare. She thought the sun on Grace's pale face would do her good. But no matter how bright the day was, hearing Grace's tragic story felt overwhelmingly sad.

"So you took the train to Montreal? Did you end up living there?"

"No. Only stayed there one night in a cheap motel. I went to a local drug store and bought scissors and dye. I cut my long blond hair and dyed it black. I knew I couldn't stay in Montreal because that's where I'd told Jack I'd be. So I went to the bus station and looked at all the places the bus would be going. I bought a ticket to Buffalo. I didn't want to stay in Canada. Buffalo seemed far enough away from Churubusco so that's where I headed."

Grace stopped speaking, playing with the loose threads on the sleeve of her bathrobe.

"And then what happened," Adele said, sitting back and letting Grace continue telling her story uninterrupted.

After showing her birth certificate to the immigration officer, where her last name was listed as Dormand, just as she'd done going into Canada, she tried to sit on the bus without causing much attention, but other passengers were curious about the guitar she was carrying, asking if she was a musician. She lied and said she was bringing it to her brother. "He's in college," she said before hunkering down in her seat and feigning sleep during the six-hour drive.

Once they reached Buffalo she found a motel a short distance from the bus station and booked a room there. She was exhausted but instead of reciting the usual prayers she'd been taught, she begged God to forgive her for leaving her family, for lying to them while asking for help on how to keep going forward because suicide seemed a viable solution. In her mind's eye, she saw how Vicky reached for her to be picked up and how Kevin clung to her. And then Jack; how the tears were streaming down his face. She'd never forget them, but how long would it be before they'd be able to forget her because that is what they'd have to do?

The following morning she went to the front desk and asked about a place that served breakfast. The clerk told her there was a diner one block over. The idea of a diner made her think of Rachel and Tim, until she got there. This one was a lot fancier and the prices were higher. She managed to get enough to eat without spending the rest of her money, but she was going to run out soon.

She hadn't really given much thought of what she would do with herself, except not be found and go to jail. That's when it occurred to her that she'd need a job. She asked the waitress who was serving her if they were hiring.

"We're always hiring," the waitress said. "We get students from the college comin' and goin' but now that school's just about over, they all head back home. Why? You lookin' for a job?"

She nodded yes.

"You got any experience?"

"I worked at my hometown diner for about four years," she said.

The waitress told her to wait a minute, then brought over a grizzly looking man. "This is Ken. He's the manager and does the hiring."

Ken looked Grace over and said, "When can you start?"

"Anytime," Grace replied.

"Come back tonight at five." He started to walk away when she interrupted him.

"How do you pay?"

He stopped, looking back at her. "You get a dollar an hour, besides tips. Cash at the end of each shift. Is that a problem?"

She shook her head.

"We're open twenty-four hours round the clock and your shift will end at one in the morning."

"That's fine," she said, and then went back to the motel to see about getting the room for the weekly rate.

Even though she was rusty, not having worked for Rachel and Tim for a few years, and things went a lot faster since they were near the bus station where people were coming and going, Grace picked things up quite fast and was amazed at the tips she made in just one night. None of the other waitresses who worked the night shift seemed all that interested in getting to know her, which was fine, but she would eventually have to come up with a story about who she was and where she came from without having any idea of what to say.

After her shift was done, it was one in the morning. She headed directly to the motel, walking at a fast clip in the dark. Just as she had done when she had the cabin, she had the key ready once she reached the door. She shut it behind herself and decided to take a long shower. After, she climbed into bed, putting her head on the pillow, and foolishly reached for Jack. She sobbed, knowing she'd never be able to rest her head on his shoulder again. What was he doing just then? He was probably waiting to hear from her, which made her stomach roil because it would be a waste of time. She then imagined Simone fuming, and hoped she wasn't taking her anger out on the kids. She also wondered if the sheriff had been by again. If so, would he believe the story that she was heading to Montreal to make it in the music business? Or would he see the ruse? The questions never stopped until she finally managed to catch a few hours of fretful sleep.

After several weeks, Grace found a monotonous rhythm to her life; she'd go to work, do overtime if there was any, go back to her room, sleep, eat when she was hungry, and repeat the cycle. She also had to keep dyeing her hair black. Then, one night there was a couple in the diner in her section. They noticed her name tag when she gave them their menus. She thoughtlessly had told Ken her name when he asked, wishing she'd changed it. But all her life she had to correct her surname and felt Grace belonged to her and didn't want to give it up. It was as though it was all she had left of herself.

When Grace brought the couple their coffees, the woman said, "I don't know anyone named Grace but it reminds us of that woman who's missing. Her name was Grace."

Grace tried her best not to let them see her handshake as she held the pad to take their food order.

"We're from Plattsburgh," the woman said. "There was an article in the paper about a husband trying to find his wife. There was a photo of her in the paper, but she had pretty blond hair." The woman's eyes went from Grace's face to her hair.

"That's awful," Grace said. "Hope she's okay. Now what can I get you?" She hoped that would be the end of the conversation, but when she brought the couple their order, the husband said, "You from around here?"

Grace forced a smile. "Sure am," she replied, placing their fried chicken dinners in front of them.

"Your husband from around here, too?" he said, nodding to her hand where the engagement and wedding bands were.

Another forced smile. "He is. Now is there anything else I can get you?"

The couple gazed suspiciously at her before saying no. She then hurried to the bathroom, trying to catch her breath and not reveal her anxiety. When she came back out, she waited on other tables while trying to avoid the couple as much as she could before giving them their bill. She started to breathe easier when they left, but something told her they might report their suspicions. She couldn't risk any such thing.

Later that night, she approached Ken and told him that she had to quit her job and go to Potsdam where her parents lived. "My father is very ill and my mom needs help," she said.

"You're kidding," Ken said. "Just like that you're gonna up and leave me?"

"Sorry, Ken," she said, "but family first." She saw the hypocrisy in such a comment but needed to play the part.

He handed her what she'd made for the day without saying another word.

The following morning Grace checked out of the motel, even though she had a couple days left that were already paid. She made her way to the bus station, having taken off her rings and tucking them in a side pocket of her suitcase.

"So," Adele said, "where'd you go?"

Grace squinted from the sunshine pressing down on her. "Can't be sure. There were stretches of going from one place to the next, working in one diner to another. I avoided going anywhere near Plattsburgh, so I kept going downstate." She took a tissue from her pocket and patted the perspiration from her upper lip.

"It's crazy that you were never found," Adele said. "I don't know that you could've gotten away with that now."

"Can't say that was lucky or not," Grace said. "No matter where I went, though, I made sure I had my black hair dye and scissors. Sometimes I wish I'd been found even though that would've meant jail."

"You don't know that," Adele said.

"And I didn't want to find out."

"But I was thinking," Adele said, "what if the sheriff went back to the house and told your husband about the body being found. Wouldn't he kind of put two and two together?"

"Part of me hoped for that. This way he'd know I wasn't running away from him or my babies. To hell with what Simone thought."

Once Adele finished writing on her notepad, she said, "So then where did you end up?"

Grace had to remind herself where she was when she woke up one morning in another motel. She looked over at the nightstand where there was a pamphlet: *Things to Do in Poughkeepsie.* She climbed out of bed and looked out the window to see there was freshly fallen snow. It was the middle of November and she'd been away now for six months. Bundled up, having recently bought winter clothing when she was in Binghamton, the last place she'd holed up at for a couple of weeks before moving on, she headed toward Main Street. It was easier to hide beneath a knitted beanie and heavy coat as she strolled past gift shops, restaurants and clothing stores. People who passed gave her a smile or nod of the head. She learned to do the same in return, seeing her breath in the cold air. Off in the distance, she spotted a blinking sign that read "DINER" and headed in its direction to see if they were hiring since waitressing was all she could do. However, just as she was passing Pub & Brewery, she noticed a sign in the window that read "LIVE MUSIC." In smaller print: "8-1 p.m. Must be 18 or over." She continued toward the diner to get something to eat and see if they were hiring.

Once she was seated, she was amused to see that there was a small jukebox at the end of her table, reminding her of the big one Rachel and Tim had in their diner. Oh, how they loved putting in change and having Kevin push the numbers for any song he'd want to hear. The reminder made Grace feel sick with sadness. Hastily, she flipped through the selections, without recognizing many of the song titles.

She decided not to ask about a job when the waitress brought her the check for a grilled cheese sandwich and cup of chicken noodle soup. She had enough money to hold her over for a while. She paid and then went directly back to her room. No matter where she went, the guitar was with her, but she hadn't touched the strings, finding it too painful. This time, however, she took it from the corner, tuned it and started strumming before she broke into song. She knew she would need to practice some more before trying to be a part of any pub scene and could she do so incognito? Without much debate, as eight o'clock approached, she freshened up and made her way to Pub & Brewery.

She weaved through a crowd that appeared to be about her age, some younger, while she looked for a place to sit. All the tables were taken and trying to get a drink from the bar meant having to push through a swarm of boisterous patrons. Instead, she edged her way toward a wall near the restrooms and waited for the live music. She didn't have to wait long. Suddenly, "See You Later, Alligator" exploded in the room and everyone started bouncing and jiggling. This was nothing like the tavern at the Summit Hotel. Once that song ended, another immediately began: *So you met someone who set you back on your heels, goody goody!* The crowd joined in with the "goody goody!"

Grace stretched on her toes to get a look at the performers, but they were on the other side of the room and difficult to see. However, she could tell that they had more instruments than just guitars and the guitars were electric. She was out of her element. This crowd didn't appear to favor the twangy country sounds she loved.

Disheartened and feeling antiquated at the age of twenty-four, she pushed her way through the noise and mayhem to get outside. Visions of Jack, Kevin, and Vicky accompanied her back to the motel while she hummed "The Tennessee Waltz." She landed on her bed and cried herself to sleep.

The following morning she made her way back to the diner. The aroma of eggs, toast, and syrup filled the air. She ordered breakfast then asked the waitress if they were hiring. Without saying a word, the waitress left and returned a few minutes later with a sheet of paper, saying, "Fill this out. The manager'll call you if he's interested."

Grace looked at the paper requiring some information that she couldn't provide. She filled out what she could, name and experience, using the name on her birth certificate, Dormand, but that was about it.

After the waitress came back, putting pancakes and bacon on the table, Grace handed her the paper, saying, "I'm staying at the motel down the street. I don't have a phone number or address yet. I'm new to the area."

The waitress looked over the sheet of paper. "Well, looks like you have a lot of experience. I'll give this to Billy. He's in the back."

Grace took her time picking at her pancakes, hoping the manager would come out and offer her a job. She mindlessly flipped the tabs on the jukebox. A nickel would buy you two songs. She was happy when she discovered Patsy Cline's "Walkin' After Midnight," and pressed G8, then decided to give someone named Frankie Lymon a try and pressed B5 for a song called "Love is a Clown." She hummed along with Patsy while looking toward the kitchen, waiting for the manager to appear. Then Frankie Lymon came on. He had an unfamiliar sound. Certainly nothing that she could replicate with just an acoustic guitar. Sam at Summit Inn never asked her to change her style, the 'busco crowd preferring country music *and only* country music. And Rachel and Tim's jukebox was filled with only country music.

By the time the songs were over, and she took the last sip of her coffee, she figured she'd leave but come back later to see if the manager had a chance to look over the application. She waited for the waitress to bring her the bill and when she did, she said Billy asked if Grace could wait for a few minutes.

Eventually, a man approached the table. He was average size with a hint of a belly and black hair. He stuck out his hand, introducing himself. "I'm Billy. Billy Smith." He sat down across from her in the booth.

"Grace," she replied.

"Well, Grace, looks like you certainly have experience, but I wonder how long you plan to be in the area. Dotty told me you said you were staying at the motel down the street."

Grace nodded. "I just got into town. Always wanted to come here. It's so beautiful."

"Where you from?"

Without hesitation, she said, "Buffalo. I plan to get a more permanent place and stay here."

Billy nodded. "Sounds good. I don't have a position open just yet but in a week one of my waitresses is leaving so you could fill her slot. Would that work for you?"

"Sure," she said.

"Okay. You come in next Wednesday, around this time and Dotty'll get you set up." He stood, then said, "Oh, are there any hours you can't work?"

"No, but how do you pay?"

"A dollar an hour, cash, plus tips. Is that a problem?"

"No."

He nodded. "That's what I like to hear."

Grace took advantage of the time before working to practice playing her guitar. She listened to the radio in her room in an attempt to learn new songs. She even tried to write a couple of her own. Two nights later she went back to the pub and discovered that the live music this time was a country music band. It was an older crowd, one that jam-packed the smoke-filled room. She managed to get a seat at the bar and sip her Coke, enjoying the entertainment, even recognizing some of the songs.

It was as though she were in another world, one that didn't allow thoughts of family, sheriffs, and judgmental mothers-in-law. It was the most at peace she'd been since she left Jack. She figured it was the music that did it. Still, she wasn't brave enough to see if the pub would hire her to perform so she planned to put in as much time as Billy needed her for waitressing.

Soon she was a familiar face at the diner with her jet-black hair where she brought in generous tips and regulars who acknowledged her with a smile. The first time that cops came in and were seated in her section, she panicked and asked one of the other waitresses to serve them, saying she needed to hurry to the bathroom. Eventually, though, when cops came in, she steeled herself, gave them a friendly hello and served them, pouring their coffee without spilling a drop. Maybe no one was looking for her anymore, she thought. Or maybe her look was enough to throw them off.

She found a one-bedroom apartment in the upstairs of an old Colonial that she rented by the month. This Grace wasn't a woman who'd escaped a nightmare but a woman who was building a new life and she began to feel settled, as settled as she could feel as long as she put out of mind the people who mattered most to her.

CHAPTER 23

The diner was open on Thanksgiving Day and Grace was the only waitress not only willing to work but do a double shift. She welcomed the distraction so she wouldn't have to think about what Jack and the kids were doing. Donna, one of the other waitresses who had a family, was put on the schedule and Billy didn't want to hear any complaints or she'd lose her job. Even though she was angry with Billy, she barely said a word to Grace during her entire shift. In reality, Grace felt she could have handled the few customers who did come in by herself, but knew it wasn't up to her to let Donna go home.

The following day, Grace was off. Even though it was bitterly cold, she needed to get out of her apartment and decided to walk along Market Street, which was festooned with holiday lights, the sidewalk filled with shoppers wishing those they passed a Merry Christmas. She stopped at a hobby shop when she spotted a toy trainset chugging around a Christmas tree in the large front window, thinking how much Kevin would like it. Then on a distant shelf, there was a baby doll with a pink bonnet and frilly dress, the perfect gift for a little girl.

"Honey, are you okay?"

Grace looked over to see an older woman studying her curiously. That's when she realized she'd been crying.

"Oh, oh, yes," Grace said, pulling a tissue from her handbag and wiping her nose. She muttered, "Allergies," though it was far from hay fever season, and hurried down the street to head back to her bland, tiny apartment.

When she approached the Colonial, the family who lived downstairs were outside putting up lights around the windows. She stopped and watched the three children, ranging in ages of five to ten, help their father by holding the strings of colorful bulbs. They muttered a shy hello to her as she passed them, as she went inside and climbed the stairs to her floor. Oh how she yearned to be with her family. Even though it was the middle of the day, she crawled into her bed and remained there until she had to get up for work the following morning.

According to Dotty, Billy always gave a holiday party for the staff and that year would be no different. He used the back room that was usually reserved for the Elks and Knights of Columbus meetings. Grace was stunned to learn that he would close the diner at 8 p.m. sharp on December 22nd, a Sunday night, so that all the staff could be a part of the festivities. Grace had no desire to go, but Billy told her, with a smile and wink, that it was mandatory she attend or her job would be on the line. "I think you need some fun," he'd said.

That Sunday night when she walked into the back room, already buzzing with activity, she found tables filled with trays of pasta, meatballs, chicken wings and more, a sparkly Christmas tree in the corner and garland draped from one side of the ceiling to the other. But what had her curious was a microphone in a stand and a guitar leaning against the wall. She went to Dotty, who was clad in a red sweater dress, and asked about it.

"Oh, Billy invites a friend of his to come and play. He's pretty good!"

That night it was the most Grace talked with the staff and them with her, some asking about her relationship status, others curious if she had any family in the area. She managed to give as little detail as possible. "Too busy to be in a relationship," she said, and "No, I have family back in Buffalo but not sure when I'll be seeing them."

She planned to leave long before the festivities were over but when Billy's friend showed up, got his guitar and started singing, she decided to stay a bit longer. He began by leading the crowd in "Santa Claus is Coming to Town." The Christmas songs continued for a while until he told the crowd he needed a drink. They began to boo him in a jovial manner. On impulse, Grace said loud enough for some to hear, "I could do a song."

Billy turned to look at her, an eyebrow raised. "You wanna sing?"

"I'd have to borrow his guitar."

His friend gave a consenting nod, calling over, "It'll give me time to enjoy some of this food!"

Suddenly, the room became quiet as the staff watched Grace approach the mic. She picked up the guitar. "I think I need a break from all the holiday music," she said, and then after tuning the guitar to her liking, started singing:

> *I go out walkin' after midnight*
> *Out in the moonlight*
> *Just like we used to do. I'm always walkin'*
> *After midnight, searching for you . . .*

She was brought back to when Rachel and Tim had first heard her singing and remembered their impressed expressions. Oh, how she missed them and yearned to hear their voices, see their faces. Similarly, she now had everyone's attention; they were swaying, their mouths dropped open. Once she finished, the applause was thunderous. Billy boisterously shouted, "Who the hell knew our quiet little Grace had such an amazing voice!" He looked at his friend and said, "Sorry, buddy, but you been upstaged. Do another, Grace!"

By the time the party wrapped up, Grace had become the topic of conversation, Billy exclaiming repeatedly that she needed to get herself to the pub and tell them she wanted to sing for them. "They need some fresh blood there," he said. "Hell! I'll tell 'em for you. They hear it from me, you'll be booked."

Dotty tugged on Billy's shirt. "But you might lose a waitress, if you do that."

When Grace went the couple of times to the pub, she imagined herself on the stage performing for the crowd, but started to doubt herself when Billy was making it a possibility. After all, performing at the tavern in 'busco was small potatoes compared to how it would be in Poughkeepsie. However, she had to admit that singing did lift her spirits.

"Let me talk to Ray," Billy said. "He owns the pub. I'll see what I can do. It'll have to be after Christmas, though."

"That's okay," she said. "It'll give me more time to practice."

Early Christmas morning, she was awakened by squeals of delight from the children who lived below. Unlike Thanksgiving, the diner was closed on Christmas Day, leaving her time to only think about Jack, Kevin, and Vicky, wondering if they were opening gifts just then. She longed to hear their voices and not those of the children coming up through the floorboards.

She climbed out of bed and dressed for the chill outside and went downstairs with change in her pocket. There was a phone booth a couple blocks over. She passed no one;

everybody probably cozy in their homes in celebration of the day. She reached the booth and took a deep breath as she dropped the coins in the slot and dialed the number. She had no intention of speaking but just wanted desperately to hear Jack's voice when he picked up. But it wasn't Jack who picked up. It was Simone.

Grace dropped the receiver back into the cradle, stumbling out of the booth. She made her way back to the apartment, where she spent the day in bed, listening to the joyful sounds from below. It would be years before she decided to call Jack Finley just to hear his voice again.

True to Billy's word, a couple of days after the New Year, he had Grace go with him to the pub, telling her to bring her guitar. It was late afternoon when they walked in, the dusky-looking room almost empty, except for three men sitting at the bar.

Billy called over to a man behind the bar. "Hey, Ray, here's the girl I was tellin' you about."

Ray looked to be in his forties. He reached over the bar, shaking Billy's hand, then said to Grace, "So Billy tells me you're one talented gal. Since you got your guitar, why not play something for me?"

Grace wasn't sure if she was supposed to go to the stage where the performers normally played or stay where she was. She decided to stay where she was and strapped on her guitar.

Billy said, "Do that Hank Williams number."

Grace took a deep breath and began:

> *Hear that lonesome whippoorwill*
> *He sounds too blue to fly*
> *The midnight train is whining low*
> *I'm so lonesome I could cry*

Billy grinned with pride, looking over at Ray, who was bopping his head. The men at the bar turned their attention toward Grace and once she was finished singing, they all applauded.

"She has tons more songs, Ray," Billy said. "Think you can fit her in here?"

"I'd be a damn fool not to," Ray said. "I might be able to squeeze you in this Saturday night, unless you're busy."

"She ain't busy," Billy said. "Are you, hon?"

Grace shook her head.

"How much you pay?" Billy asked.

"Well, we're trying her out here so how about seven dollars an hour and I'll give her two hours."

"She makes more than that with tips at the diner. You'd better rethink your offer."

Ray scowled, then said, "All right, twenty dollars for the two hours. If she draws a crowd, I'll have her back and we can renegotiate."

Billy concurred without asking Grace if she agreed. He said, "We'll see you Saturday night. What time should she be here?"

"Be here by ten. You'll play till midnight. Not a bad slot to be in."

"Grace, *Grace*."

Grace was back in her bed with Adele sitting next to her. She had no memory of coming back to her room.

"You kinda wandered off. You were telling me about how Billy got you a job at the pub. How'd it go?"

Grace shifted in her bed, scrunching up her face. *Billy?* She hadn't thought of him in ages. "Ended up becoming my manager," she said aloud.

"Your manager?"

"For over ten years. Had big hopes for me. Well, himself, since I didn't want to be famous. Didn't want to be discovered. Just liked singing." She closed her eyes, too tired to say anything more while hearing Adele say, "I guess that's it for today. To be continued."

Part Three

CHAPTER 24

The year was 1968. It had been more than ten years since Grace first performed that Saturday evening at the Poughkeepsie pub. Due to the crowd she managed to draw, Ray kept her on. After negotiating the terms of payment, Billy decided he would be Grace's manager and get her more gigs while keeping a percentage of the profits.

So much had changed and so much hadn't. Fast as the world was moving, for Grace it felt stagnant. When she wasn't performing, her time was spent thinking of Jack—in her mind's eye still looking like the young man he was when she'd left, and of five-year old Kevin and two-year old Vicky. She tried to picture what they looked like now but couldn't. Instead, they were still the little ones she'd left behind.

Meanwhile, Billy had big plans for her, not knowing that she didn't want big plans, at least those where her face would be recognizable to anyone still searching for her. Billy made her go back to her original hair color, saying he couldn't understand why she'd ever changed from the blonde beauty that she was to that horrid black dye. "It's not the look you want. You're a country singer not a hipster." He also had her buy Western shirts and skirts with fringe, gingham dresses that cinched at the waist and a cowgirl hat to complete the ensemble. She rarely wore the hat since it made her feel foolish.

Working at the diner was a thing of the past for both Grace and Billy. He bought blank cassette tapes, a tape recorder, stacks of envelopes and put together press kits, extolling Grace's musical talent. The only fights they had was when he began sending those press kits to venues far north of Poughkeepsie, much too close to Grace's hometown. Grace had to make up a story about having been in an abusive relationship and not wanting to cross her ex's path ever again.

"Think I'm scared of some asshole?" Billy said. "I won't let anyone come near you."

Quick to reply with a lie, she said, "Won't matter when he uses a gun to punish me."

Billy had a look of alarm. "A gun?"

She nodded. "Said if he ever saw me, it'd be the last time anyone would see me alive. Please, Billy, can't we just keep going south?"

That was the end of the disagreement and Billy then researched venues along the route toward the Grand Ole Opry and sent them material hoping that they'd want her to perform. He also looked for local radio stations and sent them the material, as well; no matter if he got a response or not, he and Grace would show up at those venues and radio stations, hoping to get the attention of whoever was in charge; sometimes it worked, sometimes not, which meant it was taking much longer than Billy anticipated to build Grace's resume of performances without getting much air play on any radio stations, local or otherwise.

It was as though he believed in her more than she believed in herself, even though the years rolled by without the big break he was looking for. But he did manage to get her paying gigs and, having purchased a towable trailer, they made their slow and steady way toward Nashville. Grace didn't know what she'd do once they got there, not wanting to be "discovered" as Billy kept saying would happen. But at least they were putting distance between her and the scene of the crime, even if it had been years since she'd put the bullet into her uncle's chest. For Grace, however, it felt like just yesterday when her life had been dramatically derailed.

By day, Billy would drive the Chevy truck towing the popup camper and she'd be in the passenger seat gazing out at the scenery, smoking one cigarette after the next—a habit she'd picked up from performing in the smoke-filled honkytonks. At night, if they didn't have extra money for a cheap motel, they'd open the camper and she'd sleep on one side while he slept on the other. He never made a move on her, said it wouldn't be proper being her manager and all, for which she was grateful. As far as she was concerned, she was still Jack Finley's wife and would always be. She couldn't imagine being with another man but couldn't help thinking there was another reason Billy didn't put any moves on her. She found out that reason one night when she finished performing at a small venue in Charlotte, North Carolina, and walked in on him and another man. Startled and confused, she went into the truck and curled up onto the seat, falling asleep. The following morning, neither spoke of the incident. They folded down the camper and continued on toward what Billy considered was Mecca. She didn't say anything but gazed at the passing orange and red autumn leaves. In New York, when the leaves changed color, she'd need a jacket or sweater, but here it still felt like the height of summer.

The closer they got to Nashville, the more her stomach churned. Billy talked about bringing her to some recording studio on Music Row he'd heard about and getting some producer to hear her sound. As they drove through the Smoky Mountains, Billy reached over, patting her on the arm, saying, "Don't worry, hon. They'll love you."

That's what she was afraid of.

Finally, though, they reached Nashville. Billy slowed down to a crawl along Broadway. He pointed out Ernest Tubb's Music Store, as well as other sites, driving up and down streets. "Look at that!" he shouted, as they drove by the Ryman Auditorium. "I can't believe we're here!"

"Me either," Grace intoned.

"That's where the Grand Ole Opry takes place," he said, glancing at her. "Won't it be something seeing you on that stage performing for that huge audience?" When she didn't respond, he said, "Come on, Grace. You have to show some excitement, or they aren't gonna be interested. Personality, darlin'."

Was there a sudden twang to his voice? She looked out the window, rolling her eyes.

Soon they pulled into a motel parking lot. After they got their room to share with double beds, Billy took out his map, mumbling. "Victor Studios has to be nearby." After a few minutes, he blurted, "Here's McGavock Street." He looked up at Grace. "That's where it is. How about we take a stroll 'round town and get a lay of the land."

"I could eat something," Grace said, crushing the butt of her cigarette in the ashtray.

A couple of days later, Grace was at Victor Studios with her guitar. It wasn't the same guitar Jack had gotten her. That one she'd stored for safe keeping. Instead, she bought a new one, but it was just a guitar without any history that she could hang on to.

It had taken some persistence, but Billy managed to finally get her that desirous audition. Before they walked into the studio, he touched up her lipstick and straightened her cowgirl hat, telling her she needed to dress the part to be taken seriously.

"And I want you to sing 'I Fall to Pieces.' That shows your range."

There was no debating Billy, so once she was standing in front of an unenthusiastic man named Jerry, who was in charge of the auditions, she began singing. However, she didn't get very far into the song before she was stopped.

"That song's been done, hon," Jerry said, his tone exasperated. "Have any of your own stuff?"

"My own stuff?" Grace said. "Not really." She never had the heart to share any of the songs she wrote, believing they were too revealing.

"*Not really.* What's that mean?"

"She's working on stuff," Billy said in a panic. "Ya know, getting it just right. But thought you'd appreciate her voice. Don't she sound a lot like Patsy Cline?"

Jerry shrugged. "We don't need another Patsy Cline."

"Grace," Billy said, "how about singing him that Kitty Wells song."

"How about not," Jerry said. "Listen, you gotta have your own sound if you want to make it in this business. Your manager here tells me you've been playing in different venues along the eastern seaboard and doing all right. Let that be your bread and butter."

"Come on, Jerry," Billy pleaded, "you know she's good."

Jerry took a deep breath. "Sure, she's good, *Billy*, but the thing is country music is in somewhat of a standstill. Music comin' out of San Francisco is getting more airplay than what we're getting."

"What're you talking about?" Billy snapped.

"Folk, rock. Protest songs. Buffalo Springfield, The Byrds, that kind of music."

Billy looked at Grace, pressing his sights on her as if to get her to read his mind. "Sure, she can play that."

Grace replied with an incredulous look. She had no idea who those bands were.

Jerry stood, pointing them to the door. "Listen, anyone we sign on has to be really special. Sorry, but this little lady is just average."

Billy appeared crestfallen, his face a bright red. He took Grace by the arm. "Come on, we don't need this." He pulled her out the door and onto the sidewalk, muttering, "*Average!* He wouldn't know talent if it hit him in the face." He let go of her arm and stared at her. "Why didn't you fight?"

"Fight?"

"For a chance. Why didn't you keep singing so he could get the full . . . the full experience?"

"Billy, I'm just as happy doing what he said. We're doing okay."

"Living out of a camper?" he shouted. "I wanna do more than *okay.*" He stomped down the sidewalk. "I'd think you'd want to, too. For Christ's sake, we've been doing this for years now. This was supposed to be your big break and you don't seem to give a damn!"

Grace started toward him, telling him to stop shouting, while people blatantly stared as they passed them on the sidewalk. Billy came to a sudden stop.

"Wait. Maybe San Francisco *is* where we need to be. Maybe country music *is* over."

"What do you mean?"

"You know the saying that insanity is doing the same thing over and over and expecting different results?"

She shrugged.

"Maybe I've been approaching this all wrong."

"What do you mean?"

He started walking again, babbling about needing to do research, get a better handle on things, needing to fake it until they made it, and soon they were checked out of the motel and packed up, heading West with Billy turning the radio dial going past country tunes while looking for rock stations. Now Grace had to listen to songs by Janis Joplin, Joni Mitchell, and The Mamas and the Papas.

"You can sing just like them!" Billy said. "Well, make it sound like you, though."

Meanwhile, they'd do stopovers at bigger towns along the way where Billy would get Grace gigs, where there would be over a hundred patrons, others where there would be a few drunks at the bar. Sometimes Grace would play just for tips and other times a set fee, with Billy always getting his share. He also insisted she'd weave in some of the folk songs she learned while still performing the country classics but adding a rock sound to some of them. If they did well at a particular venue, they'd stay on for a few days more; if not, they moved on to the next town. Sometimes Grace wondered if it would have been easier turning herself in all those years ago and going to prison, since she felt trapped by her situation anyway.

Once they got to Oklahoma City, Billy started shopping for another camper, an upgrade. "Our overhead is low, so we can swing something better," he said. He ended up trading in both the truck and what had been their home, one that showed wear and tear, to an RV almost twice the size. It had a working kitchen stove with an oven and a bathroom so roomy that Grace no longer rammed her elbows against the stall when she took a shower. It had four beds, two that were converted from kitchenette seating. And they would no longer need to close the camper in order to travel. They ended up staying in Oklahoma City, living out of the RV for a couple of months since Grace had a successful gig at a pub called the Main Event, but Billy still wasn't going to give up the big dream.

One afternoon after she had taken a walk, Grace found
Billy sitting at the kitchenette with a stack of press kits ready to
be sent out while music was playing from the radio.

"Not sure if this matters anymore," he said.

"What do you mean?"

"Times are changing, Grace. You can't keep singing the
same old songs."

"I'm not! I now include 'Me and Bobby McGee' and
'Monday Monday' and I'm learning other songs."

He looked to be thinking, shaking his head. "You gotta write
your own stuff. That's how you'll make it in this business."

"I told you, I don't know how!"

"Learn! Write about 'Nam and all those boys going off to
war," Billy said.

"I don't know anything about that," Grace snapped.

"How could you not? Heard of the draft, haven't you? The
protests?" Billy slammed his fist on the table. "Too many of
our young men are going over there and dying. For what?" he
shouted.

It suddenly occurred to her that Kevin could be one of those
boys in Vietnam right then. Her memory of him was of a gentle
child who refused to even step on an ant. The idea of him being
in harm's way almost paralyzed her. She edged down on the seat
across from Billy, staring out the window.

"Try writing a song about that, Grace!"

Barely above a whisper, she said, "No. I can't."

His jaw tight, Billy said, "Then write a goddamn love
song." He paused, before adding, "Guess not. Never heard you
say you'd been in love before. But if you were and your heart
got broke, write about that!"

Grace got up and went over to one of the beds and climbed
in under the covers. "Wake me when it's time for me to go play
tonight."

CHAPTER 24

Before long, it was October, the year 1970. They were driving through Arizona, heading to Sedona. Billy had managed to get what he called a nice gig for Grace at a 300-seat venue called Stage Sedona.

"This will be one of our biggest gigs yet," Billy said to Grace, who was behind the wheel of the RV. He chuckled, then added, "Didn't hurt that I mentioned how you'd performed in Nashville."

Grace took her eye off the road for a moment, giving Billy a scowl. "You said what?"

Billy shrugged, putting his feet up on the dashboard. "I just padded the press kit a bit. I didn't lie. You did perform in Nashville."

"For less than a minute, Billy! And I got turned down."

"Semantics, darling. All semantics."

She put her sights back on the road, mountains in the distance the color of burnt sienna. She wanted to say something more, but a disc jockey came on the radio, his tone sober, announcing the sudden death of Janis Joplin from an accidental drug overdose. It had only been a month earlier that Jimi Hendrix had died. Neither Billy nor Grace used drugs, but they had been in places where it was free-flowing.

"Hear that?" Billy said, straightening in his seat.

"I heard. It's so sad."

"It is," he said, "but maybe there'll be room for you now. Keep practicing that new raspy sound."

Grace didn't respond; just stared ahead as she drove, remembering that October was the month when she and Jack had married. She wondered if he recalled the anniversary. When they pulled into a gas station to fill up, she said she wanted to buy some snacks and headed into the market. Instead, though, she went to the phone booth, making sure Billy wasn't paying attention, and for the first time in years, she fed change into the slot and punched in numbers she'd never forgotten. Her heart pounded double-time as the phone rang. She looked at her watch. It was almost four in the afternoon in 'busco. She hoped Simone wouldn't be the one to pick up. *Simone. Was she even still alive?*

"Hello?"

Grace gasped at the sound of a young girl's voice. *Was it Vicky?*

"Hello?" the girl repeated, her voice shaky.

Grace wanted to say something, but no words would come. *How could they? What could she possibly say?*

She sucked up some air and before she got to speak, the girl shouted, "I hear you breathing, Brad! Leave me alone!" Then she hung up.

Grace stood numbly in the booth, the phone still in her hand. She'd hoped to hear Jack's voice. Perhaps next time. Hearing the young girl's voice was addicting and she knew she would be calling again, even if it were just to listen to her.

"Why didn't you say anything?"

Grace was no longer standing in the phone booth but lying in her bed at the nursing home. "What?" she said.

"Why didn't you tell her who you were? I mean, I would think she'd always wonder where you were."

Grace mumbled, "I was afraid."

Adele said, "But so much time had passed, the sheriff couldn't still have been looking for you." She paused, then added, "Did you ever try to find out if they figured out it was your uncle who was murdered?"

"I had no way of knowing, but I wasn't afraid of that."

"What were you afraid of?"

"That she'd have no idea who I was. I didn't know what she'd been told. I didn't know if Jack remarried. I didn't know anything except that I just wanted to hear all their voices, to know that they existed, even if I didn't for them."

Adele flipped the page in her notebook. "So, Billy got you a pretty big gig in Sedona. Did they find out he lied about Nashville?"

Her set list had consisted of songs that were constantly being played on the radio. The crowd at Stage Sedona treated Grace like a sideshow while they guzzled their beer and partied. Sometimes Grace wondered if they could even hear her while she sang, attempting the raw sound that Billy insisted she do. She was stunned that the crowd didn't give reverence to Janis Joplin's passing when she began "Me and Bobby McGee." Billy sat in the corner looking frustrated, but she wasn't sure if it was with the rude audience or her lack of enthusiasm. She tried to be engaging, she really did, but it was so contrived that she ended up not caring anymore and just kept singing until her evening gig was over. To Billy's surprise, the venue manager didn't complain, and each night handed over the agreed fee.

After she was done for the night, she'd head to the RV while Billy said he was meeting up with a friend for a drink. Oftentimes, she'd wake up the following morning to see that he wasn't in his own bed. During the day, she'd walk around town while occasionally stopping at a phone booth and feeding it coins, hungry to hear the voice she longed for. Most often, the phone would just keep ringing, while other times a young girl would pick up. After she would say hello and Grace didn't reply, she'd slam it down. Another time there was the young girl's voice demanding that she stop calling, making Grace wonder if she knew it was her long-lost mother and wanted nothing to do with her. Never once, though, did a man's voice come through the receiver, forcing Grace to consider the unthinkable.

One afternoon while she was strolling along Main Street, she spotted Billy sitting with a man at an outdoor café. She wasn't sure if she should go over and introduce herself or just keep walking. Something told her that the man, slim with short brown hair, was more than just a friend to Billy who noticed Grace and waved her over.

"This is Harry," Billy said. "He owns a candle shop down the street."

Grace forced a smile and said hello.

"Feel free to check it out," Harry said. "Let the girl behind the counter know I said to give you a twenty percent discount."

When it was obvious they had no intention of inviting her to join them for a beverage, she said thank you and continued walking.

Soon, the two-week gig was over, and it was time to keep heading toward San Francisco, their newest destination where she was to be discovered. Billy was once again counting on it.

CHAPTER 25

Adele raced down the hall, couldn't get to Grace's room fast enough, stunned at what she'd discovered. After her previous session with Grace, she decided once again to take advantage of her school library's resources and did some research, keying in specific words. Even though she was working on deadline, as Mr. Wilson referred to her assignment, she decided to leave no stone unturned, a phrase her teacher used several times during the last couple of weeks.

She rushed past Mary's empty bed, finding Grace in hers lying on her back, her eyes closed and mouth opened. She was snoring lightly. Adele scraped a chair over near the head of the bed, leaned in and whispered in a sing-song tone, "Grace, you awake?" She waited a second, but there was no response. She repeated herself, not once but twice until Grace gave a snort with a jump, looking over in Adele's direction.

"Aren't you tired of me yet?" Grace mumbled.

Adele drew closer and said, "I . . . I . . . have some information for you. I think—"

"What do you mean?" Grace tried to sit up.

Adele stood and plumped Grace's pillows, helping her get comfortable, before she sat back down and leaned in close enough so that Grace could hear her every word. She wasn't even sure where to begin, but pulled a printout from the *Press Republican*, a Plattsburgh newspaper. She took a deep breath. "Listen to this. It's an article dated August 21, 1958." Adele read:

Body Identified at Previous Murder-Suicide Site

Coroner Shatelle confirms that the body that appeared on the Dormand property in Churubusco, NY was that of Homer LaBarge who went missing approximately at the same time that Ernest Arthur Dormand murdered his wife, Evelyn Francis neé Cooke, and took his own life on that same property. At the time, LaBarge and Dormand ran a bootlegging operation. Sheriff Clark reports, "By all appearances, Dormand killed LaBarge, buried him, then didn't want his wife to turn him in, so he killed her, too. Guess he couldn't deal with the guilt. Either that or didn't want to be responsible for his baby daughter, and took his own life."

Adele put down the news clipping for a moment to see Grace's face scrunched up.

"Do me a favor," Grace said. "Could you read that again?"

"There's more, but okay."

After Adele re-read the article, Grace said, "But it wasn't Homer. It was my uncle. I never knew any Homer."

"Grace," Adele said, "there's more. This is the part that surprised me." She read:

Simone Finley neé LaBarge is quoted as saying, "My brother got mixed up with Ernest and look where it got him." Mrs. Finley went on to say that she thought her brother had high-tailed it to Canada when in fact he'd been shot and was wasting away in the ground. "And without any last rites," she said, her tone angry.

Grace sat straight up, staring at Adele. "Her brother? He knew my father? She never said a word about that. Not one word. I don't even think Jack knew."

"You know what Mr. Wilson thinks?" Adele said. "He's my teacher. He thinks that maybe Simone thought it was her brother who killed your parents and then went into hiding."

Grace looked to be digesting the information.

"But who knows where he really ended up?" Adele concluded.

"And maybe he really *did* kill them. Maybe my father wasn't who I thought he was this whole time." Grace began to shake, punching her fists onto the bed. She started screaming, her words jumbled and unclear.

"Grace! Grace!" Adele said, jumping up and trying to calm down the old woman. "It's okay, it's okay."

A nurse came running in. "What on earth is going on?"

Adele backed away. "I don't know. I thought—"

"What did you say to her?"

Tears came to Adele's eyes. Grace's reaction wasn't what she'd expected. Out of the corner of her eye, she saw Mary roll in the room in her wheelchair, stretching her neck to see what was going on.

"No, no, no," Grace repeated.

Another nurse came in and managed to get Grace's hysteria under control.

"How could she?" she muttered before drifting off.

Adele took a step closer, her breathing labored. "Is she? I mean, did she?" She couldn't bring herself to say the word.

"No," the nurse said. "She's fine, exhausted, but fine. I think you'd better go, though."

Adele nodded and started to walk out the door when Mary said, "She talks all the time. If she says anything that I think can help you for your project, I'll let you know."

Adele looked across the room to see Grace was settled but still mumbling. She thanked Mary and said, "I'm so sorry I upset her. That wasn't my intention."

Grace and Billy arrived in San Francisco at the end of October, parking in a lot in Haight-Ashbury. Grace felt like she was on another planet seeing the way people were dressed, wondering if maybe it was just Halloween garb. There were headbands, ponchos, short shorts, skirts and bell-bottoms so long they dragged along the sidewalk, tie-dyed shirts, moccasins, and everything in between. Without hesitation, Billy guided Grace into a clothing shop and insisted they buy some new outfits so she could dress the part. It was time to ditch her gingham dresses, puffy-sleeved blouses, sensible dungarees, and cowboy boots, he said. He also told her wearing make-up no longer seemed to be necessary for this crowd.

While he was going through some racks of clothes, Grace asked, "So where am I scheduled to perform?"

Without replying, he handed her a floral A-line dress with a peace sign just as a young girl came from around the counter and began to pull some other items from the rack. "How about these? They'd look smashing on her." She handed Grace a pair of pants that couldn't seem to decide what color they wanted to be. "They're called psychedelic. Very popular now," she said.

"Go ahead," Billy said. "Try those things on."

"Our dressing room is right over there," the girl said.

Grace tried the clothes on, not at all sure they fit her right. It was difficult to tell. Billy called into the dressing room, "So, let's see!"

She came out wearing a long flowing dress, her expression uncertain.

"So cute!" the girl said.

"Is it supposed to look like this?" Grace said.

"Sure. It's the style now."

Grace shrugged and saw Billy looking her up and down. He also shrugged, relenting to the new fashion.

"So, I guess I could wear this at my next gig," she said. "Where will I be performing?"

Billy cleared his throat. "I haven't gotten anything scheduled yet."

"What do you mean?"

"Listen, from what I understand, people play in each other's homes or on the street. We'll set you up on a street corner and you'll play for tips."

Grace glared at Billy. "Are you serious?"

"Hey, you're the one who didn't care if we didn't make it big. I sent out the press kits, but when I followed up with calls, they said they were booked months out."

"So why did we come all this way?" She tossed her arms in the air and then wandered back into the dressing room, gazing at the woman in the mirror. Living the life she was living had aged her. Her eyes had lost their sparkle, frown lines were permanently etched into her forehead and her lips were thinned. And all those Styrofoam cups of coffee and cigarettes on the road had yellowed her teeth. Would Jack, if he were still on this earth, even recognize her if they passed each other on the street?

Later that night, they bought tickets and made their way into the Fillmore West. A band called Jefferson Airplane was performing. Grace looked at posters on the wall promoting upcoming acts. It seemed they were all groups, no solo performers, from what she could tell, and with strange names—The Grateful Dead, Quicksilver Messenger Service, but there was also a sign with Janis Joplin's photo. Billy pointed at it, shouting over the music, "That could be you!"

She scowled. "Dead?"

He rolled his eyes. "No, the next big thing!"

She turned her back and saw a man she recognized standing off to the side. "Billy," she shouted, "isn't that the guy from Sedona?"

When Billy looked, he didn't seem surprised. "Harry!" he said with a grin, walking over and giving Harry a lingering hug before the two of them returned to where Grace was standing, the crowd getting tighter around her.

"Good to see you again," Harry shouted. "Nice outfit!"

Grace was wearing a tie-dyed blouse with fringe down the sleeves and bell-bottom pants. She felt silly but from what she could tell she wasn't out of place. She said loud enough over the music, "Shouldn't you be at your candle shop?"

"I own it," Harry yelled. "It doesn't own me." He nodded toward the stage. When do you go on?"

"I don't. I'll be on some street corner tomorrow."

He lifted an eyebrow.

"Not like that. Your buddy here," she motioned to Billy, "didn't get me any gigs in this town. He thinks I should just play for tips on some street corner."

At some point, Grace had gotten separated from Billy and Harry, while she tried to enjoy the music and someone kept passing a joint her way. She shook her head and eventually made her way out the door and back to the camper. She stripped out of her unfamiliar clothes and climbed into bed, hoping sleep would come without the nightmares that often haunted her.

The following morning, she sat quietly in the camper's dinette while sipping black coffee and smoking a cigarette.

"Hey," Billy said, coming up the steps. "How's it going?" He was alone.

She looked away and said, "Where's your buddy?"

"Harry? He's sleeping in. We had a late night. So, you ready to do this?"

"I guess."

"If we don't get there soon, someone else will take your spot. I found out it's *the* spot to be discovered."

After she slipped into her attire for the day—what she'd worn the night before—she and Billy headed over to the corner of Haight and Ashbury Streets. Grace had to almost run to keep up with Billy while he kept remarking about the "cheerful" sun and "crystal blue" sky, as if the weather had bearing on her success.

"Good, no one else is here yet," Billy said, once they reached the corner. He opened her guitar case, handing her the instrument, then put the case on the sidewalk, leaving it open. He took out his wallet and tossed in a couple of dollars.

"Why'd you do that?"

"Get the ball rollin'," he said. "Seed money. Now start singing,"

One look around told her there wasn't anyone to sing to and said as much.

"Just start and then they'll come."

Several songs in, a guy with a ponytail and grungy looking jeans approached Grace. She ceased singing when he put his hand up to stop her. He said, "You're playing everybody else's stuff. Not cool. Play your own or give someone else this spot."

Billy strolled over, letting the guy know that he was Grace's manager.

"Then you should know better having her play other people's stuff. John and Denny would have something to say about it."

"John and Denny?" Billy said.

"Yeah, *the* Papas of the Mamas and Papas. Either she plays her own stuff or let someone else have this spot."

Grace put her guitar back in its case without looking at Billy. She then handed him the two dollars he'd put in and made her way back to the camper. The next day they were on the road while Harry returned to Sedona.

Billy resorted to his connections back home, calling up contacts, saying, "Yup, she performed all over the country from Nashville to San Francisco." She couldn't hear what the other person was saying, but could guess when Billy replied, "Well, we want to give Poughkeepsie our thanks for helping make her a breakout star. Sure she is! Well, I can't help it if your radio station doesn't play her!"

Eventually, though, he wore the contact down and told Grace she was booked at a holiday festival in Poughkeepsie for Thanksgiving weekend. The drive was long without any stops other than for gas and groceries, the two of them taking turns at the wheel. When they pulled into Poughkeepsie at mid-afternoon, winter had arrived full force, several inches of snow covering the ground. While Billy went to the venue where Grace would be performing to confirm the details, she did what she hadn't done in weeks and made a phone call.

Trembling from the cold, she closed the phone booth door and fed the slot with change and waited, her breath visible in the small space. The phone rang three times before someone picked up. It was a young girl's voice. Grace shook from both the cold and fear. She desperately wanted to say something but before she had a chance, the girl said, "Listen, asshole, this is Brenda. Brenda Hannigan. Stop calling Vicky! You're freaking her out, Brad!" Then the phone was slammed down.

Brenda? Grace had no idea who Brenda was, but why would she? Quite likely, the Finley household was so far removed from how she'd left it. Kevin and Vicky were young adults now. She wasn't even sure she'd recognize them. That feeling that often overwhelmed her was coming back. All she wanted to do was crawl into bed and pull the covers over her head. Billy referred to when she got like that as her depressive state of mind. No matter how hard he'd try to get her out of it, nothing worked. She couldn't help but think that maybe it was time to stop making those phone calls and torturing herself.

CHAPTER 26

Grace lay in the quiet of her room, having no idea what time it was. It had to be somewhere in the middle of the night with how silent it was. She had never lived for the past because it was too painful, until that young girl intruded on her life. Now it was all she could think about. However, after the recent revelations, she wondered what would have been different had she stayed with Jack. She rolled on her side, and curled up, trying to keep the truth at a distance. Instead, she allowed herself to continue going back in time.

She had a steady gig at the pub in Poughkeepsie and was often hired for local parties or other celebrations. Billy, who occasionally would disappear for days, eventually concluded that Grace was not going to be the big star he'd hoped she would be, but they managed to bring in enough money to survive. But then one night he showed up at the pub and during her break told her that his cousin who lived in Syracuse was a fireman looking for someone to perform for their field day.

"It's the last Saturday in August," Billy said.

"Think it's worth the drive?" Grace said.

"I think it'll get you more exposure. You've been stuck here for months. And it'll give us a chance to sell more cassettes."

Billy had thought it was a good idea to record Grace and sell the cassettes at the pub and local music store, an opportunity to make some money, he'd said. It had been weeks, though, since they'd sold any copies.

"It's decent money," Billy said. "And it'll give me a chance to see my cousin. He's a good guy."

It wasn't as though Grace really had an option and it was set.

They arrived in Syracuse the last Saturday in August to find the town abuzz with activity. There were carnival rides, vendors selling all sorts of food, games to win stuffed toys and a bandstand.

"That's where you'll be," Cal said. Cal was Billy's fireman cousin. You go on at seven tonight. We advertised it in the paper and everything." He looked directly at Grace. "That must've been awesome playing at the Grand Ole Opry!"

Before Grace had a chance to correct the mistake, Billy clapped Cal on the back, thanking him and asked if he could get him something to drink while leading him away from Grace.

Grace decided to get herself a hot dog before going back to the RV to freshen up. She no longer wore the clothes Billy had her buy in San Francisco, but usually relied on a pair of jeans and t-shirt; therefore, there wasn't much to freshen up. They'd parked behind the bandstand so after she got her hot dog, she went to the camper until it was time to perform.

Around 6:45 Billy walked in. "You about ready?" He looked around. "God, this place is a mess."

She crushed her cigarette in the overflowing ashtray, then said, "Just what did you tell your cousin about me?"

"I just padded the truth a bit. Besides, you could've performed there."

"Billy—" she began before he interrupted her. "You ever gonna clean this place up?"

She gave him an insolent stare. When they first got the new camper, Grace took pride in it, always straightening it up, wiping down countertops, shining the woodwork; however, the last few months there'd been a shift and she had no desire to do much of anything. It took most of her effort just to get out of bed. Once again, she was in her depressive state.

"Where's the cassettes?"

Grace shrugged.

"Jesus Christ," Billy said, going over to the cabinets and opening them and slamming them shut until he came across the box of cassettes. "You go on in ten minutes." He then stomped down the steps and out of the RV. Just as he was shutting the door, she caught a glimpse of a familiar face. *Harry.* Had he really come all the way from Sedona to see Billy?

She lit another cigarette and smoked it down to the nub before crushing it with the other nubs. She pushed back her stringy blonde hair, grabbed her guitar, and went out to the side steps of the bandstand where Billy and Harry were standing. Harry acknowledged her with a nod.

"You ready?" Billy said.

She peered out into where an audience should be. "Where's everybody?" she said. There were a few people in the front row, but most of the other seats were empty.

"You start singing, the seats'll fill up," Billy said, leaping up onstage. He went to the microphone, tipped his cowboy hat to anyone watching and called those strolling by to come on over.

"Just like Cher," he said, "she goes by one name only. She's toured the world and has agreed to perform for us tonight. Ladies and gentlemen, please give a warm welcome for Grace!"

Harry muttered, "good luck" as she went up the steps and onto the stage. She noticed the people in the front row were goofing off with each other and not paying any attention to what was happening onstage. She set the mic to her height and said how good it was to be in Syracuse, and then started singing, "Busted flat in Baton Rouge . . . waitin' for a train . . ."

She kept singing but spotted a pretty young girl, hair so short it could've been a boy's cut, edging closer and closer to the stage, making her feel somewhat unsettled. She eventually concluded the song by singing, "Hey, hey, hey, Bobby McGee, yeah."

"Thank you," she said, as if there'd been a generous round of applause before looking down at the young girl standing near the front of the stage with a pocketbook strap draped from her shoulder and holding a shoebox. Grace didn't know what to do about it, so all she said was "Hello."

The girl looked to be confused, maybe even star struck. Grace used to have a few groupies years ago, but it hadn't been long before they lost interest. She looked up at the few people finally gathering and said, "Looks like I got a fan."

A couple of chuckles came from the small audience.

"Uh, you got a request?" Grace strummed her guitar waiting for the girl to speak.

The girl shook her head, then said, "I got the clipping."

Grace paused. "I got the *clipping*? Never heard of that one."

"From the *Syracuse News*. Didn't you send me the clipping?"

Grace's heart began to pound, realization setting in. She glanced over to see if Billy was in the back but couldn't tell. She hoped he'd gone off somewhere with Harry. Her mouth dry, she said, "Can't say I know what you're talking about, but I have to get back to performing or I'll lose these folks."

"I'm Vicky."

Grace panicked, wasn't sure what to do, so she said, "How do you do?" and began strumming the guitar with more vigor. "The next number—"

"I'm your daughter!" the girl shouted.

Grace stopped strumming and blurted into the mic, "Back in a few," before running offstage. To her dismay, she passed Billy, who shouted, "What's going on?"

Grace ran into the camper, slamming the door, feeling as though she were going to pass out. She grabbed her cigarettes, pulled one out and lit it without much thought. The door swung open. It was Billy.

"Can you tell me what the hell is going on?"

"I . . . I . . . don't feel so good," she said.

"Well, you'd better start feeling good 'cuz we won't get paid otherwise, and it'll be an embarrassment for my cousin."

Just then, there was a knock on the door. Grace hoped it was Harry or even Billy's cousin. The knock grew persistent. Billy went over and swung opened the door to see the young girl standing there.

Before she gave Billy a chance to say anything, Grace said, "Come in," feeling a jumble of emotions. Standing before her was her daughter, a daughter she'd yearned to see for years, a daughter that Billy had no idea about.

Vicky looked around, appearing appalled at what she saw. She said, "Could I talk with you for a few minutes?"

Billy huffed, "She's supposed to be on stage."

"Billy," Grace said, "please just give us a few minutes."

"This is bullshit!" Billy brushed past Vicky, saying, "She's gotta get back on stage!"

The minute he went outside, Grace shoved some magazines off one of the seats, motioning for Vicky to sit. She did, placing the shoebox on the kitchenette table.

Grace stared at her, wanting to rush over, pull her into a hug; tell her why she'd left. Instead, anger bubbled up inside of her. Seeing her daughter only reminded her of everything she'd been forced to give up. She caved inside, refusing to reveal her sins to the beautiful young girl who, thankfully, looked undamaged. She crushed her cigarette in the ashtray brimming with butts and took out another. She offered Vicky one.

Vicky shook her head, looked to be in shock.

"Good," Grace said. "Glad you never picked up the dirty habit." She brought a lit match to the cigarette, attempting to steady her hand, and inhaled. As smoke billowed out, she said, "Always pictured you with long hair."

Vicky didn't say anything but reached into her purse and pulled out a yellow envelope, sliding a photo from it. "Would you know where this was taken?"

Grace took the Polaroid, gazing at it. She used the counter for support, leaning into it. It was as though time stopped. There she was sitting on a stone wall, with a spray of waterfalls in the background. She was wearing a pair of red slacks and a white sleeveless turtleneck. It was one of the outfits she'd purchased from Pearl's when she was making money singing at the Summit Inn. Her legs were crossed at the ankle, her head tossed slightly back, as if she'd been caught laughing. *Laughing,* something she hadn't done in years. Jack had taken the photo. It was a Sunday afternoon. They'd gone on a picnic to the chasms. It was one of Jack's favorite pictures of her. *Jack.* The very idea of how she'd left him made her feel she had no right to ask how he was.

Grace collected herself as best she could, and said, "Haven't a clue. Not even sure who took it." She nodded toward the shoebox. "There more in that box?"

Vicky shook her head. "It was the only one Kevin was able to save. Grandma threw out the rest."

Simone. "Not surprised. She was a tough old bird." She needed to distract herself, so she began picking up the clothes that were scattered on the floor and tossed them on the bed.

"So, uh, so how'd you find me?"

"The clipping," Vicky said. "You sent it, right?"

She went back to the table and crushed another cigarette. "I never sent you any clipping."

Tears suddenly appeared in the young girl's eyes. She looked to be trying to make sense of everything. Finally, she said, "I've been wondering about you."

Grace had to turn her back for a moment, gather herself, chastise herself to keep from getting emotional. Again, she wanted to blurt the whole story, but how could she tell her daughter that her mother, a Dormand, after all, was a murderer and ran away like a coward?

"Have you, you know, ever wondered about me?"

She gripped the counter. "Every day. You and Kevin." She sputtered, "How is he?" She wanted to say, *and how is your father*, but too afraid that would have put her over the edge.

"Kev . . . Kevin died."

It was as though someone slammed her against the wall. Had she heard correctly? Was it in that damn war? She started to empty the dish rack, something she hadn't done in days. Keeping busy was a distraction she needed. Finally, steeling herself, she said, "He was always such a good little boy."

"He was an incredible brother," Vicky said, the words coming out strained. "He tried to protect you."

"Protect me?"

"He tried to make me believe that you loved me."

Grace wanted to scream, *I did love you! Do love you*, but certain the words would tear open the truth. She thought of what Kevin's life would have been like had it been known what his mother had done, and how he would have had to live with it, she blurted, "I didn't want that kind of life for him." After all, she recalled how people judged her for her father's murderous deeds.

"What kind?" Vicky said.

"Huh?" She realized she'd spoken those words aloud and had to cover up for it. "Farming. I mean, night and day. It's such a rough life and he was such a gentle little boy."

Vicky's face turned red. "He loved it! He gave up everything to try and make it work."

Even though Grace helped on the farm, enjoyed gardening and canning what the ground yielded, she said, "Your father and grandfather tried, too."

"Maybe if you'd stayed," Vicky said, "things would have been different."

Oh, how she wanted to tell her daughter how many times she wanted to come back but why she couldn't. "I . . . I was going to come back. After I made it in this business," she lied. She saw how Vicky was looking at the mess she was living in and quickly added, "But look at you. You grew up to be so beautiful. You have your father's eyes."

Vicky gazed at Grace, studying her.

"That's a compliment, by the way. Your father was a very handsome man." She choked back tears, thinking of Jack. "He's the one who bought me my very first guitar."

"The same guitar you had when you left?"

"Huh?"

"That's what Kevin remembered. You walking out with a suitcase and guitar. And Dad crying."

Grace wanted to tell her she'd been crying, too; still was, but didn't think it would matter.

There was a rap on the door followed by Billy flinging it open. "Grace, we're not gonna get paid you don't get back out there."

"Okay!" she said, hungering for more time with her daughter.

"Grace . . ." Billy's tone was threatening.

"I'll be right out!"

"Is he your boyfriend?" Vicky said.

She didn't know why, but she shrugged. "What about you? You must have a long line of boyfriends." It was daunting thinking how little she knew about this young woman before her. She looked at her daughter's features, seeing so much of herself in them from her younger days. "You remind me of me."

Vicky shifted on the bench. "We're nothing alike."

Grace nodded. "Funny, I forgot about that first guitar." She pointed to the one leaning against the counter. "This one's a beauty, though, don't you think?" *Why did she say such a thing? She hadn't forgotten about that first guitar but kept it under the bed, tucked away with the memories. Was she scrambling for small talk to keep her daughter with her for as long as possible?*

"Didn't seem to impress anyone tonight."

Grace smiled sadly. Before Billy came back to yank her out of there, she grabbed a scrap of paper and pen from the table. "Here's where you can reach me," she said, giving the Poughkeepsie post box address. "I'm not always on the road. I really want to stay in touch." She did, but wasn't sure how that would work. She tried handing the note to Vicky, but she ignored it and stood, going over to the door, her pocketbook hanging from her shoulder.

Please don't leave. Please. Grace said aloud, "Vicky, you stopped answering the phone."

"What?"

"I had this real strong need to hear your voice. I'd call and . . . and . . ." She paused, before pushing the words out. "And you'd answer. I wanted to say something but then you stopped answering."

A tear slipped down Vicky's face before she brushed it away. "It was you calling?" She stared off. "And not Brad," she said, barely above a whisper.

Grace took a step closer, wanting to pull her into a hug.

"Please don't," Vicky said, pushing the door open before she turned and said, "The guitar was nothing more than an excuse."

"What?"

"You didn't want to be a mother, but you couldn't just walk out without some sort of justification." Vicky purposely looked around the small space, at the unmade bed, the dirty dishes piled in the sink, the overflowing ashtray. "I'm glad you left. It's made me who I am today. Kevin made me who I am today." She dashed out of the door, leaving the note, picture and shoebox on the table.

Grace crumpled onto the floor, sobbing. In her mind, she heard, *Once a Dormand, always a Dormand.*

Moments later, Billy came rushing in. "Grace, come on!"

"I can't," she cried, crawling over to the bed. "I just can't."

"Are you fuckin' kidding me? What did that kid say to you?"

She pushed some clothes to the side and, once again, slipped under the covers.

"Who was she?"

"Leave me alone."

"You're never gonna get a gig again, Grace. Never!"

It didn't matter. She had no desire for anything. Kevin was dead. There'd never be the possibility of seeing him again. Never. And her daughter hated her, something she'd tried to avoid by leaving. And what about Jack? Where was he?

Billy thundered out of the camper. She overheard him apologizing to whatever crowd had gathered that the show had been canceled before he stormed back in.

"I'm through!" he shouted, pulling out his duffle bag from the closet and shoving clothes in it. He went to the bathroom and gathered more items before he went to the safe they had under the counter. "I'm taking my share and getting the hell outta here. You take the RV."

She sat up, staring at him. "What do you mean?"

Harry poked his head in. "You ready?"

"Sure am," he said and left without another word.

Grace awoke to the sound of people shouting orders and vehicles running. By the way the sun was shining through the window, she'd slept throughout the night. There was a knock on her door.

"Grace, you okay?" The door opened. It was Cal. "How ya feelin'?"

"Been better," she said, sniffling. "Billy left."

"I know," Cal said. "It's up to you to move this vehicle off the field. We're cleaning up."

Once he left, she swung her feet to the side of the bed and stumbled toward the bathroom, unable to get the image of Vicky out of her mind. Moments later, there was another knock on her door. This time louder. She shouted, "I'll move it!"

"I need to speak with you." It was the voice of a young girl. *Vicky!*

Grace rushed down the RV's narrow aisle and opened the door only to find a redheaded girl standing there.

"Yes?" Grace said, disappointed.

"Can I come in?"

"Who are you?"

"A friend of Vicky's. I'm Brenda. Brenda Hannigan."

"Is she okay?" Grace stood to the side, giving Brenda entrance.

"She's a wreck," Brenda said, coming up the steps.

"So am I," Grace replied.

"Who cares!" Brenda shouted. "All these years she thought you were someone special, making up stories about you. Turns out you're nothing but a murderer!"

Grace lurched back. *So, somehow they knew?* "I . . . I didn't mean—" she began.

"Those phone calls you made freaked Vicky out. She thought it was Brad trying to hurt her."

Grace hesitated. "Brad? I . . . I don't know what you mean."

"The night Kevin died, he was racing to get to her. She was babysitting and someone was trying to break in. She was sure it was Brad Hunt, the one who tried to rape her. All those times on the phone when you didn't talk, she thought it was him all the time calling to torment her. So when someone was trying to break into that house, she just figured it was him. And called Kevin for help."

Grace tried to grasp what she was saying. "I just wanted to hear their voices." She thought for a minute, then said, "So he was trying to break into the house? Is he the one who killed Kevin?"

"No! It was just a mistake. Kevin got killed on his way trying to get to her." Spitting and sputtering, Brenda said, "Why didn't you just say something? Kevin would be alive if Vicky knew it wasn't Brad always calling her. She wouldn't have been so scared!"

Cal appeared at the door, shouting, "Grace, you gotta get off this property. And now!"

Grace looked from Cal to Brenda.

"I just thought you should know it was you responsible for Kevin dying." She headed down the steps, calling behind her, "You needed to know that!"

"But I don't understand."

Grace opened her wet, crinkly eyes to see Adele close to her. "Understand what?"

"Who sent that clipping to Vicky?"

Grace slowly shook her head. "I have no idea."

"So Billy just gave you the RV?"

"Yup."

"What happened after that?"

"I left," Grace replied weakly. "Never sang again. Didn't have the heart."

"So what'd you do? I mean that was about thirty years ago, right?"

"Don't you have enough stuff for your article?" Grace said, her tone tired.

"Just a few more questions, Grace, please," Adele said. "What did you do all those years?"

"Started waitressing again. Traveled here and there. Utica. Albany. Kept my nose to myself."

"Must've been so lonely."

She shrugged. "Got myself a cat or two over the years."

"How'd you end up here?" Adele said. "I mean, you're not that far from Churubusco. I don't understand."

"Once my body couldn't lift all those dishes, going back and forth to the kitchen, I decided the best thing to do was go up into the mountains to die."

"Coyote Hill?" Adele said. "That's just so sad. Did you ever try to see Jack again? I mean—"

Grace gave Adele a hard look. "How could I do any such thing? I was responsible for his son's death. Vicky hated me. Instead, I just thought about those few years when we were as happy as we could be. Over and over again that's all I thought about. So I drove the camper up to Coyote Hill and parked it there. It was close to dyin', too. Found most of the shanty in a pile." After a moment, she said, "That's also where I found a big marker stuck in the ground with my aunt's name carved in it. Guess that's where my uncle buried her."

Adele hesitated then said, "So did you ever go back to your cabin, where you buried him?"

"Not a chance," Grace said, wheezing. "Far as I'm concerned, my biggest sin was leaving my family, not shooting him."

"But . . ."

"Listen, they should've left me up there to die. I'm done talking. Now go write your article and leave me alone," Grace said, closing her eyes.

CHAPTER 27

Adele had only one day left before Mr. Wilson expected the article or she'd get a failing grade, but she felt there just had to be more to Grace's story. She went to the nursing home's administrator's office to get as much information as she could. Mrs. Stewart, a sturdy, gray-haired woman, was the one in charge.

"Yes," she said, "I heard you have been around quite a lot the last couple of weeks. Have quite an interest in Miss Dormand."

"I'm just wondering how she ended up here," Adele said, sitting across from her desk.

"You're not related to her, are you?"

Adele shook her head.

"Then I really don't have the authority to give you much information."

"But she's all alone. No one ever visits her," Adele said.

Mrs. Stewart paused then said, "What are you going to do with this information?"

"I'm writing an article for a school project. I have to hand it in tomorrow and I know my teacher will want it to have some sort of conclusion."

Mrs. Stewart got up and went to the filing cabinet. After going through some files, she pulled out a folder and brought it back to the desk. She opened it and scanned the papers before looking up at Adele.

"She was admitted here two winters ago," she said. "Some snowmobilers found her living up in the mountains. They broke into her camper, not expecting to see anyone living there. There was no heat, hardly any food. She was barely alive. Had frostbite. Somehow an emergency crew got her out and brought her to Alice Hyde Hospital."

"Guess that's how she lost some of her toes."

"We had no way of knowing who she was. There was some paperwork that was found in the camper with the name Dormand so we figured that might be her name. We looked for anyone with that last name in the area but found no one. The Oklahoma license plate on the camper was researched and apparently it belonged to a William Smith. Do you have any idea how many William Smiths there are? So, when we registered her here, we gave her the last name Dormand, and she didn't correct us. Of course, she didn't talk much. Well, not until you showed up." She gave a light laugh. "She apparently has been quite entertaining to Mary with the stories she tells."

"But it's so sad."

"What is?"

"That she has no family, no one to come see her."

"It is," Mrs. Stewart said, shutting the folder. "Well, what I told you should help somewhat with your article."

Later that night, Adele sat at the kitchen table typing up the article on her laptop while her parents were in the living room watching television. She decided to title the article, "Before She Was a Finley." Mr. Wilson told her to have it emailed to him no later than eight o'clock the following morning.

"How's it going?"

Adele looked up to see her father heading to the cookie jar on the counter. She said, "Not great. Mr. Wilson wants it to be concise and for me to keep my opinion out of it." She brought a palm to her forehead, looking discouraged. "Dad, I don't know if I can be a journalist."

"Why?"

"I'm not sure I can ever forget this woman. She got such a bum deal and my heart breaks for her."

"It's that bad?" Her father took a bite out of a chocolate chip cookie.

"Yes! Like I said, Mr. Wilson said that a good reporter reports and doesn't allow themselves to get emotionally involved." Adele's bottom lip trembled. "Dad, I love that woman and wish I could do something for her."

"Like what, sweetie?"

"I don't know. Just something."

He went to his daughter and hugged her. "Give it some thought. Maybe something will come to you." He kissed her on the head.

"Thank you, Dad," she said.

"For what?"

"Everything."

The following morning, instead of meeting her friends at the lake as she'd promised she'd do once she emailed her assignment, Adele got into her car and took the half hour drive to Churubusco. The town could barely be called a town, but she found one square block where there was a Catholic Church and across from it a building with the sign: Churubusco School House Apartments. She turned onto Smith Street and soon came upon a fire department. Across from it she spotted an abandoned building. The garage door was wide open to the fire department, and she spotted some men sitting around a folding table, coffee cups in front of them. She parked the car, climbed out and called over, "Excuse me."

"One of the men stood. He was built like a truck and had a full beard. "Ya lost?" he asked as he approached her.

"No. Not really. I just have some questions."

"Can't guarantee ya I'll have any answers but shoot away." He motioned for her to come inside where two other men were sitting. He introduced them. "This is Chester," he said, motioning to a gray-haired, trim man with a twinkle in his eye. "And this is Mel. I'm Danny. What can we do for ya?"

Adele took a deep breath. "I'm wondering if you know of anyone named Jack Finley."

Danny grinned. "Sure do. Lives on Whalen Road. Bout a mile from here." He pointed toward the left of the fire department.

Mel piped in. "He's an old fella but you won't find a nicer soul."

"Had a tough life, though," Chester said. "Poor fella." He looked at Adele. "You related to him?"

"Oh no. I, I met someone who knows him." She then looked out of the garage and down the street. "Where's the railroad?"

All three men laughed. "Oh, that's been long gone," Danny said. "It used to run along Looby Road."

"And," Adele said, "wasn't there a diner somewhere around here?"

Mel scrunched his face, looked to be thinking. "You mean LeClair's Diner?" He pointed across the road at the empty building. "That was it. Closed up years ago after Rachel died. Tim couldn't manage it on his own and he moved to Canton, I think. Had family there."

Adele found it almost charming the way everyone seemed to know everyone.

"So what's a young girl like you doing asking so many questions?"

"Just some research for an article I'm doing," she said. She'd already turned in the article, but they didn't need to know that.

"That so?" Danny said. "Did you know that the schoolhouse down the road is one of the oldest in the country? It's an apartment building now, but once was a schoolhouse."

"Really?" Adele said.

"We may be a small town," Chester said, "but we got lots of good people here." He got up and went over to a counter and poured some coffee into his cup.

Adele hesitated before she said, "Did you know the Dormands?"

Mel, who looked to be up in age, shook his head sadly. "Tragic, tragic, tragic. No one really got to the bottom of that one."

"What's she talking about?" Danny said.

"Over near the Poupore property. A fellow and his wife were found dead," Mel said. "Big story back in the day. Thank God, we haven't had any other big stories like that in a long time."

"Would you like some coffee?" Chester asked her.

"Oh, no thank you," she said.

"Won't cost you a dime," he said with a grin.

Adele smiled. "No, no thank you. I think I'll go see if I can find Mr. Finley."

"Easy enough to find his place," Danny said, walking out to her car with her. "Just go down this road about three miles and you'll see Whalen Road. Make a right there and his house will be on the right."

"Does he live alone?"

"I believe so. But he has family nearby. His daughter and son-in-law own that resort Lake in the Woods not too far from here."

"Thank you," Adele said, climbing into her car.

Soon, she was pulling into the driveway of the house she figured had to be Jack Finley's. Across the field she saw a smaller house, remembering what Grace had told her about two houses being on the farm. And a short distance away, was the barn.

She got out of the car and went up to the front porch door. There was no doorbell, so she knocked and waited. When no one came, she knocked louder and kept waiting. Finally, an old man, bent over, shuffled onto the porch. He squinted, trying to make out who was on the other side of the glass door as he opened it.

"Hello," Adele said. "Are you Jack Finley?"

"Sure am," he said. "What can I do for you?"

EPILOGUE

All Grace did anymore was sleep. It was as if she'd relived her
  horrid life over again and wanted nothing more than death to
come and take her. Hadn't she been punished enough? Something
stirred her awake and she felt her hand being held. Slowly, she
opened her eyes. It took her a moment to realize that an old man
was sitting next to her bed. His face was lined with wrinkles and
deep crevices while his gaze was soft on her. He leaned in and
whispered, "Grace Finley. I finally got you back."

It felt like her heart had stopped. Perhaps death had come
after all. In a whisper, she muttered, "Jack, that you?"

He brought her hand to his lips. "It is."

Just then, a woman, standing behind Jack appeared.

"Mom, I'm here, too. Me, Vicky."

She gasped, tried to make sense of what was happening. Once
again, she started to believe death had indeed come for her.

"This girl, here," Jack said, "came to find me. Told me the
whole story. Oh my, sweetheart," he choked on the words, "I
am so sorry."

Girl? Grace shifted her focus to see Adele standing at the foot of the bed.

Words of forgiveness were exchanged amid apologies. Blubbering regrets blurted. Tears were shed at the mention of Kevin. "It was no one's fault," Jack said. "It was an accident."

Grace wasn't sure she believed that.

Eventually, Jack, looking off into the corner, said, "Would that be the guitar I got you?"

Grace nodded. "I could never let it go. Fought like hell to keep it when they took me out of the camper." She pointed to the nightstand. "Vicky, the shoebox is in there."

"Shoebox?" Vicky said with hesitation. She went to the nightstand and found it.

"I read those letters over and over," Grace said. "Sometimes I think they saved me."

"What's she talking about?" Jack said.

Barely able to speak, Vicky said, "I used to write her letters and have Kevin mail them for me. But they always got returned." She leafed through a stack of envelopes, yellowed with age, some addressed just to "Mommy" others to "Grace Finley."

"One of my favorites," Grace said, "was the one with all the spelling errors."

Vicky pulled it out and showed it to Adele:

Dear Mommy. I luv yu. I hop yu com home. I am lerning to cook. I will make super for yu. Luv, Vicky, your dauter.

"Oh!" Vicky said, pulling something from the box. "Are these your rings?"

Grace nodded.

"Vicky," Jack said, "give me those." He took the engagement ring and wedding band from his daughter and slipped them on Grace's finger."

"They're loose," Jack said, "but right where they should be."

"Mom," Vicky said, "we're going to bring you home."

"Home?" Grace said, her eyes brightening.

"Yes," Jack said. "You're coming home with us. Where you belong."

Her voice quivering, Grace whispered, "I love you, Jack Finley." She'd never stopped.

Just then, Adele's cell phone rang. She passed Mary, who was sitting on the edge of her bed, dabbing tears from her eyes, and ran out into the hallway. It was Mr. Wilson calling to tell her he'd read her assignment and gave her a B plus. Even though when she began the project, she was hoping for nothing less than an A, the grade no longer mattered. She felt, though, she'd gotten the conclusion she'd been seeking so instead of going back into the room, she headed down the hall to leave, but then stopped and turned around, returning to the door where the plastic slot notified visitors whose room it was. Maybe she wasn't the kind of reporter who didn't get emotionally involved, after all, but she decided to make one last move and reached into the plastic slot, slipping out Grace's name. She then took her pen from her purse, scratched out "Dormand" and printed "Finley" above it before slipping the tag back into the slot. She then headed back down the hallway.

Now she could go to the lake and meet up with her friends.

ACKNOWLEDGMENTS

It's always risky acknowledging those who were instrumental in this writing journey of mine since I may unintentionally leave someone out. Naturally, first and foremost are my adult children, Jason, Corrie and Natasha. They've been on this ride with me for as long as I can remember and I thank them for their constant encouragement. Then, of course, there's my sister, Connie, who has always been eager to read anything I've written. I hope she knows how much that means to me. Even though I dedicated this book to Judith Vaughan and Peggy Zieran, they also need to know how grateful I am for their authenticity, a word we always keep at the forefront when doing our Wildflowers Podcast. Then there is Rory Vecsey who has been a champion of my writing for several years now. I hope she knows how much I appreciate her support. I also want to thank journalist and friend, Arthur Kent, who often reminds me not to be tempted to stop writing, in spite of how challenging the publishing industry is.

With that in mind, thank you, too, to David Wilk for making *Before She Was a Finley* a part of the Easton Studio Press and All Night Books family.

Printed in the USA
CPSIA information can be obtained
at www.ICGtesting.com
JSHW020832260724
67032JS00001B/1